Jana .

Air and Angels

Air and Angels

BY

Susan Hill

SINCLAIR-STEVENSON

First published in Great Britain by
Sinclair-Stevenson Limited
7/8 Kendrick Mews
London SW7 3HG

Copyright © 1991 by Susan Hill

British Library Cataloguing in Publication Data
A CIP catalogue record for this book is available from the British Library.
ISBN: 1 85619 052 8

Typeset by Rowland Phototypesetting Limited, Bury St Edmunds, Suffolk.
Printed and bound in Great Britain by Clays Limited, St Ives plc.

Prologue

THE RIVER was crowded, and the lawns that sloped down to the river, there were young people everywhere, and the sun shone, as it properly should on such a scene, as it shines in stories, sparkled on the water and on the upturned young faces, and the parasols (for parasols were once again in fashion). And then, suddenly, there was a stir in the midst of it all, where the crowd was thickest, and some of the young men raised a boat high, high above their heads, to a great shout . . . 'Hurrah' . . . 'rah' . . . 'rah', and water cascaded out of it onto their heads and shoulders and down their arms, in a brief silver stream. The crowd parted to let them through and they advanced slowly up the lawn in triumph.

Though what precisely the triumph was, or whose, he could not be sure. For there had been so much noise and confusion, so many people, such a succession of triumphs, all that long, hot, golden afternoon.

For years, all the young men had looked alike to him, and he knew none of them any more, they blurred together with his memories of the young men of the past. Though at least they stood still in age now, at least they no longer seemed, as they once had, to be becoming disconcertingly younger and younger, until he had feared they might turn into small children and then to babies and so finally disappear backwards altogether.

But they had remained simply boys. (Though they were young men in their own eyes, and perhaps that was all that counted.)

Then, standing half inside the entrance to the marquee, but

looking out onto the throng on the lawn and the crowded river, for a moment he panicked, clutching a cup of tea and a bowl of strawberries, quite alone, seeing no familiar face among so many. He wandered a few paces into the undersea light of the tent's interior, where they sat in groups at small green tables that were set too closely together, and where the heat and the steam from the tea urns, and the babbling voices, seemed to rise and hover in a dense, visible cloud just above their heads.

He fled, and collided with others, pushing in through the doorway, and stopped, panicking again, trying to clutch onto the sense of his own identity, and his reason for being here; and then, in trying to rescue his bowl of strawberries and steady himself by raising his cup to take a sip of tea, the tea spilled and slopped over and the saucer somehow spun out of his hand onto the grass.

So he waited and let the crowd swirl around him, and gradually he felt calmer and knew once again why he was here, as he had been here every May Week of his adult life. Though he was still entirely surrounded by strangers. There were so few left who were not.

And out of a painted sky the sun shone and shone.

But *he* was known to them. Or at least, to some. They saw an old man, who had once been handsome, and was still tall and upright, still had a full head of hair, springing up thickly, though entirely white. For although it was more than thirty years ago, before any of these young men and women were so much as born, the story – or at any rate, a public version of it – was known and remembered, and sometimes alluded to, had become one of the legends of the place.

So, milling about on the lawn, looking down to the river, on their way in or out of the marquee for the tea and strawberries, some whispered his name to one another.

'Thomas Cavendish . . . the Reverend Thomas Cavendish . . . Did you never hear . . . ?'

On the other side of the lawns, Georgiana caught sight of him, lost him as the crowd milled around, then saw him again, as he shambled forwards, an old man who had spilled his tea and was being jostled. And a sudden dart of the purest anguish struck her through the heart, so that she all but cried out loud at the pain of seeing him as he was, and thinking that she had not wanted him to come to this, had wanted something quite other for him, had dreamed of . . .

But, glancing up and catching sight of him again, she saw, too, how fine a figure he still was, and how the shadow of his former handsomeness lay over him, and for a few seconds then, saw him not as her only brother on this May Week afternoon, not in time at all, but timelessly, as an immortal. And became inattentive to the chatter of Professor Bulmer's moustachioed widow (for Georgiana had companions, there were plenty of faces here that were familiar to her).

I used to challenge him, she thought, aware of how much had gone before. But now, I simply accept. What does he think of, or feel? What does he believe in?

But she did not know. Perhaps she had never known, only assumed.

For no reason at all that was apparent, a picture came into her mind and she saw him on another summer afternoon, in another place and a lifetime ago.

She was a small child, standing at a window watching out for him to come back from fishing with the son of the tinker, Collum O'Cool, fretting because she herself had nothing to do, and the deathly silence of after-lunch and her parents' rest lay thick as a blanket over the house.

Then, as she willed and longed for him to come, there he was, striding ahead of the little, dark, nut-faced Irish boy over the grass, a bag and a rod slung from his shoulder. Looking up, he saw her at the window, stopped, and beckoned, and she went flying from the room and down the stairs and out of the front door to meet him, and he lifted her up and swung her through the air, she saw his face, laughing up at her and smelled the sea-salt, fishy smell on him. And behind them stood Collum O'Cool. She had been five years old and her brother Thomas fourteen, and the Irish summers were immaculate in the memory.

Fifty yards away, by chance or the curious process of telepathy acting between them, he too stood, and dreamed a vivid, momentary, waking dream of Ireland, and it brought with it the overwhelming desperation he had known so often in his later life.

He saw himself in a boat, the little, low-bottomed boat of Collum O'Cool, who was rowing them far out on a grey sea, at first light. Behind them, the low shoreline, the house, and the violet shadow of the mountain, grew small and distant, as if they were being blotted out of a picture, and above them there was only sky, and all around them only sea, and the two merged together on the horizon towards which they rowed, and the only sound was the creaking oar and the slap of its blade into the water and the thin whistling that Collum O'Cool made through his teeth.

A great surge of excitement and joy, a wave of exultation in the space and the freedom, and their own progress away, far away, from house and land and people, surged through him, so that he wanted to shout and sing, to stand up in the little boat and reach out in rapture to embrace the sky.

He felt the ripple of the memory of it now, as he stood watching more young men with boats on the jostling river, but it was not felt as pleasure but as frustration, a longing for freedom again, and the days of the past, for sea and sky and space, and the Irish summers of boyhood, or the Scottish holidays, or the bleached winter dawns on the Norfolk marsh. He felt rage at the cramping and confinement of old age, and of this low-lying, miasmic, oppressive place.

From the river, more shouting. Puzzled, he stared down

at a saucerless teacup and a bowl full of strawberries – a fruit
he especially disliked.

The Professor's widow was chattering again, talk seemed to
issue from her as effortlessly as breath.

'Yes', Georgiana said, and then 'No', and 'Yes, indeed'.
But otherwise could be inattentive.

From somewhere behind the white boat-house, music, a
band.

In a moment, she would detach herself politely and go to
him, for she wondered how he had ever come to be over
there alone. He hated these occasions, had always hated them.
But always came. Even that first summer, after it all.

She thought, I am keeping an eye on him, as if he were a
small child. But *he* used to look after me.

Brightly the band played on, and everywhere people were
smiling. It was, after all, simply the most perfect day . . .

When she looked over to him again, she saw that he was
standing a little apart from the crowd, and that he was quite
motionless, frozen, staring ahead to where the bridge spanned
the river. She followed his gaze, and saw his absolute intent-
ness, even at this distance. Saw what he saw.

And she knew at once what was in his mind, what he felt
and thought, for how could she ever have forgotten? In
those seconds of seeing him so transfixed she understood
completely that the anguish had never lessened but was as
raw as it had ever been and would remain so and the only
thing that would ever alter it was death.

He had looked up vaguely from his saucerless cup and bowl of strawberries and seen her.

The low bridge arched over the water and the girl stood alone upon it. One hand rested on the rail and the other held a parasol (for parasols were once again in fashion).

Her hair was dark, and the white dress brushed her ankles.

She was looking towards the boats, which were some yards away, so that her face was turned from him, and in the shade cast by the willows. She was completely still.

It was her.

Of course, it was not.

But the shock made him gasp for breath, and time went spinning out of control, and the past came racing, like a wave, up the lawn towards him, and broke over him, and he drowned in it . . .

He felt Georgiana's hand on his arm, knew that it was hers, and let her lead him away, and did not once look back. After a while, the young woman on the bridge lifted her arm and waved to one of the laughing groups and the picture was broken, and then she moved, ran lightly down and was lost among them. But he did not see her.

And in any case, who was she?

His sister nodded and smiled and spoke here and there, saying goodbye. But he was far away, immersed in the past. In the cab home, driving between the high walls of the college buildings, softened by sunlight, he was quite silent, sunken into himself. She kept her hand on his arm, but knew better than to speak.

In the quiet, late afternoon avenue, the shadows were long.

(6)

There was no one about, and faintly, from the Backs, the music of the band came floating, and the distant cheering.

'I think we should like some tea, Alice.'

For urn tea really was not the same.

But Thomas shook his head and went down the hall and through the door that led to the conservatory, and closed it behind him.

For some time after it had gone cold, Georgiana sat over her tea beside the open french windows that gave out onto the garden. Occasionally, the house creaked in the silence. From the kitchen, a faint clang, and the rolling of a saucepan lid across the floor.

She thought, Alice is getting old, along with us, she needs a rest. Perhaps she would really like to retire. But put the thought out of her mind at once, dreading change and up-heaval, the whole business of beginning again with someone new. Though in many ways Alice had become less than satisfactory.

From the conservatory, there was no sound. Perhaps he slept. Slept, or dreamed his waking dream. But there was nothing that she could do for him, she could not go to him or reach him. Had never.

Trees lined the garden and stood, stately at the far end of it against the sky, this part of the town was rich in trees, and just now they were at their fullest and freshest and best, the limes, the walnut, the horse-chestnuts and the great, dark, heavy copper beech, whose branches swept like outspread skirts to the ground.

She saw a table covered with a white cloth, and laid for tea beneath it, and herself pouring cup after cup, and Thomas talking earnestly to one of the young men, pacing beside the flowerbeds. And other young men sitting cross-legged on the grass, awkwardly balancing cups and plates, laughing too loudly at her jokes.

(7)

Florence, elegant in grey, teasing them.

But Kitty was not there.

And the monkey puzzle tree that she loathed. But they had never bothered to do anything about it.

Now, the lawn was empty, the young men did not come here any more. But she still took care of the garden. The flowerbeds were stuffed with fat, pink, blowsy peonies, and the rose Albertine cascaded over the wall; the front of the borders needed attention. She would go out later, cut some of the flowers to fill a bowl, snip dead heads and clip the whiskery grass. Fidget. But for now she sat on, looking out at it all, the picture in the frame, and thought of the other garden, this morning, and Florence lying staring at it, but unseeing, unknowing. Uncaring? And her skull pink and shining beneath the sparse, downy white fluff, what remained of her beautiful hair. Oh and the Home was the best place for her, the only possible place, that was clear. They fed her well, she had become quite fat, she who had always had such a good, such a disciplined figure, though full, and set on a broad frame. Now, the fat spread in flabby rolls, pale as raw dough beneath her chin.

They kept her clean and moved her bed to give her a view of the other side of the garden and a glimpse of the street, people walking by. She had refused to get up for almost a year.

But there was no love.

Whichever way her bed faced did not interest her, and when she spoke, she raved and knew no one.

'Why have you let this woman in here?' she said, of Georgiana, and rang the bell furiously. 'Get rid of her.'

'Is it Christmas yet?'

'Why did no one bring me breakfast?'

'They let a cat in at night to pee on my bed.'

'Thomas? Thomas who?'

'My teeth ache.'

A Home, Georgiana thought, leaving that morning. But not a home. Yet what else is there? Demented, senile, the woman who was Florence but was not Florence had to be cared for and protected from herself, and from matches and gas taps and boiling water and wandering out naked into the street.

Remembering, and trying not to remember, blotting both the past and that morning's visit from her mind, Georgiana wept, as she regularly wept; for the loss of her friend and the waste and her own helplessness, and guilt lay like lead in her chest.

On the lawns that led down to the river, the crowds were thinning at last, though slowly, for people were reluctant to go, and so bring an end to the glory of the day. One by one, the boats were brought out of the water and carried in.

Somewhere, refusing to catch the eye of her Mama, lost in the centre of a group, the girl stood, her shoulder just touching that of a young man with a blond moustache, her eyes shining with the thought of the ball to come, and of dancing out of the marquee onto the moonlit grass. One of any number of pretty girls with dark hair and a white dress (the parasol folded now and put away).

The band had stopped playing, but the sun, lower in the sky, still shone benignly and there was no cloud to mar the perfect end to the perfect day.

I must get up, she thought. I cannot sit here, doing nothing. For she was very conscious of being the only one of them who still could 'do' things, this or that, find some purpose in life.

Yet she sat on, feeling her age more and more. Thought, where might it all have ended if it had not ended here? With my brother old and shambling and dropping his saucer and spilling his tea, and Florence, angry and demented and all unknowing, unaware.

And she herself, spinning in circles of busyness and usefulness and sociability, for fear of the alternative.

Looking up, then, she saw that the sun had gone off the lawn, slipped down behind the monkey puzzle tree she had always hated.

And Kitty?

Part One

1

AN AFTERNOON in November. Mist rising off the water, water dripping from the trees, and the cobbled lanes and passageways greasy and treacherous. Not quite four o'clock but already dark. Here and there on the street corners, braziers, and beyond them, black shadows.

The gas lamps flared, haloed in mist, and in so many college rooms, the lamps were lit and young men bent their heads over books or the toasting of muffins.

Thomas Cavendish leaned back in his chair, watched this one particular young man, shuffling papers together at the table. His name was Eustace Partridge.

There is something wrong, Thomas thought. The boy had been vague, tense, had lost his train of thought several times, made elementary mistakes in the translation. It had happened before, the previous week, but that for the first time.

'Is something troubling you?'

The boy stood up, startled as a young horse, flushed, sent Munro's *Homeric Grammar* flying to the floor.

'You seem rather unsettled.'

'No. Thank you, sir. There's nothing wrong, absolutely not. Of course. Thank you.'

He darted a glance across the table, apologetically, Thomas thought, as if to say, I am lying and you know it, and there's nothing to be done. I'm sorry.

'I'm sorry, sir.'

'Very well.'

He nodded his dismissal and Eustace made for the door.

'The boy has', his school High Master had written, 'one of the finest minds it has ever been my fortune to encounter. He is in every way exceptional.' So he had arrived in the college, garlanded, the Masterman scholar and set fair to sweep the undergraduate scholarship board. A runner, an oarsman, and of alarming beauty, fair-haired, Grecian-featured.

Thomas went to the window and watched him go at a half-run across the court and under the archway. And suddenly, remembered another early evening standing looking out onto these buildings, the chapel tower, the court, the same horse-chestnut tree, set in the middle of the lawn. The first evening.

He had been surprised by the size of the rooms he was put in, had paced up and down the sitting-room and touched the furniture reverently, stood facing the blazing fire, and then with his back to it.

The servant had brought a jug of hot water and a bowl, clean linen.

'Dinner is at seven in Hall, sir, and if you would care for a glass of sherry now?'

He had examined the books all round the room. Plato. Lehr's Aristarchus. Plautus. Tulse's Commentaries on the Epistles of St Paul. On another shelf, the complete novels of Sir Walter Scott.

Then, he had gone to stand at the window and, after a moment's hesitation, opened it wide and leaned out, and the smell of the damp, dank November air, of river and earth and coal smuts and fog, had filled his nostrils and gone deep down not only into his lungs but into the deep and permanent well of memory, so that over all the years that were to come, though there would be so many other evenings, in cold winter or high, drowsy summer, when the smell of Cambridge below and beyond and all round him, was quite different, it was this, exactly this, this autumnal mist and smoke, that became for him the one reliable trigger for nostalgia.

He was not a man who, on the whole, yearned for his youth; he had often felt uneasy then, being young had not suited him in some essential way, he had felt ill at ease with it, as though he were wearing someone else's suit of clothes. With the coming of middle age, he had relaxed and begun to feel settled in and with himself, and in a right relationship to the world.

Now, at fifty-four, standing at the open window of this other set of college rooms and smelling the damp, he remembered again vividly but without any yearning how it had felt to be eighteen years old and up for the scholarship examination. And how, smelling that smell, and hearing the sweet, gentle sound of the chapel bell begin to ring across the dark deserted spaces, a passionate desire to belong here, settle here for life, had risen up in him. The emotion had been so strong that it had taken him aback, for he had never been given to any kind of passionate feeling, to yearnings and ambitions.

'I have to,' he had said to himself, and gripped the ledge, 'I have to. I *must*.'

And so he had. So that now, all those years afterwards, he filled with a great, indulgent tenderness towards his younger self, and for the passion of his own longings.

From across the court that same sweet chiming of the bell. He took his gown from the hook behind the door, turned the lamp down and left the room.

Eustace Partridge set his books down on the table in a neat pile. Disarranged them. Sat down. Stood up again. Knew that he had to go out again, as he had been out every night for the past week, to walk anywhere, restlessly, aimlessly. To think, and try not to think.

But, going to the door, he heard the chapel bell for Evensong, and realised that now he must wait, or else meet others on his way and be obliged to speak, and so he simply stood in the middle of the room, eyes closed, clenching his hands, willing the minutes away.

In the grate, the whitening embers shuffled and slipped down upon themselves with scarcely a glow at the core. But he made no move to put on fresh coals and so restore a blaze. Only stood in the darkness, as the bell rang relentlessly on.

2

IT IS one of the handsomest houses in the old residential district of Calcutta, with a drive and gravelled paths that are swept and raked three times a day, lawns, flowerbeds and fountains, and a flight of steps up to the porch, lined with geraniums in pots.

On her bed under the mosquito net, in the middle of the afternoon, Kitty drifts pleasantly in and out of sleep and a half-dream, half-recollection of the great snow-peaks of the Himalayas, glimpsed across the blue-shadowed valley, and it seems as if, in her dreams, she can smell, even taste, the coldness, and that the mountains are near, near, only a leap away. If she could simply take off, lift her skirts and fly. She has often stood like this, since she was a small girl, and dreamed of flying, longed and longed to fly, itched with the frustration of feeling her own leaden clumsiness, of being bound in the confines of flesh and bone.

And, putting her hand up to her face, she can feel the air that blows across with snow on its breath, it is blissfully cold on her cheek.

But, coming to, half opening her eyes, sees that it is, after all, only the curtains, blowing a little in the slight breeze that comes in from the garden – for Kitty does not close her shutters, and she keeps the window open.

It is the Cold Weather season now, to everyone's relief, they are back from the Hills. But it is still hot enough, in the middle of the afternoon, and besides, rules never change, she is obliged to come to her room and lie down on her bed and sleep.

Try to sleep. And it is pleasant enough to lie in her trance, here, and yet elsewhere.

Everyone else sleeps, Kitty thinks.

And yes, a corridor away, Lady Moorehead, fully dressed in coffee-coloured muslin with cream lace, sleeps nevertheless on her day-bed, sleeps peacefully, deeply, stilly and quite without dreaming, under the gently revolving fan. But her shutters are tightly closed, and the room is shadowy.

In a more modestly proportioned room at the side of the house, as befits her station (though the Mooreheads are kindness itself, they treat her with great respect, offering friendliness, if not exactly friendship, she had never been made to feel at all inferior, although naturally it is quite understood between them that she is), not asleep, nor even lying down, but sitting quietly, pen poised over a letter she is writing, Miss Amelia Hartshorn thinks of the Hills too, and with greater nostalgia and affection because she knows she is unlikely ever to see them again.

From somewhere just behind the house, a sudden wail, and then the brief noise of screeching, quarrelling voices rises and falls; and at once it is quiet again, and the heavy, sleepy stillness of mid-afternoon has scarcely been disturbed. Miss Hartshorn has almost learned to ignore such ripples upon the bland surface of everyday life, though always aware that the raised voices and screams and wails that may mean nothing more significant than a spat between the cook and the boy over utensils, may equally well signify riot, sickness, madness or sudden death.

In her innermost heart, she is still terrified of this bright, passionate, impenetrably strange country. She has merely learned to overlay her fears with apparent calm and indifference.

'The flowerbeds are very gay again,' she bends her head to write, 'they sow seeds one day and it seems they are all but up the next! I am still unused to the sight of hibiscus and plumbago and bougainvillea, cheek by jowl with pansies, asters, petunias and snapdragons.'

Kitty dozes, to the plashing of the fountain beneath her window. But in the Hills, there is always water, the ceaseless tumbling of it, down between the tree trunks into the river that flows far below. And the river forms the background to everything, though after a day or two there, one simply ceases to notice it.

In the end, between the fountain and the slight stirring of the breeze, she does fall soundly asleep. Come in to her some time later, Lady Moorehead is taken aback by the extreme whiteness of her daughter's skin, its delicacy. But above all, by the fact that she looks so young, so child-like again in sleep, and touches a finger to her cheek, and then bends to kiss her. Kitty stirs, but does not wake, and Eleanor Moorehead leaves the room quietly troubled, and rendered indecisive all over again by the subject that has been so preoccupying her, and about which she had all but made up her mind to speak to Lewis that night.

For what has flared up anew within her, fierce and fresh, is helpless love for her child, and the desperation of having Kitty, and only Kitty, as the focus of all her hopes and longings.

In her room, she sits again, without calling for the shutters to be opened, upright and tense, and thinks that time is cruel. It is a thought she is not particularly aware of having had in relation to herself before, so that the truth of it strikes her all the more forcefully.

3

THE VERGER was lifting the taper to light the candles on either side of the altar, and as they sprang to life, so did Giorgione's great picture that stood behind it. Pools of light fell here and there, on the sallow face of the potentate and the nut-brown face of the shepherd, upturned in adoration and on the gilded Offerings, and the serene young Madonna, the waxen-fleshed child and the roseate cherubs. Outside the lighted areas, the remainder of the picture was in gloom, though it was a coloured gloom, deep brown and indigo and the red-brown of old, dried blood.

It was a formal expression of religious sentiment, a glorious, distant thing. There was nothing personal, nothing intimate about it, and it neither invited nor repelled belief, it was simply a statement. Here, it said, is the Word made flesh; bow down and adore.

Only in the ecstasy of the expression of one kneeling figure, of no importance, in the bewilderment and humility and rapture that transformed it from an earthbound human being to one potentially immortal, did Thomas ever catch a glimpse of the glory of it all, only this obscure and shadowy corner moved him to more than dutiful admiration.

Now, in cassock and surplice, seated in his stall, he looked up at it again, and thought, yes, I see it. It is still there and it will never fade or be unavailable to me. In that one face . . .

The choir stood to sing the Magnificat. In the body of the chapel, a dozen worshippers knelt in the dimness. But the music and the voices would be raised, the worship conducted, regardless of whether there were eight or eight hundred in the congregation, and that pleased and satisfied him, that things were ordered as they should be.

He himself felt no religious fervour. What uplifted him, moved him to praise and wonder, was all elsewhere and had long been so, in a world quite outside this building, these people, this order of service. He had never truly felt even the young believer's ardour. He did not feel guilty about this. He was suspicious of the emotional. He had accepted what he had always been taught to be true, and had decided to commit himself to it, and in any case, it was all so much a part and parcel of the rest of his life, of his studying, his teaching and his official position in the college. He could not have told where religious belief and feeling began or ended, nor had he ever thought it necessary to brood upon those matters.

The notes of music dropped beautifully, clearly, separately, out of the air. 'Now Lord, lettest thou thy servant . . .'.

Only, he regretted the loss of something, he could not have said what, some yearning, some pure, spiritual ecstasy.

> Like as the hart panteth after the water brooks,
> So panteth my soul after thee, O God.

What he felt, here in this place, was a deep contentment, a sense of the rightness of things, and he thanked God with something approaching passion then, for his own good fortune, for his life here within these walls, and for all the rest that lay outside them. And at once, he felt a warm spurt of pleasure, thinking of the house, the conservatory, his study and what they contained, all waiting for him, and of the work ahead that was to be done, the new ideas that crowded in upon him daily. And all of this had been given to him in addition to the rest, and freely, and was more than he had any right to expect.

The rumble of benches, as they knelt to pray. Thomas bent his head and closed his eyes, and behind them came, all unbidden, the image of the boy Eustace Partridge's secretive, troubled face.

'Oh Lord . . .' for he had a duty to pray for him, though, knowing nothing whatsoever of what might be wrong, he could only pray unspecifically, committing him to God's care, and asking for wisdom and peace on his behalf.

On his own behalf, he prayed for nothing. His life was serene, and as he wanted it to be.

Behind the candles, the Magi adored, and the shepherds, and the Virgin sat for ever imperturbable, and the naked infant received its homage with an ageless, expressionless face.

Eustace Partridge lurked in the shadows beneath the high walls, guilty-seeming as a footpad or a vagrant; but he had committed, and would commit, no felony, and if asked his reasons for being here, would have had no answer. 'Is something troubling you?' his tutor had asked. He wished he might have told him, that he could unburden himself to someone, anyone, and so relieve this terrible waiting and not knowing, this tension and dread. But after all, what was there he might say? Nothing, for there might *be* nothing, it might not have happened or be going to happen, his world might continue as before and he would be reprieved. Or else there would be news, tomorrow or next week (surely it could not be much longer than that? But he realised that he did not know, and was appalled at the extent of his own ignorance).

Or else there might be silence, and silence would be as good as good news.

He shook his head to clear the buzz of confused thoughts and speculations. He knew he should go back to his rooms and work, or sleep, or else knock someone up, Hanson, or Agnew-Brown, and get drunk.

But he simply went on standing in the shadows, in the mist and chill, like a boy who has broken a vase and run away and dares not return home to confess.

And that was how he was inside himself, as miserable and

vulnerable and frightened as he had been at the age of four or eight or thirteen, whenever he had been faced with the prospect of having to see his father. For if it had all gone wrong, that was what he would have to do, face them all, one by one, or together, but worst of all, face his father.

I am a grown man, Eustace thought, and yet it is still like this.

Someone turned out of the college gateway and walked quickly away down the street towards the river. Eustace shrank back further into the shadows. But he thought that his tutor had not so much as glanced in his direction.

In the end, he went back to his rooms and ordered up supper, and when it came, to his own surprise he wolfed it down, and was comforted by the warm food and drink, as an upset child is soothed by a bowl of sweet pudding.

Georgiana, in her small sitting-room, at a round table covered in a dark green chenille cloth, the light of the lamp encircling her, and the pile of papers in front of her.

Ten minutes before, Alice had come in to see to the fire, which was burning sluggishly, as fires always did at this damp back-end of the year. But then, she had said, 'No, Alice, thank you, don't draw the curtains.' Though there was nothing to be seen outside. Only, she did not like to be closed in as early as this, to have the winter evenings seem any longer.

She turned back to her work.

'Bazaar' she had written.

'Sale of handiwork.'

'Subscription ball.'

'Lantern lecture?'

Where she paused, wondering if it were true that the Misses Tufnell were really friends of Lady Leonora Fletcher, who had crossed Afghanistan by mule, and if so, whether she might be persuaded to come and speak about her travels in public. According to Florence, they knew her well, might even be on visiting terms, though someone else had doubted they were more than acquaintances, and not even recent ones at that.

And would people pay to come?

'Donations' she wrote, and looked at the word and felt depressed, thinking of all the hours of list-making and letter-writing.

'Dear Lady . . . Dear Duchess . . . I wonder if I might bring a cause with which I am closely associated to your kind attention?'

Well, it would have to be done, though perhaps she might manage to foist much of the letter-writing itself onto others. But it was a sure way of raising at least some of the money.

At the meeting of the Committee for Moral Welfare, on the following day, they were to be told exactly how much they needed, either to build a new house, or, if that were to be too costly, buy and convert an existing property, for use as a Home for girls and unmarried women who were with child, to live in during pregnancy and confinement, and for the period immediately afterwards.

Florence had found a manor house, in a secluded situation in a village seven miles outside the town. None of the others had yet been to see it – it was empty, and slightly derelict. But Florence had been forceful about it for some weeks and was sure to be even more forceful tomorrow, since the Committee was meeting in her own home, which always gave one a certain advantage in pressing points.

But others felt it would be more practical for the Home to be established within the town itself.

It had all been taking up much of Georgiana's time during the past months, and now that the project did, at last, seem to be coming to fruition, it would take up even more. It was time she gave gladly, believing passionately in the cause. For Georgiana always had a cause to which to devote her energies.

Now, looking again at the pencilled note, 'Lantern lecture?', her mind strayed to Lady Leonora, who had been, she knew, the insignificant fourth daughter of a minor duke and who, at the age of twenty-nine, still at home, and plain, with dwindling prospects, had decided to take up travel. Now, seven years on, she had been, as well as to Afghanistan, to India, Pakistan and Persia, and was rumoured to be planning a journey to the Amazon Basin. She travelled alone, used native bearers and guides, and had put herself into innumerable situations of danger and discomfort. She excited admiration and disapproval in equal measure, had been disowned and subsequently, as her fame had spread, reclaimed by her family.

And Georgiana envied her and sometimes, as now, indulged in fantasies of emulating her, of going away from here, somewhere – she thought idly of mountains and deserts and of seeing places previously accessible to no Western woman. And the mist closed in across the Backs and pressed up the dark garden towards the house, and the clock chimed six and then ticked softly on, and looking up, she thought that she must wash and change and then go to speak to Alice about a duck for tomorrow's dinner.

The fire was beginning to glow a little at the core as she dreamed her brief dream, and all the time knew that she would do no more than take a walking holiday in Switzerland. If Florence could be persuaded.

After supper she might go and talk to Thomas about the Committee meeting, ask his opinion on the subject of the house purchase, for there were persuasive arguments on both sides, though she herself was inclining to agree with Florence, that the young women would be better off cared for somewhere discreetly in the country.

And then, they might all three discuss it at dinner tomorrow. She wondered how she might broach the subject of 'dinner tomorrow' to him. And so, tapping her pencil on the pile of papers as she sat in the light of the lamp, turned her mind to contemplating that.

Thomas crossed the bridge and walked briskly down the avenue, under the dripping trees, light of step and of heart. But behind him in the shadows had been Eustace Partridge, though he was sure that the boy had not seen him. He wondered again what might be wrong, and what he himself ought to do, and was mildly irritated by it all, liking the tenor of his life to remain even, and people to behave predictably.

There was no one about. As he reached the corner, he stopped. Ahead, the avenue of houses, set behind their drives and lawns. But beyond them, the fields began, and just at this point, there was something in the air, a smell of the open countryside, and a particular wind that blew off the far Fens. That was what had made him pause. For he felt pent up on these lowering days of early dark, needed to get out under wide skies and across the marshes. He closed his eyes and the air smelled colder, fresher. One day next week, he thought; he could take the train on Friday evening and stay at Clawdon Quay, be up and out in the boat before dawn. Yes.

As he passed the gate of the house fifty yards from his own, a cat came slinking out from the bushes and followed him. He stopped at once and turned on it, hissing, but it did not retreat, only stayed beside him and then began to weave around his legs. Thomas shuddered, and pushed at it with the side of his foot. But the sleek, coiling body evaded his movement, and the eyes stared up at him without blinking.

If he could have killed anything in his life, it would be a cat. He was not in any way afraid of them, he simply hated them, for what they were and would do.

Above all, he did not want a cat to follow him to his own house. In the end, because the creature sat down beside him and he could not get rid of it, he crossed the road, and recrossed it some yards further up. Looking back, he could see the cat watching him, topaz-eyed, out of the darkness.

Georgiana, still sitting in the circle of lamplight beside the fire, heard his footstep and the opening of the front door, and started, and for some reason felt guilty. She did not like idleness in others, and was ashamed of being caught out in it herself.

But I was not idle, she said, I was preoccupied, what with the Committee and the question of the Home, and whether, after all, it would be best to order a duck for tomorrow's dinner or – in case that should seem too much as if she were wanting to make an occasion of it – fall back upon a simple fowl.

She began to sort her papers and put them together.

But she heard his footsteps retreat across the passageway, and then the closing of his study door. He was not going to come and see her, and would have no idea of what she had, or had not, been doing.

Well then, a duck after all, she determined, and *let* us make it an occasion.

And went off to the kitchen, to speak to Alice.

4

NOW THE house stirs again.
Kitty must be dressed in several layers of uncomfortable clothing (her second-best white with
the high frilled collar has been laid out) and go out with
Mama to take tea at the club. She must submit to having her
hair pulled back and plaited (for she is not yet sixteen and too
young, Lady Moorehead feels, to be allowed to wear it up,
or loose).

But for the moment, she stands at the window and watches
the play of sunlight on the fountains, and suddenly, feels
energy, her own youth and confused desires, *life*, well
up inside her, and does not know what she might possibly
do with it, and in a great flurry, rushes out of the
room and through the passages and the cool hall onto the
porch.

So that her father, just returned home, calls out, 'Kitty,
Kitty – where are you going at such a rate?', laughing. But
she waves and runs on into the garden, and perhaps does not
hear him.

Only, stopping somewhere, down one of the gravel paths,
beside the lawns where the grass is the vivid green of the new
season, Kitty runs out of steam and stands stock-still again,
irresolute, and a little foolish.

'Kitty might still be six years old.' Lewis has come into the
room, laughing indulgently.

'She is almost *sixteen*!' And she says it with such passion
that he swings round in surprise to stare at her.

'Don't worry about her.'

'No. But then, of course, I *do*, I fret over her the entire time.'

But then she smiles brightly and rejects his outstretched hand, not wanting to have this conversation now, when she is not completely prepared for, or relaxed about it.

'Are you coming to the club?'

'Later.'

'Yes. Well then . . .'

Lewis waits, lets her call the tune, as always, thinking again, she is too rare for this place, for me, still unable, even after nineteen years, to believe his own luck.

At the door, she hesitates.

'Lewis . . .'

But it is all jumbled in her head – Kitty – her restlessness, which was plain for all to see – her being still a child and almost a woman – her cleverness – what ought to happen – what she herself wants – what Miss Hartshorn . . . and that was another thing – Miss Hartshorn.

'And now we shall be late for tea.'

She turns away and it is the same, abrupt impatience of movement that he had recognised in Kitty, dashing down the steps. He shivers, taken for a second by an appalling dread of losing either of them, and it cannot be a cloud crossing the sun, for clouds do not stray in that occasional manner here.

5

I T WAS quite a dark room, not large, and the conservatory led directly out of it.

On two walls, his books – ornithology, with some geology and botany lower down, and, here and there, a little literature. But the theology and classics, tools of his daily trade, had no place.

His maps were raked below a specially built table, on which he could spread them in a frame, and beside them, the cabinets of birds' eggs, arranged beautifully in their drawers. Above, and taking up every other available space, the drawings and water-colours and identification charts of all the pale, delicate sea-birds, graceful of wing and leg, the colour of pebbles and waves, of sky and cloud, shore and shell.

Thomas stepped inside and closed the door and for a moment stood quite still, and felt the familiar satisfaction and pleasure, and the absolute sense of his own identity.

The fire burned sweetly, the lamp was lit, the room waited.

But first, he must see to the birds.

In summer, the whole outer wall of the conservatory slid back, and then the aviary was open to the sunshine and the outside air, and belonged more to the garden than the house. But now, the heat was on and the moisture that rose from the small pool in the centre, with its trickling fountain, made the air steamy to breathe.

He switched on the lights, and at once the cages came alive

as the tiny birds began to flit and flutter from side to side, flashing emerald and orange, black and saffron and scarlet wings, and the humming birds hovered, whirring softly in mid-air, and the cheeping rose from the cage like a cloud.

He went to the far end and carefully unhinged the door and let it swing open.

For several moments, the birds fluttered about in agitation. But then, first one, then others, flew out and straightaway up towards the roof, and then down again, to alight on the branches of the tree that grew up from the floor, where the earth had been left exposed in an area surrounded by a stone ledge.

He began to go methodically round, replenishing seed and water dishes, cleaning and tidying, and once or twice paused, as a bird came close to his hand, or darted into the cage and out again, and froze stock-still as a zebra finch settled briefly on his shoulder.

And, coming in to tell him that dinner was ready, because of course he had not heard the bell, Georgiana saw him from outside, and watched in silence, knowing that he was entirely content, that there was apparently no room for anything else in his life, and wished that it were not so, thought for the thousandth time that it could not, surely, be right.

Thomas glanced round, sensing her there, and gestured for her not to open the door.

'Dinner is ready,' she mouthed at him. But he only nodded, and went on with the bird cages.

Georgiana turned impatiently away, thought, he has never needed me, not as, since the day that I was born, I have needed him.

As a child, barely able to walk, she had followed after him, in and out of rooms, up and down stairs. He had been endlessly tolerant of her. When he had gone away to school at the beginning of every term, she had wept, days and nights of abandoned, desperate tears, had felt as if the solid ground had given way beneath her.

The plain truth is, she said now, that he needs no one. No one at all. Well – he should be *made* to need . . .

She returned to tell Alice not to wait, but to serve dinner, thinking, let him eat it cold.

'He needs no one.'

But he arrived at the same moment as the soup.

He wiped his mouth fastidiously, before laying his napkin down. 'Really,' he said, 'there seems no doubt about it, Georgiana, and nothing to discuss.'

'You are so dismissive. Why must you be?'

'No.' He spoke quite kindly. 'Not that I hope. Of course, I know how conscientious you are and that you want to do what is right. You are concerned.'

'Then why cannot you be concerned?' She rang the bell rather too hard. 'Oh, I know what you are going to say – that it is no business of yours. But I want to make it your business – at least for the moment.'

'Yes.'

He was silent, and at once she felt ashamed of her own abruptness. For why should any of it be of interest to him?

'I'm sorry for raising it.'

'No,' he said evenly. 'You were right. You've a duty to weigh all the considerations carefully, of course.'

'Well – it is important, Thomas, not just some idle women's business to fill up my time. I want you to know that.'

'I do know it.'

'I value your opinion – and your good opinion of me.' Oh, she thought, as she spoke, yes, that is the one thing I have valued, have longed for, all my life.

'You know perfectly well that you have that.' He was laughing.

'Don't tease.'

Alice came in, with a Queen of Puddings.

'It is simply that there seems to me nothing to be gone

over. It is perfectly clear that your Home will have to be in the country. How could it be any other?'

But the moment he spoke so decisively, she saw with extreme force and clarity the strength of all the arguments against it.

'They would need to be near the doctors – and perhaps within reach of their families, who would want to visit.'

'Would they?'

'Some would. Or at least, they ought not to be made to feel they were being deliberately cut off from them.'

'Isn't it more than likely the families would think otherwise? Would want them as far out of sight – mind even – as possible.'

'Besides,' Georgiana ploughed on, 'in the country, they would only have one another for company and – and influence – which might, of course, be all for the bad.'

'Too late to worry about that by then, I should say – wouldn't you?'

'And then . . .'

But she had foundered and he knew it, and waited calmly for her to finish.

'The fact is,' he said, 'it would be a charity to these – young women, to put them in a Home in the country. They would be spared the prying eyes and the malicious tongues. They might even salvage a little of their reputations by being out of sight until they can return. And besides, surely the air would be healthier.'

'Well – perhaps you are right. At any rate, I am grateful to you for letting me talk it over.'

'And you will talk it over again at your Committee.'

'It will have to be decided, yes. But most likely we shall have to spend too much of the time talking about money.'

Thomas got up from the table. 'It is disturbing that the subject should have to take up anybody's time at all.'

'I daresay. But I'm afraid that, human nature being what it so often is . . .'

'Yes.'

'Are you going back to the study?'

He hesitated.

'Only so that I may tell Alice where to bring the coffee. And perhaps I may join you a little later?'

For she had still not broached the other matter.

Thomas nodded. 'Whatever you wish, of course,' walking briskly to the door.

Out in the dark garden, among the dismal rhododendron bushes, the cat which had made Thomas so agitated, prowls, and will soon slip even nearer to his house, confident of mice, but also sensing rarer prey.

And in other corners, other cats, yowling for lust as well as blood.

Out on the marshes miles away, a thousand wild birds roost, secret among the sandbanks, the hollows and the fidgeting reeds.

But in India, the gaudy birds that are two a penny, shriek and cackle all day, and flaunt themselves.

And in other hiding places, very different creatures, warm, pliant girls and urgent, persuasive young men, press together against tree trunks, in outhouses and boat-houses and alley-ways and even on the memorial bench in the pretty little overgrown garden behind St Botolph's church, and whisper and kiss and attend only to the moment, never to their futures, which Georgiana and her Committee may sooner or later oversee.

She did a thing that she had not done for years.

In a drawer of one of the back bedrooms, lay oddments of uncompleted sewing, and she rummaged about until she found something acceptable, a cushion-cover, half embroidered, and with the remaining silks and needles stuffed inside. She did not remember it, had no idea at all whether it had been a project of hers from girlhood, or even of some nursemaid or companion half a lifetime ago.

It was not unattractive, a modest circlet of pansies and violets interlocked in shades of mauve and blue, with white. And perhaps she should make an effort herself to provide some things, if they were to have a Sale of Work.

But that was not the real reason. She felt awkward, suddenly, wanting to sit with Thomas, wanting to talk to him, and to broach the subject of tomorrow evening, yet hesitant and embarrassed. Fearful of his reaction.

But how perfectly ridiculous, she thought, I am a grown woman, intending to invite an old friend to dinner, and that is all.

And took up the bag of embroidery and swept calmly through her brother's study and out into the conservatory.

Only that, of course, was very far from being 'all'.

He sat in a basket chair in the shadows, the birds busy here and there secretly among the leaves.

He said, 'But you never sew! You are not that kind of woman.'

And what kind of woman am I? she might have asked, or what kind of woman is it who sews? But did not, only threaded another needle clumsily, inexpertly, as he watched

(35)

her. And set aside the consideration of what kind of woman she felt herself to be – aspired to be, perhaps – until she was alone and brave enough to face it.

Instead, she simply looked across at him, and said, 'I have asked Florence to dine with us tomorrow evening.'

'Ah. Then I shall be dining in Hall.'

'Don't be ridiculous!'

'I shall be dining in Hall.'

Georgiana stood up, letting the embroidery drop to the floor, and began to pace up and down, annoyed, discomforted, angry beyond bearing.

'Please sit down, you will agitate the birds.'

'*How* can you be so churlish? How can you be so ill-mannered?'

'You had much better sit down again and try to be calm.'

'Florence is my friend. She has been a very *good* friend to me.'

'I know it, and I am glad of it. I would not have it otherwise, naturally. But you know perfectly well that I will not tolerate your machinations.'

A small, quick, scarlet bird was keeping pace with her, crossing and recrossing in the air, as she crossed the tiled floor.

'She has everything you could want.'

'But I do not.'

'Everything you could hope for. Beauty. Intelligence. Money. Presence.'

She stood immediately in front of him, her heart pounding.

'Georgiana . . .' For he hated her to make a fool of herself. 'Why must you say all this?'

'Suppose it is simply that I am tired of being your house-keeper.'

She had shocked him.

'I sincerely hope that is not how you see yourself! Of course that is not the case and you must know it, this is your home as much as mine, it has always been your home.'

'And if I were to wish to leave it?'

Thomas stared at her.

'Do you?' he asked quietly, at last.

'If I wished to . . .'

She turned away, went to the window and stood, looking out into the dark garden, but saw only his reflection, tall as a crow, behind her in the lighted glass.

She said, 'You would need a wife.'

'I should not.'

'Then what, pray?'

'You know full well.'

'Oh . . .' She spun round, furiously impatient. 'Oh yes, I know – those college bachelors . . . old men . . . *soup-stained*!'

She left, and the embroidery lay where it had fallen to the floor, until the next morning, when Alice picked it up and returned it tidily to the back bedroom drawer, and it was never touched again.

And after a while, the little birds settled, the agitation over.

But he could not settle. So that, in the end, he went out, to the far end of the garden, where the grass gave way to scrub and the night air smelled of the pine needles that had been pressed underfoot into the earth.

And the cat slunk back into the deepest shadows and was gone, and he had never been aware of its presence.

Georgiana, getting ready for bed, felt battered by emotions that washed up against her, receded, broke over her again.

She was annoyed at herself, and angry with Thomas, embarrassed and frustrated. But the strongest feeling was of shame and the loss of pride.

She, too, was unsettled. Went to the window and opened it, closed it again, fidgeted in drawers, brushed and rebrushed her hair.

Above all, she did not want to forfeit his good opinion of her, that mattered, as it had always mattered, more than anything.

But how should I go about things? she asked of her mirror image, holding the brush for a moment in mid-air. And felt herself to be inept at the business of life, unable to grasp the subtleties of it. I am clumsy at it, like some gauche girl.

What I want is his happiness – *their* happiness, I want what would surely be best for them both.

But at once saw through herself and her own manipulations.

She turned out the lamp and lay, wide-eyed, and suddenly, bleakly, she saw them, all three, as barren for ever, dry, joyless people, and saw them as growing old like it, too, to no purpose, while the girls they were so conscientiously feathering a nest for . . .

But she knew it would not be as comfortable as that.

A flurry of rain against the window, and her thoughts stirred about, hearing it, until they rested lightly upon the time of year, the month, the date, and the recollection that it was Nana Quinn's birthday. Ninety-one? Two?

At once, the old woman's face was before her, and the bent back, draped in the brown shawl, and Georgiana was a child again, peering into the hollow that was Nana's mouth, fascinated by the mumbling gums that sucked bread into a pap before she could swallow it. She could smell the smell of her, a rich, peaty, fleshy smell, not scented like that of her mother, or acrid, like the maids.

And thinking of her, in that beloved place, she was at once entirely happy, cocooned again in childhood, hearing the lapping of the water on the shore outside and the soft sweep of the rain, with Thomas asleep only a room away, and his promise to take her to see the swan's nest to hold fast to.

Smiling, she fell asleep and did not for one moment think of saying any prayers.

But, hours later, Thomas prayed, read the Divine Office, dutifully, and then the 104th psalm for his own pleasure, and the words were sonorous to him and steadied his mind and heart again at last.

6

THE COMMITTEE for Moral Welfare was touring the house in the country, led, upstairs and down, in and out of rooms, by Florence, who had organised it all.

There were seven of them, and Dr Whyte-Simon, co-opted for the morning for his professional opinion.

'Bedroom.' Florence strode along a narrow corridor, pushing open doors with the ferrule of her umbrella. 'Bedroom. Bedroom.'

They had been maids' attics, and perhaps a nursery, too. Wooden bars were nailed across the windows.

'It smells very damp,' someone said.

Yes, Georgiana thought. Damp. Mice. Decay. Aloud: 'Must they be made to feel they are coming to a prison?'

Florence turned and cast one of her most brilliant smiles over her shoulder. She wore a silver-grey coat, tight-waisted, with a full skirt, and her deep red hair coiled and piled elaborately.

She said, 'Well, of course, we would be completely refurbishing it all.' With a sweep of the hand.

'But how much might that cost?'

Miss Quayle, the rich brewer's daughter.

'It needn't be prison-like. But we are not providing them with an *hotel*.'

'There is a back staircase, of course, down to the kitchens.' And Florence moved them all on, and Miss Quayle's voice came back up the stairwell, peevishly complaining.

The dust settled.

Georgiana hung behind in the long attic, and tried to see it with more hopeful eyes, freshly painted, light, airy. Beds with white coverlets, she thought, a cabinet each for possessions. And the little cribs.

Beyond the small, barred, dirty window, the flat, flat countryside, field after brown field, without dip or undulation, or the softening shelter of any trees, and the dun-coloured sky reached down to meet the land at the horizon. She imagined it here in February and March, the wind cutting across the flat land and into the house through every crevice, the low, heavy-bellied clouds, the rain, rain, rain.

There was a drive, overgrown with weeds and a scrubby hedge, and the gardens were a ruin of nettles and thistles and the remnants of a few hollyhocks, shrivelled and blackened in the damp cold air.

Beyond the house and drive, the lane, leading to a straggle of cottages, a mile away.

She felt total despair, in the place, the situation, and in what they were planning, despair for the young women who might come here.

A tiny spider let itself down on its spinning thread in the air in front of her face.

What would we be thinking of, to bring them here?

It is . . . *desolation*.

She heard Florence's voice below, energetic, persuasive. And saw her married to her brother, installed in their household, dominating them all. Saw, too, how handsome they would look, admired across rooms, together.

While I . . .

The world unrolled, tantalising, before her.

But in the yard at the back of the long grey house, among the broken paving-stones and the old roofless stables, the miasma of depression and disillusionment clung close to her as cobwebs again, and Florence's enthusiasm and determination could find no chink to penetrate.

We are barren, Georgiana thought. And I would never dare to go.

From the doorway of the cottages, labourers' wives and solemn children stood frozen-still, and stared at them, as they drove by, back towards the town.

Florence and Georgiana sat side by side, in cocoons of separate thought, looking out at the November fields. While in Dr Whyte-Simon's carriage, the talk was vigorous, and all of money.

Florence's mother, old Mrs Gray, sat in the window-seat and ate fruit muffins and read the newspaper through a strong magnifying glass brought up very close to her face.

Rain curtained the Backs.

A cobbler had been brought to trial for murdering seven women after tattooing them with an awl. Evidence of the mesmerising charm of the man, as well as details of some of his extraordinary habits, was given by his wife and two other women, who had been his mistresses.

It was all remarkably absorbing, and she was confident of remaining uninterrupted, for the outing of the Committee for Moral Welfare would doubtless be followed by yet another meeting somewhere, yet more talk.

Their house was one of the handsomest and best positioned in the town, and very much too large for them. They had been moved into it after the death of her husband, the former Warden, possession granted by favour of the College until some future, unspecified date. Which she took to mean, once she herself was dead.

And Florence then?

Two grown men walked along the path towards the bridge in gowns, without coats or umbrellas, heads inclined together, talking, talking. Philosophy, she thought, or Thucydides, or inorganic matter. It was all talk, here.

She had lived in Cambridge for more than half a century, and it had never ceased to interest her.

But she had never been happy. Never belonged. Only made the best of it, and pursued her own thoughts, and looked round occasionally, in bewilderment at finding herself here at all.

Passion, she supposed. Love. Yes, that was what had brought her. She remembered a passion that had made one a foreigner to oneself. And then one awoke in a strange country.

But at least the rain had always been familiar. She had grown up in a castle in the Scottish Highlands. Remembered mists and mountains and travelling great distances in extreme cold, discomfort and excitement to other castles, to eat huge meals and dance reel after heady reel.

And solitude. The open air. And rain. Rain without cease.

He had been a visitor to neighbours, sixty miles away. Within a week, he had proposed to her, two months later, during his next vacation, they were married.

She had scarcely been back.

Now, she rang the bell for a second pot of tea.

At the Old Bailey, the trial of the cobbler had been adjourned. He had sat, head up and defiant, throughout the evidence of the three women.

Passion, she thought. Passion.

She would not have wished to end her life in this place, nor chosen to have her only daughter married and widowed and in possession of a small fortune by the age of twenty-one, without, apparently, having known anything approaching passion. And now, how would she get through the rest of her life?

The cataracts made her eyes water, she was obliged to put

the newspaper down, and after that, simply to look out of the window at the rain. But she had been an onlooker all her life, and so found it no hardship.

The day passed. The rain fell. There were no visitors. At seven, she rang the bell and said she would take an egg on a tray, as it seemed clear Mrs Bowering would not be in to dinner.

Beside himself with dread and the tension of waiting, unable to work or sleep, or to unburden himself to anyone, Eustace Partridge took a train to London. He had no idea what he might do there.

As they passed out of Cambridgeshire, towards the end of the afternoon, the rain eased and a shaft of late sunlight gleamed on the back of a pheasant, flurrying out of a hedge bottom into a field, and, seeing it, he longed to be out, striding on up to the ridge. His fingers tightened on an imaginary gun.

It was the only thing that he shared now with his father. Though usually, they merely walked and stood and shot and called up the dogs, there was never any conversation. But that did not trouble the Major.

He had no idea if he would ever be allowed to go back there, no idea at all of what might happen to him, and to his future. He had been a disappointment enough, refusing to go straight from school into the army. When the letter of acceptance and congratulation had come from the Senior Tutor of the College, his father had held it at arm's length.

'Cleverness,' he had said, 'cleverness is all very fine. And what about the rest of it?'

Cleverness. But that would not save him now. He had not been so very clever.

If.

His troubles buzzed about like bees trapped inside his skull.

Outside, the afternoon dwindled away to nothing. By the time the train reached London, it was dark.

But in London, there were street lamps, and there was noise, there were people going about with a purpose. Cabs. He took one as far as the West End, and began to walk down towards Piccadilly.

In his college rooms, a letter, come by the late afternoon post, lay on the oak table, awaiting his return.

7

I T IS late afternoon. Time, of course, to be at the club again. Where Kitty has been for an hour or two already, playing tennis with the Swainson girls. But Lady Moorehead has been out visiting and only just arrived.

And Miss Hartshorn does not come at all, she feels uncomfortable at the club, unwelcome (though a point has always been made of welcoming her), out of place (though a place has always been found for her at once). She stays at home, making notes at a wicker table in the shade of the verandah, a pile of books at her side. Tomorrow, she intends to continue their study of the Lakeland poets.

'Kitty is much admired.'

Lady Moorehead turns her head in surprise. She is drinking a glass of iced tea, sitting beside the Sub-Collector's wife.

'Kitty?'

She looks over, towards the courts.

'They have so much energy!'

The girls do not play well but they play with tremendous enthusiasm, flinging themselves about in every direction after the most hopeless of balls, to shrieks and peals of laughter.

'You have not been watching as carefully as I have.'

Eleanor Moorehead follows her companion's gaze, to where one of the handsomest of the young officers is standing, viewing the game.

'He has been all eyes for Kitty.'

'What nonsense!'

'Well, I shouldn't dismiss him, he is very highly thought of. His name is Penderly and he is a viscount.'

'And Kitty is a child. No young man should be looking at her at all.'

'Oh, don't worry, my dear, Kitty has not noticed.'

'I should hope not. If he does not turn away soon, I shall have to go over and speak to him.'

But as she says it, several more young men arrive, and he does move, to join them.

'There – not so much as a backward glance. So that is that.'

'Well, she will have plenty of rivals after tomorrow. The Fishing Fleet is due.'

'Oh, that is such a vulgar expression.'

'Accurate, nevertheless.'

The women smile. Marjorie Marchmont has only sons, and so is blessedly free of the problems of finding eligible young men for daughters to marry. For that is the purpose of the return of the Fishing Fleet of young women, come out from England for the winter to visit their parents, and in the hopes of making a good catch.

'Of course, there is no harm in having a girl marry and settle rather young.'

'Now here they are, all hot and excited, and you are to stop this talk.'

I am being teased, thinks Eleanor, and I cannot take it, not about Kitty. And looking at her as she comes up, flushed and with her hair all anyhow says, oh, but she is quite beautiful. And her heart almost stops.

'Child, child, now sit down quietly and have some tea, you are steaming like a pony and it is not at all becoming.'

Kitty laughs and sits down at her mother's feet in a cloud of white muslin and shining hair.

'It is all so much *fun* for you girls nowadays.'

Kitty stares at Mrs Marchmont. But says politely after a

moment, 'Oh yes, of course, it is great fun.' Yet the life seems suddenly to have gone out of her and her eyes are far away.

In the notebook that lies beside her, Miss Hartshorn has written:

Poems referring to Childhood
Poems founded on the Affections
Poems of the Imagination
The Period of . . .

Here, she has laid her pen down. It is quiet. There is only the soothing play of the fountain, some distance away. She feels more relaxed and more accepting of this place and of her own being here than ever before. She supposes it has to do with her decision. (For she is to leave, though neither Sir Lewis and Lady Moorehead, nor Kitty, yet know it. She has only written of it to her friend in Warwickshire.)

She has almost fallen asleep. From the kitchens, a gentle, rhythmic crooning, like an ayah's lullaby for a baby. But there is no ayah and no baby, it is the cook's old, blind grandmother, who sits outside all day, rocking herself and alternately dozing and singing.

And the singing weaves itself into the half-dream Amelia Hartshorn is having and is aware that she is having, and gradually, even the continual alarm bell that has gone on ringing deep within her without pause ever since she arrived in India is, if not stilled, at least grown so muffled and faint that she feels safe enough to pay it no attention.

Then there is something. The slightest sound. A shadow falling across the grass. She opens her eyes. And it is as though she has been turned to ice or stone, with fear.

The syce stands a yard or two away from her. He has come up, barefooted, soft as a panther.

Her mouth and throat are paralysed.

All of her horror and loathing of India, her revulsion from its sights and sounds and smells, and everything she has ever heard and believed about it, every rumour, whisper, story, superstition, rises up within her like a terrible bile. Only, because she is paralysed, it sticks in her gullet and cannot be vomited out.

His eyes are upon her intently; and yet somehow, not quite upon her. She sees a glaze over them, and a wildness in them. She remembers the times she has spoken to him sharply, imperiously even. Though it has only been in brave imitation of those around her, as she has tried desperately to behave in the proper way, even while knowing that it will never be natural to her. For she, too, is in the position of a servant, and the servants know it.

The garden is silent. The singing has stopped.

The man stands absolutely still, and now, she sees that he has something in his hand, a stick or a club. She stares in fascination at his long, brown, naked foot, which is slightly raised, as though he is about to step forward, wonders, in a strangely tranquil way, if this is to be her last sight on earth, this one man's foot, on the grass of Calcutta. For surely he means to kill her. His body quivers with intent.

Yet they are in the open, outside the house, and it is broad daylight.

But there is no one about, and the shutters are closed. She imagines hidden eyes, gleaming between the chinks. Perhaps they know. Perhaps it has been long planned.

All this goes through her head in the frozen instant before the syce leaps, lunges, his arm raised, and brings the wooden club hard down. She hears the slight swish through the air.

(48)

Behind her head, the snake drops from the verandah, stone dead onto the grass.

The man grins, a great, white grin of triumph, and pleasure.

8

FOR MORE than a week it had rained, the river was swollen and running fast, the Backs and the towpaths became flooded.

So that it was quite easy for the girl to wade into the water and drown, a little before midnight.

The body was found at dawn, by a ferryman. It was caught by the dress in the waters below the mill, and washed to and fro, and the dress clung close to the girl when the grappling hooks dragged her to shore, and clung, too, to the swelling of the child that was within her.

She had been the daughter of a drayman, living in a yard at the back of Silver Street, as the local newspaper, to Mrs Gray's edification, reported.

Georgiana and Florence were in the breakfast room writing appeal letters, the whole table had been cleared and given over to it.

But Alice had brought a tray of tea and buttered biscuits, and the evening paper, which made an excuse for a respite.

And so, reading the paragraph over Georgiana's shoulder, Florence reached out and tapped it with her finger.

'It is for *that*,' she said with passion, 'it is so that poor, wretched girls do not have to do that in their desperation. *That* is why we are here, and why we must raise the money.'

For the general response of the Committee to the house in the country, had been rather negative. And now they themselves were growing weary of writing the ingratiating letters, with the endless rain pattering on the windows. The room was stale, it did not seem to have come fully light all day.

Georgiana asked, 'How is Mrs Gray?'

'Oh, Mother has gone to visit some poor old woman in the cottage hospital. She is dying I think. Her husband was one of the college butlers, in their day. And then she is to pay a call on some newlyweds, just returned from their honeymoon tour – Vita Phipps's daughter. She will enjoy that. She will *scrutinise* them!'

'Then you will stay for supper?'

They looked at one another, and the glance held for a moment.

But Florence only said, 'Thank you' very smoothly. 'That would be pleasant.'

'Well, it would mean no need for any more interruptions. We can go on with the letters until just before.'

'Yes,' Florence said. 'So we can.'

But she stared out of the window and made no move to sit down at the table once more.

They had been watching the Painted Bunting, which had head fathers of a clear and most exquisite blue. It had come forward to sit on a branch very close to them.

But now, Florence had left the conservatory and was standing again in the study.

'But it is here,' she said softly, gesturing around her, at the frames of drawings, one below the other, on the walls, 'that your real love lies.'

Thomas stood in the doorway. 'The sea-birds. Yes.'

'And is your catalogue near to completion?'

'Oh, no. It will take me years, it is a life's work. Especially as, of course, it is *not* my life's work, properly speaking.'

'Only that of your heart.'

He smiled.

'It is the names,' she said. 'They have such beautiful names.'

And went along, reading them out aloud in her strong voice.

'Fulmar. Shearwater. Cormorant. Avocet. Turnstone. Kittiwake.'

'But then, of course, "spoonbill, gannet, shoveler, scaup and loon".'

She inclined her head, smiling.

Thomas crossed the room, and opened one of the chests.

'Look at these. They are new to me, they came from London quite recently.'

The portfolio, tied with black tape at all four corners, contained several dozen water-colours, of the whole sea-bird placed centrally, and sketched in around it, details of wing and beak, nest and egg and individual feather, together with a silhouette of the bird in flight. They were delicate, painstaking, opalescent in the beauty of the pale colours and fragile pencil lines.

Georgiana, stepping into the room, saw the two of them, framed together, heads bent, beside the lamp, and would have turned away again, leaving them alone. But seeing her, Thomas stepped back and gestured to her to come, and so the picture was broken.

She said, 'You have never shown these to me.'

'No.'

And she saw him as a boy again, sailing out with Collum O'Cool, the sea-birds soaring and swooping overhead around the boat, saw her brother looking up at them, the joy open on his face.

Coming in that evening, he had joined them at dinner without demur, and been more than civil. The talk had grown quite lively. Florence always listening to him with careful attention, before startling him by some remark.

But he respects her now, Georgiana thought.

He went to the bookshelf, and took out his copy of John Clare's notebooks, and now he read aloud from them, as they stood looking at him, his voice soft with pleasure.

The bittern, called here around the butter bump, from the loud noise resembling that word, haunts Whittlesea Mere, lays in the reed shaws. About the size of the heron. Flyes up right into the sky morning and evening, and hides all day.

'It is all very fine to play the scientific scholar.' He looked down in reverence at the book. 'John Clare was not a scholar. But I would give my arm to set it down as he does. And yet it is clear.' He tapped the page. 'The observations are exact. It is all here.'

Passion, Florence thought, hearing him. It is simply that. And at that moment, completely understood and respected him, and recognised the truth about him, too.

9

LEWIS AND Eleanor, late at night.
'She says she had been planning to leave in any case.
She had intended to tell us quite soon, but now, of
course, she wants to go at once. By the next available boat.'

'That is the shock. I daresay she will see things differently
in a day or so.'

'You really must take it seriously, Lewis. She is quite
adamant.'

'But these things happen in India every day. And after all,
she is perfectly all right. Sadu saved her life.'

'She knows that. But she says that she has hated it –
India – everything about it and the life here, from the very
beginning. She says she is terrified.'

'Shock. Shock and hysteria.'

'We cannot oblige her to stay. Oh, it is all very difficult.
She has really tried so hard with Kitty, tried to find things to
interest and stimulate her. She says Kitty is far cleverer than
she knows.'

'Perhaps . . .'

'Yes?'

'If things had been different. If Kitty had stayed at school
in England . . . But it is too late to repine about that now.'

'Oh, it was my fault, I know that.'

'My dear, I am not saying so. You know I have never
blamed you.'

'I was the one who couldn't bear to be parted from her,
who took her all the way Home and brought her straight
back again.'

Kitty had been eight years old. They had stayed in a quiet house on the Sussex coast for three months, and looked at school after school until, at last, one had seemed to suit. Eleanor had quite made up her mind. Only to realise, the day before Kitty's first term was to have begun, and when she herself was packed ready to return, that she could not possibly leave the child there. Nor could she herself have stayed. Other women did that, chose the children and abandoned their husbands, to a bleak life of work, the club, polo, for years upon end.

But Eleanor had cared too much about her marriage. And too much about her child, and so, had chosen them both. She and Kitty had travelled back to India joyfully together, and shortly afterwards, the procession of governesses had begun.

'There is no question of anyone's being to blame. You did what you felt was right.'

'And you?'

'If it had been a son . . . but Kitty has done very well, and I adore having her with us, you know that.'

'But now?'

'Now . . . I imagine she will have outgrown a governess altogether before very long, so perhaps it does not greatly matter. Her mind will be full of other things.'

'Yes. Tennis parties and gymkhanas and . . . and *chat*. But we have always agreed that we wanted more for her.'

'Well, I am not sure that I want a bluestocking for a daughter.'

'And *I* do not want a butterfly.'

'Well, I imagine if Miss Hartshorn seriously intends to leave and you think it best, we will find a replacement.'

'Yes. Perhaps that is the answer.'

'Have you something else in mind?'

'Kitty is so unsettled just now. You must surely have noticed. Her head is full of dreams.'

'All fifteen-year-old heads are full of dreams, of one sort or another.'

'And I do not want to have it turned too soon by some young man. She is very pretty.'

'Well, it will be turned sooner or later. Perhaps she had better begin to get used to it.'

'There *has* to be more to her life than . . .'

Than I have had. But she does not say it. And it is not so clear as that. She herself has been happy, has wanted nothing more.

Uneasy with the way the conversation has turned, he smiles, comes across and puts his hands on her shoulders.

Says, 'But I daresay when Miss Hartshorn has calmed down, she will decide to stay here, after all.'

For a moment, she is almost blinded by rage at his obtuseness.

Amelia Hartshorn lies, stiff, still, wide-eyed. From the garden, through the shutters, the night sounds of India. And through her head, reeling endlessly, silently, terrifyingly, the events of the previous afternoon, every detail seen, heard again, every fibre of her body reacting, over and over.

They have been kindness itself. Lady Moorehead has sat with her, listened, murmured comforts. The servants have brought fruit and iced tea, tiptoed about.

And the syce saved her life of course. And it is over, and perhaps they will not sympathise with her for very much longer.

It happens every day here, after all.

And through it all, she prays. Prays with a fervour she has not known herself capable of, a single-minded desperation. Prays for a place to be found for her on a boat soon, soon, to be gone from here. Prays for Home.

She cannot sleep and so, will not dream. But beneath the endless repetition, running through her head, is Home, England. She catches glimpses of it and tries to grasp them. But they fade. India is more powerful. India overcomes and obliterates, its appalling brightness, the blazing colours, the chattering, the smell, the horrors, the craziness, the bedlam of India, fill her head like the terrible, inescapable cry of the brain-fever bird.

And so she lies rigid, praying her passionate prayer, and so the night passes.

Kitty sleeps and dreams no dreams. But, waking at dawn, has a vivid recollection of walking with her mother along a flat, hard, shining beach in the rain. Watches the line of her footprints fill up at once with water, hears the sound of the sea and the cry of the gulls, remembers the joy she had in that great expanse. Remembers taking to her heels and running, running, running.

England, she supposes.

And turns, and sleeps again at once.

10

FLORENCE AND Thea Pontifex sat over tea in Thea's room in the women's college. They had been friends since girlhood but, in the face of opposition, Thea had attended the university, and so, gone on to teach. Florence had watched her without envy but rather, when she herself had married Chester Bowering at the age of twenty, with a considerable sense of superiority. She had treated Thea quite patronisingly.

Thea, clear of mind and of purpose, fair and generous of heart, had gone on her way steadily, aware of, but unconcerned by, Florence's airs.

Now, feeling herself to be a woman without a purpose in life, as well as grossly undereducated, Florence envied Thea.

She said, 'You are the one person I know who is entirely contented, who has no dissatisfaction.' Though even as she spoke, she recognised that it was not entirely true, and added, 'Or at any rate, the only woman.'

Thea smiled, poured more tea. The room seemed too small to contain all of Florence's restless energy.

'It is *perfect* here,' Florence gestured. 'You see, I am simply envious.'

And at that moment, meant it, and longed for what the college room represented, and which she herself had never known; attendance at stimulating lectures, afternoons spent in serious private study, the intense loyalty among a group of like-minded young women, talk late into the night, earnest, engaging.

It was a room full of character and interest, she thought,

with books, pictures, china, ornaments, journals, music, a crowded room, personal and supremely unfashionable.

'Perhaps it is not too late. I should like to embark upon some course of study. Learning is so important, you have shown me that.'

'Have you some particular subject that interests you?'

Florence rose and began to pace about the room, tall and dramatic, between tables and chairs, the desk and the piano.

'Oh, history perhaps . . . ancient history . . . the classics and early civilizations. Or then again, science . . . the new discoveries. Or something very pure – philosophy.'

Thea bent her head and busied herself with the tray.

'Well, perhaps it is best to be clear.'

'Yes. Oh yes. I understand that, of course. You have always been so sure, and then simply gone ahead.'

'Women are not indulged here. Any indecisiveness, any wavering, a suggestion that one is less than fully committed – and oh, it is so gleefully pounced upon. We have to be all that men are, but doubly so. And yet . . .'

She stood, 'Still women. Shall we walk outside a little before it gets quite dark? The rain has cleared now, I think, and you must see the viburnum in the far shrubbery, it is a mass of pink.'

They toured the paths. There was no one at all about.

'Of course,' Thea said, glancing sideways, 'we are a very closed society here. We are so far out, and I daresay we give off a slightly frumpish air – even conventual. We have very little male society.'

They reached the shrubbery and the bush, its branches starred with the sweet-smelling blossom. Thea sensed that Florence had a need to confide in her. But after a few moments of silence, nothing had been said, so that in the end, she herself asked more about the plans of the Committee for their Home in the country.

'Perhaps we could help in some way here. We are all so very fortunate . . .'

'Perhaps.'

'It must take up a good deal of your time.'

'Yes.'

'And energy.'

Florence reached out a hand and touched the blossom.

'But I think that you are so good and right . . . and . . . and *brave* to do it. It is so very important.'

Thea's round face shone, fresh and unblemished beneath the neatly plaited hair. She was a short, compact woman.

Abruptly, Florence asked, 'Is there nothing that you long for, quite passionately? *Want*?'

'Oh, all human beings have aspirations!'

'Aspirations! I was not talking of anything so elevated. *Wants* . . . Desires.'

Florence looked round the garden wildly. It was cold and almost dark and the rain had begun again. In the buildings behind them, she felt the presence of studious, purposeful, dedicated young women.

'This . . .' she gestured. 'I could never aspire to this.'

Nor ever want it, she realised. For the air would surely suffocate her.

'I must go back. Mother is on her own.'

'Oh do, please, give her my warmest greetings. I mean to come and see her once the term is over. We lead such full lives.'

They walked slowly to the gate. Shaking hands, Thea held onto hers for a moment.

'If there is anything . . . if I can be of some help? I felt sure there was something you wanted.'

'Ah.' Florence drew away her hand, smiled a sudden, dazzling, distant smile. 'What are mere "wants" beside so many aspirations?'

And felt nothing but relief at leaving them behind, relief and a return of the old sense of superiority towards Thea, as well as – for she had told the truth – envy.

But the outing had been for a purpose more considerable than friendship. It had been an exercise in keeping Thomas

Cavendish from her mind, and as such, altogether unsuccessful.

Wants, she thought now, in the darkness of the cab. I want.

For she recognised that it was nothing so gentle or so honourable as love. She wanted him, and wanted to succeed in getting him to marry her.

Like Thea Pontifex, his life was complete and satisfying to him, and he had not a moment's need of her. She felt similarly towards them both, felt irritation, superiority, envy, anger.

In the case of Thea, none of it greatly mattered.

In the case of Thomas Cavendish, whom she wanted, it did.

Well, she would go home. She would play backgammon or rummy with her mother, who had been too much alone, she would stay up late, as the old lady liked, would be companionable, affectionate. They would chat.

If I do this, if I am not neglectful, if I look after my mother tenderly and with complete devotion, then it will come out, like a game of patience, and I will be rewarded, I will have what I want. Or so the thinking ran.

At the corner, she stopped the cab. The driver was to wait.

The blinds of the house had already been drawn.

'Oh, Alice . . .'

'Good evening, madam?'

'It's quite all right. I know I'm not expected, but perhaps you would say . . .'

'I'm very sorry, madam, but there is no one at home. Mr Cavendish is in college, and Miss Georgiana has gone out visiting.'

'Well, never mind . . . it does not matter in the least.'

She did not know what she had hoped for. Only, on the spur of the moment, had wanted to be here, to step inside the house again. Perhaps to talk to Georgiana, have his name mentioned.

Or he might have been at home.

'But I would like just to leave some papers.'

'Of course, I'll put them on Miss Georgiana's desk. She always goes to it when she gets in.'

But Florence had swept away from her, down the passage.

'No, no, Alice, please don't trouble, I'll do it. And they are for *Mr* Cavendish. Don't let me interrupt you, I know where to go.'

She closed the door sharply behind her.

He was not there, of course. And yet he was, the room was full of him. The book he had been reading lay open on the arm of the chair. She went over to the desk.

Bird notes. His handwriting was spare, abbreviated, in black ink. Not easy to read. She stared at it, trying to force it to yield up something of the man to her. She felt a curious flutter of excitement, as though she were gazing into some intensely private diary, learning secrets. But they were simply names, descriptions, measurements.

She lifted her eyes from the book, to look slowly round the room again, wanting to hoard every detail of it, to remember everything. Thought, this would be my world. I would no longer be an intruder. But there was an acute, guilty pleasure in being in here alone, as though she had in some way caught and held something of him.

Across the room, the glass doors that led to the conservatory, and the other birds. She did not understand at all the appeal they held for him.

But she saw herself, seated in another chair, beside the lamp and opposite to him, reading, belonging.

Absorbed, she had heard no sounds. Now, there was Alice's voice, quite close, explaining, protesting, and the door had opened, Thomas came quickly, angrily, into the room.

11

'BUT YOU can hardly blame Alice. You have heard what she told you, that Florence simply marched in. Alice could not stop her. You know what she is like.'

'Incompetent.'

'Florence.'

'Oh, certainly. It is becoming all too clear. How *dare* she enter my room, and pry and poke about like that. What possible reason could she have?'

'Alice said something about papers . . .'

'Papers! She wanted to push her way in, to . . .'

'Oh, to *what*, Thomas?'

The door was ajar. From the hall, they heard the slightest of noises, instantly suppressed.

'You had better lower your voice.'

They were in Georgiana's small sitting-room. She had come in, soaked to the skin, from having walked down the avenue, to find her brother raging, as she had never seen him before, Alice stiffly self-defensive, Florence gone.

'Please sit down. If we must discuss this before I am even changed out of my wet clothes, then let us do so quietly and calmly.'

To her surprise, he did sit, and, looking at him, she saw that the anger had left him, and his face was pale, weary.

'I am sorry. Of course you are uncomfortable. Don't trouble about this, please.'

'I do trouble.'

She sat opposite him. He asked where she had been.

'Being patient while Adèle Hemmings's aunt shouted at me

about fallen women. Why is it that those who cannot hear well themselves believe the rest of us are stone deaf too?'

He smiled. 'Fallen women?'

'Adèle Hemmings's aunt is extremely rich.'

'Ah – the Committee . . .'

'But it was all a great mistake. I should never have gone. I had to shout my head off trying to explain what it was all about, and then be harangued for an hour about Jezebel. It would have been a good deal more satisfactory if I had been appealing for money to rescue fallen cats. Really, the house does smell so.'

'Perhaps Adèle Hemmings's aunt has lost her olfactory sense too. We must be charitable, Georgiana.'

'There, you are laughing now, so that is better.'

'You are very brave to go off on your fund-raising. Brave altogether, in such a cause.'

'Not brave, no. But we are so needed.'

'So I realise. It is all a great pity.'

'Well. Shall I ask Alice to bring in a glass of madeira? I feel I need to be warmed.' She reached for the bell. 'And you were home earlier than I had expected.'

'Yes. A pupil did not arrive. I was already concerned about him, he sent no excuse or apology. I left a message in his rooms. The servant seemed to think he had gone home rather suddenly.'

'Some family matter then?'

'He is supposed to ask for leave of absence. But he has been disturbed, I know. Well, I shall have to get to the bottom of it.'

Alice came in with the tray. Thomas spoke at once.

'Alice, I must apologise for my curtness earlier. Of course it was not your fault.'

Georgiana waited for some moments after the door had closed, before saying, 'Thank you. That was the right thing to do.'

They sipped the sweet, dark wine. She was about to tell him some remark of Adèle Hemmings's aunt, when he said quietly, 'I want you to assure me that you will say something to her.'

She waited.

'It is intolerable, Georgiana. *I will not have this*. I cannot bear it – I do not – I am not interested in that woman – or in any. I do not want to be – hunted. Hounded. Above all, I do not want to think that you are in some sort of conspiracy about this – whispering, plotting, like silly young girls, behind my back. I have spoken of it before and I have listened to the things you have said. But please understand me now. I was angrier than I know how to express to you when I came in this evening.'

'Yes. It was wrong of her, very wrong. Of course she should not have gone into your room. But I am sure that she meant no harm.'

'We neither of us know what she meant and I do not wish to hear any reasons, or excuses. I do not wish to hear the matter mentioned again. I would just ask that you – say something – make my feelings plain. I know I can trust you to behave tactfully – to – to respect my wishes.'

'Of course. It is only – oh, that I am so sorry you feel as you do. Not only about Florence but . . . you are my brother, I should so like to see you settled – loved. You are a good man, a . . .'

But she could find no way to continue. Only said, 'I am sorry if *I* have done anything to disturb you.'

He inclined his head. 'Let us talk no more about it. I know that you have understood. And now, you had better have a second glass of wine and go up to put on dry clothes.'

Obediently, she did so.

Old Mrs Gray played her cards wth meticulous slowness, periodically looking up from them to scrutinise her daughter's face.

But Florence was giving nothing away. She was only

grateful for the pauses and that she was not required to think or to play quickly. She was still considerably upset.

There is something, Mrs Gray said, something, and soon, I shall go to bed and think about what it can be.

In the meantime, she contemplated the queen of spades.

No one tends the garden behind the house of Adèle Hemmings and her aunt, it is entirely overgrown, as the garden of some ruin or uninhabited place, and so the cats have it quite to themselves, and rustle and slink there and often pounce, among the weeds and the tall grasses, and the skeletons of years lie unburied, white and frail, and the soft, furred, rotting bodies of those more recently murdered, it is a graveyard of small mammals.

But in the house, the cats preen themselves and are cosseted, they lie sleekly on cushions and in the folds of eiderdowns, with bland, closed faces.

When it is very late, Adèle Hemmings opens the door and stands, listening to the night, and imagines herself a cat, free to walk off alone and where she chooses, wonders about possibilities, shadowy in her mind.

But she does not move, goes nowhere. Only the cats flick past her skirts and merge with the darkness.

Florence was trying to remember what it was like to be married. She had a photograph of Chester Bowering, wide-browed, with the huge moustache that made his face look so foolish. But it yielded nothing, she could not breathe life into it, make him the reality he had been.

Deliberately, she thought of walking beside him, her hand in the crook of his arm. But she had taken the arm of other men in the formal, everyday manner, many times since then, and so the thought was meaningless.

Occasionally, she had woken in the night, and it had all been absolutely clear, so that she had almost believed he had been there, she had felt his hands, smelled the hair oil he had used. But fleetingly, confusedly, and nowadays rarely, so that even the wedding photographs and the ring she wore hardly convinced her that she had been married at all.

Chester Bowering had been an American. They had returned to live in Boston after a protracted honeymoon tour of Europe and she had begun to settle into society there as the wife of such a prominent man (he was a widower and almost forty, when he had married her), into being an American.

Eight months later, Chester Bowering was dead, fallen on his bathroom floor one morning from a haemorrhage of the brain. Florence had returned to Cambridge a few weeks later, bewildered and rather rich but, otherwise, strangely untouched by the whole business. The episode of her marriage seemed scarcely to have left a mark upon her.

Now, she wondered what she had ever felt for her husband. She had no recollection of it. She supposed there must have been love. She remembered a fondness, and an excitement, and she had been flattered, certainly. Above all, there had been a reassurance about him, he had seemed, in spite of being American, safe and familiar. Nothing more. But perhaps nothing more had been necessary.

But now, there was more. Passion, she thought. Passion. Though still, she knew it was not love.

Thomas had been white-lipped with anger. He had spoken to her as to a servant, caught in an act of petty theft, had asked her coldly to leave his house. Confused, disconcerted, she had not known how to respond, had simply gone. But outside, the feeling that had flared up within her had been anger. Anger, and a bitter determination.

Want, she thought. *I want*. And calmly, turned the photograph of her husband face downwards in the drawer.

In the end, weary of thinking, Mrs Gray fell asleep, though it irritated her that she had not found a solution. There is something, she said, over and over again, something. But, waking in the middle of the night, as she regularly did, realised that she had not been able to understand what there was because her daughter had looked and behaved in a way she had never done before.

12

EUSTACE PARTRIDGE put his head in his hands and wept and the tears ran between his fingers and down his wrists.

Thomas, watching him and shocked beyond belief, had no idea what to do or say. The boy had burst into his rooms, white-faced, in the middle of the morning, had said what he had to, and then, simply, sat down and wept.

A girl was to have his child. He scarcely knew her. She was the sister of an acquaintance from school, daughter of neighbours in the country. But otherwise, it seemed, quite insignificant.

He had been home. The whole story was out. There had been confrontations with both families. And now, Thomas.

After a while, Eustace raised his head and pushed a hand through his hair, said, 'I am most dreadfully sorry, sir.'

'Yes.' Thomas could not look at him. 'Yes.'

'Of course, I shall have to go down. I am to marry her.'

'And then?'

'I . . . I really don't know. That is – there is talk of the army. India. I don't want that at all. Or there is a possibility of helping to run the estate. They are . . . it is all being discussed.'

'I see.'

'I am sorry.'

'It is hardly necessary to apologise to me.' Though of course, he believed that it was.

The boy stared miserably at his hands. You are a child, Thomas thought, glancing at him, for the face was open with misery and had somehow become a child's face again, soft, unformed.

A strange desire to console him came to Thomas, to treat him as tenderly, as lovingly, as he supposed one would treat a small boy who had come to confess some trivial offence, and burst into tears in just this way.

But the offence was not trivial, though commonplace enough. And it disgusted him, he could neither understand nor sympathise with it. Above all, he felt, somehow, personally rebuffed, and was angry. So that in the end, rather than trust himself to speak at all, he simply sent the boy away.

Eustace Partridge went hopelessly, to stare out of the window of his room down onto the college courtyard and across the roofs of the town, in despair that through a folly he scarcely understood, or even remembered, he was to lose everything.

But the bitterest shame had been having to speak to Cavendish, and the bitterest disappointment too, for he had believed that his tutor not only thought highly of but warmly towards him. He had seemed to be an ally and a friend. The contempt on his face, the way it had closed against him, had shown him that there was no one on his side, and that he had no supporter, after all.

He remained at his window, brooding, regretting, and already felt quite detached from his surroundings, as though the college and its life and purpose already excluded him.

Of his future, and of the pert, pretty Mary Wimpole, he could not bear to think at all.

In the end, Thomas saw the Dean, and the Dean, who was a broad-minded and tolerant man, heard him out patiently, soothingly. Though Thomas could not be soothed.

'It is the waste, the foolish, unnecessary waste. He was a pupil I was proud to teach, he had one of the finest brains it had been my good fortune to encounter. There was excellence, there was achievement, and then, there was such promise.'

'You speak as if the boy were dead.'

'He is dead to me.'

'Try to see it this way – that this incident, and the disgrace of it, have ruined his life. To us, it is merely a passing disappointment. We have been let down. But he has failed his whole self. And so, we must be charitable.'

'He has thrown everything away – and for what?'

'Perhaps for a good wife and family, a happy life? We cannot tell. The situation could have been considerably worse. At least the girl is marriageable.'

Later, he spoke to Georgiana, not only of Eustace Partridge, but of the Dean. She said, 'He has a forgiving nature. He is a man of tolerance.'

'He took an easy attitude – a *lazy* attitude.'

'You are hurt. You feel that you have been personally betrayed.'

'He has betrayed us all, let us all down, for some idle passion. No – not even that, he said as much. He has not even that excuse.'

'And is there no possibility of his staying up to complete his degree? Could his father not . . .'

'The father is a boor and a philistine. I daresay this is all in character. He will like nothing better than an excuse to take the boy away. He has a dim view of scholarship.'

'Try to be forgiving.'

But he felt that his heart had been turned to stone and all his hopes and expectations dashed and he could not forgive.

Only, much later, he was overcome with remorse, and a picture of the young man weeping in his rooms came to his mind with such force that he put on his coat again and returned to college, meaning to see him and speak gentler words.

Georgiana had said, 'I hate it when you are so hard. That is not the brother I know.'

He bowed his head, against the wind and rain, and in acknowledgement of his own lack of charity.

The boy's rooms were in darkness, and when he sought out the servant, it was to hear that Eustace Partridge had already left the college.

Returning to his own desk, he wrote a short, anguished letter of contrition and, after addressing it, walked across the court and into the chapel. There, he knelt in the darkness and poured out his heart, prayed for the young man and his lost future, for the young woman and the unborn child, commended them all to God, and then turned his attention inward and searched his own soul, asking for the grace to have a right judgement in all things, and for the gifts of mercy, of humility and of love.

And the air seemed to seethe around him with the prayers of the centuries, they pressed in upon him, and he felt touched and uplifted by them, and as if his own prayers and his solitary voice had joined others, to become part of the fabric of the building. Relief filled him, and gratitude, he had a more immediate sense of the holy and live-giving than for years, and was profoundly comforted.

Three days later, he took the train to Norfolk.

13

OTHER GIRLS sit out on the verandah, sewing, writing diaries, sketching, gossiping, giggling. Drinking sodas and lime. And perhaps, later, a piano lesson.

But their mothers sit, too, and write endless chits, about that evening's dinner or the stores, or send messages, by the boy, about dances and dress patterns (for now the young women have arrived from Home, everyone is very much concerned with fashion, and refurbishing last year's dresses and ordering new. The returned girls are quizzed relentlessly for details of the latest collars and trimmings, hats and hems, the local dressmakers driven frantic with orders, toil and toil.)

And other women on other verandahs hasten to reply.

But Kitty does lessons every morning.

(And if they have ever disagreed about it, Eleanor has told Lewis that at least if Kitty is educated, she will make a better companion for a husband. Though she knows there is more to it than that.)

'Men don't want clever women. They don't want that sort at all.'

He has been tetchy, at the end of a day, gone off, irritably, to his bath.

But they talk on, through the open door. Only the boy has got the water at the wrong temperature, or else the soap does not lather.

'Kitty is going to marry. It goes against all natural thinking that she should be *clever*. Let her have fun, be admired. So long as she does not damage her reputation. George Springer's girls . . .'

She lets him grumble on, hearing the regular sluicing of the water down his back.

And of course, when he is out and dried and dressed, it has all been smoothed away. Then, they agree about Kitty after all, discussing George Springer's buck-toothed daughters, and having higher aspirations for their own.

For she is all they have.

Miss Hartshorn is much recovered.

(Though the terror will disfigure her dreams, sleeping and waking, perhaps for ever.)

But she is up and about and anxious to put on a brave face and be back to work, at least for the time being.

So here is Kitty, sitting beside her, listening.

It was a threatening, misty morning – but mild. We first rested in the large boat-house, then under a furze bush. The wind seized our breath. The Lake was rough. There was a boat by itself, floating in the middle of the bay below Water Millock . . .

When we were in the woods beyond Goldbarrow Park we saw a few daffodils close to the water-side. We fancied that the Lake had floated the seeds ashore, and that the little colony had so sprung up. But as we went along there were more and yet more; and at last, under the boughs of the trees, we saw that there was a long belt of them along the shore, about the breadth of a country turnpike road. I never saw daffodils so beautiful. They grew among the mossy stones around and about them; some rested their heads upon these stones as on a pillow for weariness and the rest tossed and reeled and danced, and seemed as if they verily laughed with the wind that blew upon them over the lake; they looked so gay, ever glancing, ever changing. This wind blew directly over the lake to them. There was here and there a little knot, and a few stragglers a few yards higher up, but they were so few as not to disturb the simplicity, and unity, and life of that one busy highway. We rested again and again. The Bays were stormy and we heard the waves at different distances and in the middle of the water, like the sea.

Miss Hartshorn falls silent, and for a long time they sit together, and the vision of the daffodils, the landscape of the Lakeside, of all England, lies between them, and they are speechless in contemplation of it.

And India stretches away all around, irrelevant, disregarded.

Kitty has a sudden picture of herself in a railway train, flashing across England, through the wet, green, flat fields that run towards the coast, sees her own feet sticking out in front of her, beneath a blue serge coat. Sees her shoes, black-buttoned, with a scuff on each toe. Sees the very marks on the floor of the carriage.

The volume of Wordsworth's poems is open on the wicker table. Miss Hartshorn looks down. Will say 'And then, of course, there is the poem itself. Her brother's poem. But that came later, that was not written until 1804.'

And she will take it up and read it aloud. (She reads rather well.)

But not yet. Now, they are still too much in the midst of it all. They sit on.

'Oh, I want to go there, to be there, to see for myself. To walk beside the Lake, climb the crag, stand in the rain, feel the cold wind on my face. To read more, read the others. To see their graves. I want it all so much.'

Kitty's head is a confusion of disconnected fragments. Names. Places. Hopes. Dreams.

But she says nothing.

From the house, a burst of singing, half-chant, half-melody.
 Silence.
 Eyes closed, Kitty recites.

>   I wandered lonely as a cloud
>   That floats on high o'er vales and hills,
>   When all at once, I saw a crowd,
>   A host of golden daffodils . . .

(For she has memorised it long ago.)
 Hearing her, Miss Hartshorn weeps.

Eleanor sits opposite the young woman whose child has died of cholera, the previous day. The fan goes round and round, round and round in the ceiling, and the room is rather dark.

 The first few, formal murmurs having been made, there is nothing at all that she can think of to say.

 But the mother talks.

 'He seemed *perfectly well*. Nothing was wrong. When he went to bed he was . . . normal. Oh, and I have been so careful, ever since he was born . . . stood over the servants . . . had everything boiled . . . made sure that the food . . . but someone has been careless . . . I can't . . . I have been so strict with them. About . . . things for the baby . . . everything. I don't think they like me, but they know . . . I ordered them . . . Herbert ordered them . . . and he was never allowed to drink the milk in any other house . . . we carried our own . . . he . . . the ayah *knew*.'

 Her voice went on like a slow-flowing river, monotonous and repetitious, over stones.

 Flick-flick, flick-flick, flick-flick went the fan, around and around.

 There were swathes of faded and patched English chintz and cretonne covering the Indian chairs, and water-colours

(76)

and oil paintings on the walls. Ben Nevis. Sheep at Evening. Salisbury Cathedral. But the furniture, the whole room, still looked, as always, Indian.

And little brass and ebony tables everywhere.

'It happened so quickly. It was hideous. But he seemed so *well*.'

She got up, wandered about the room. Smiled vaguely. Sat down again.

'The doctor was half-drunk. Though Herbert said . . . But he didn't seem to care . . . even be interested. It was almost as if he were . . . we were . . . as if it was some *native* child. I told him we had done everything . . . asked if there was . . . he shrugged. He simply shrugged.'

She stared in a sort of panic, huge-eyed, at Eleanor.

'I haven't cried. I cannot cry. It has all happened so quickly.'

Yes, Eleanor thinks. And watches the fan go around and around. That is how it is here. Children, babies, playing, sunshine, healthy one day, dead the next. Cholera, typhoid, dysentery, malaria, septicaemia. Snakes, scorpions, mosquitoes, rats.

India. Danger.

First Miss Hartshorn. And now this.

She has lived, been very happy, here, for twenty years. And for almost sixteen of them, since Kitty's birthday, has been fearful, constantly shadowed by anxiety over her safety. She has exposed her only child to all these risks, to this ever-present, lurking danger, and all for the joy of having her with them, and because she could not have borne the separation.

And it will go on, she thinks, it will never be over.

The young woman, whose name is Myrtle Piggerton, rings for tea. But then leaves the room abruptly.

Eleanor sits in the bamboo chair, under the flicking fan, and sees the future. Sees Kitty married to some young soldier or civil servant, and sent off to a remote station. Kitty lonely, bored, frittering away her life among a lot of dull, provincial women. And with nothing but the appalling dangers of pregnancy and childbirth ahead of her. And afterwards, the whole cycle would merely begin again.

Harry Piggerton was an only son, the first-born. He was not quite two years old.

The young woman comes back. Apologises. But is dry-eyed still.

Then, sitting across the room, after the servant has brought in tea, and hard little coconut cakes, she tells Eleanor about the child's birth, trying to draw her into the great, stifling conspiracy of female suffering.

'Yes,' Eleanor says. 'Yes. I know. Of course. I understand.'

But she does not. Only remembers, before Kitty, having been told that it would be unendurable pain, and so, of course, expected it.

They were in the hills, her room looked out onto the valley and the line of mountains beyond. She had felt at peace, and strangely detached. It was very early morning, the tree-tops rising out of the mist, the rooks caw-cawing.

And the pain had been really nothing to speak of, short-lasting and quite endurable, she had almost enjoyed the rigours of it, as of a good, hard walk uphill, straining every muscle, but exhilarated.

Afterwards, she had looked down at her fair, small, perfect daughter, and the joy of it, the passionate love and commitment of the moment, haunted her still.

For no particular reason that they could determine, there had not been any other child.

So that, when women talked, she kept silent and felt apologetic, as if a suffering had quite unfairly passed her by.

Now, she stands, feels obscurely guilty again, facing the dry-eyed, distraught young woman. Thinks, and this is another suffering evaded, and nothing truly bad has ever happened to me.

'No . . . won't you stay? We could sit on the verandah . . . Herbert won't be home for . . . oh . . . the boy will bring us a drink.'

But she makes an excuse. And it is true that there is a dinner tonight and the Viceroy will be present. She intends to look magnificent.

'You see . . .' The young woman takes Eleanor's hand, grips it. 'Now I have nothing.' And she looks desperately about her, at the mean little bare-earthed garden, the fence, the flagpole on the nearby government building, the vulture, raking the sky.

Yet she has always seemed the most devoted, the most conscientious, of the younger wives, even Lewis has remarked upon it.

And will be so again, Eleanor thinks, driving away, will do her duty, and make the best of India, will bear more children, and perhaps with greater ease, and will love them, agonise over them, and eventually, one way or another, lose them. But what she has said this afternoon, for all it is the truth, was revealed in shock and grief and distress, and will be soon denied, or even forgotten.

She turns her attention to the evening ahead, and how she intends to look magnificent.

But the dry-eyed young mother of the dead little boy, and her fears for her own Kitty, get in the way.

14

FLORENCE HAD had a small table set in the upstairs bay window. She intended to sit at it and read seriously, to educate herself.

She had already written to Thea Pontifex.

'Of course, I am an historian,' Thea had replied in her plain, round hand. 'I cannot pretend to guide you in any other area, except perhaps a little in literature, which has long been my other love.'

There followed a short list of General Introductions to the study of English history and the Constitution. At the end of it, was an appendix on The Novel.

Florence stood up. It was a fine morning. She would go into town, in search of new gloves; and afterwards, to the bookshops.

Seeing her, in the bright sunlight across King's Parade, Mrs Lacey, wife of a college Warden, held up the traffic with her umbrella. Bicycles swerved madly.

'Now at last I have caught up with you. You have been positively *striding* out.' She took Florence's arm.

'We are having a dinner on Friday. There will be a Professor of Fine Art from London, and Miss Blake, who has published poetry. I do hope you are free to come?'

Free, Florence thought. Oh yes. But looked around her in sudden panic, feeling pressed in by tall buildings, and the crowds pushing past along the pavement.

Oh, I am always *free*.

'I am short of a lady.' She pushed her face, with its little, snouty nose, close up to Florence's shoulder.

'But I think I may be already engaged for Friday. Perhaps I may let you know?'

Florence smiled charmingly, and then escaped, to walk as fast as she dared making for the side lanes, and the bridge, gloves forgotten, books unbought.

Here, it was very quiet. A chill wind cut off the water. There were scarcely any other walkers, under the bare trees.

She thought, as she thought every hour, there is *nothing* else that I want in my life, and nothing else will satisfy. I have a single purpose.

But, for the time being, had no idea how to go about achieving it, and longed, walking very slowly, looking down into the river, for an adviser, a confidante.

In the end, finding herself back among the buildings and in the shadow of his college, she went in and crossed the court to the chapel, where she stood with a few other visitors, and gazed up at the great picture, behind the gilded altar. But it meant little to her, and she passed altogether over the one, half-shadowed face of the kneeling figure, quite unseeing, unaware.

And of course, she had hoped that he would be somewhere about, and he was not, so that at last she was obliged to leave, to go back across the courtyard and out through the gates, into the clamour of the streets again, and if she had glimpsed the windows of his rooms, she did not know it, for which were they?

It was lunchtime. And she despised herself for a weak fool,

and then rushed to purchase some gloves which, on getting home, she saw that she did not like.

The bookshops remained unvisited.

But she went to dinner at the house of the Warden, and wore silk, of a startling blue, and sensed admiration.

And overheard, farther down the table, as a silence abruptly fell, the rather shrill voice of the Professor of Fine Art.

'A woman can make any man marry her, if only she will go about it in the right way.'

Florence stared at him, a flush of excitement and wild hope suffusing her neck.

At another dinner, Eleanor sits next to the Viceroy and is charming, he is quite delighted with her, and at the ball which follows, dances with her twice. And she does, indeed, look magnificent. So Lewis thinks, watching, and he himself feels glorious with pride.

Uplifted and made radiant by the admiration and interest, the flattery that surrounds her, Eleanor waltzes like a girl, as perhaps Kitty will soon waltz here, and is quite satisfied, quite fulfilled, for surely, she thinks, life can hold nothing more than this, and in the midst of it all, I am doing my duty, and supporting my husband, it all reflects upon him, I am exactly where I should be.

And whirls away, lightly, in the Viceregal arms.

Tomorrow, there is another ball, in fancy dress, for now the Cold Season is in full swing, every day there will be garden parties and afternoon drives, the gymkhanas and the polo, tennis and archery and badminton tournaments and teas, there will be regimental balls and club balls and moonlight picnics and a wedding or two, with everyone young, or pretending to be so. Charmed lives. And sadness and loneliness and homesickness and beggars and lepers, the return of the hot weather and the deaths of children, are banished out of sight, thought not always quite out of mind.

And Kitty sits in bed under the mosquito netting, and reads of Lakes and mountains and rains and mists, of shepherds and daffodils, poems she does not fully understand, and looks up now and again, to dream and make and unmake plans, and listen to the night-howl of the jackals.

15

BY THE time the trap deposited him in front of the inn, it was quite dark and blowing a strong wind off the sea.

Thomas stepped down and set his bag on the floor beside him, waiting until the horse's footsteps had receded into the roaring night, down the two-mile track into the village.

Then, knowing his way blindfold, he crossed the patch of rough ground to the quay, and felt forwards until he came up against the parapet wall.

Out beyond that, in the pitch blackness, lay the marshes and mud-flats and water, stretching out to the North Sea, from which came now the boom and crash of the waves, brought in on the gale.

At his back, the inn sign swung, creaking and straining. Below the door, a line of oily light, which once or twice fanned out brightly and wavered as someone came in or out, before disappearing again.

The wind beat about his head, and the salt taste came into his mouth, and every anxiety, every petty concern and irritation, every thought of other people in the life left behind, dropped away from him.

Now, he was the other man he had become on every visit here over the years, the same man who was descended from the boy who had gone out in the boat across the water with Collum O'Cool.

And the man of Cambridge, of court and chapel and cloister and book-panelled room, the tutor, the cleric, the scholar, hemmed in, confined, formal, had no existence here.

Now, he turned and, his eyes grown accustomed to the darkness, could make out the hulks and roof-lines of the boat-builder's sheds and workshops, the falling-down fish stores and warehouses. There was nothing else, save the inn, and the open waterlands to the sea, no dwelling of any kind, and no shelter.

The wind battered at his back, raged about him, wailed and whistled in his ears and he welcomed it, though at the same time hoping for better, calmer weather by dawn, when he meant to set out.

But for now, he let it come at him, and over him, and when a burst of rain and spray whipped his face, turned himself, to catch the full force of it.

But in the end, because he had brought the minimum of spare clothing and did not want to live for four days and nights soaking wet, he picked up his bag and walked across the yard, to push open the heavy door of the Wherry Inn.

They knew him well enough now. Though he was still a curiosity to them, and was not, could never be, one of them. But the drone of conversation faltered only slightly, as he went in, like the step of a lame man, before recovering itself and continuing on its way. One or two heads turned, then back again.

The taproom was small and close, the air furred with tobacco smoke and oil fumes from the lamps and the heavy old black stove in the corner, its funnel rising to a hole in the roof, with the smell of ale and the breaths of a dozen or more men.

Behind the bar, on ledges around the walls, stood the trophies of generations of men, these and so many like them, the cases of stuffed birds, shelduck and widgeon, grey-leg and pink-foot, whimbrel and godwit, harrier and bittern and short-eared owl. There was no other decoration, beside the wooden casks and barrels, and pewter tankards, and a yellowing coastal map. The walls were stained brown, in long tongues, darkening to black near the ceiling, with the accumulated smoke and tar of years.

One man, on a corner bench, nodded, a second, across the room, took his pipe from between his teeth and mumbled the time of day. No more.

Because of the fierceness of the weather they would have been here and immediately outside, for much of the day, unable to put out, drinking, talking, smoking, and in between, roaming restlessly about the quay and the green and up towards the jetty, to look at the sky, and out across the marshes and the water, like caged-in wild creatures, wanting to be free and away. And besides, poor weather meant a poor livelihood for these men who lived by what they caught or shot, the wild-fowlers, punt-gunners, poachers, eel-men, wherry-men.

The landlord finished his sentence, and the serving of ale, before gesturing curtly to Thomas, and going on ahead of him, up the steep staircase and along the dark, narrow passageways, keeping his head bent low, to the door of the attic room which was always his, and the only one let out.

The floorboards sloped and were bare. There was a bed, an oil lamp on a three-legged stool, a low-seated old armchair, a washstand, a single rail across the corner.

Thomas sighed involuntarily, like a man come home.

'Glass is low, sir. You'll not be away tomorrow.'

'So I fear.'

The lamp flared, flickered, steadied itself. The shadow of the landlord loomed like a giant upon the wall.

'Supper at six, if it 'ud be convenient.'

'Perfectly, thank you, Mr Jebbings.'

The man nodded, and left, and his footsteps sounded like thunder, down the stairs.

All night and for the whole of the following day, it blew a gale off the sea, roaring and booming about the inn.

He had stood at the window and watched the dawn come up with great, inky clouds piling together like fast-moving ships against the reddening glow.

By noon, the restless frustration of the other men was upon him. He went out two or three times, to pace about, over to the quay, up as far as the boat-sheds, head bent into the wind. His body felt tense, he could settle to nothing, had unpacked his books, but did not read; thought, with guilt, of Cambridge, and the work he had abandoned, and of Georgiana, too much alone.

Now and then, a solitary bird appeared on the near horizon, low-flying, battling against the wind, blown up like paper before dropping down in search of shelter.

In the end, in the waning light of late afternoon, he went out again, struck off west, to walk six miles or more inland, and as he went, and as the dusk crept in around him, the roaring of the sea at his back faded, so that, gradually, he could hear the soft, rhythmic tread of his own footsteps on the marsh grass, and began to be calmed by it.

He saw no one at all. Ahead, the leaden sky reached down to touch the ground, which darkened to brown and peat-black as it receded from him. Here and there, water gleamed in small pools and tongues. But then, the marshland dried up and gave way to heath and sandy scrub, and eventually to a thin belt of woodland, where he rested out of the wind.

And, in the last few yards, when he was almost into the trees, a short-eared owl, which had been lurking, silent and motionless down close to the ground, so that he had all but stepped on it, rose suddenly on whirring wings and swerved, he saw the fierce glare of its eyes, before it made off in ghostly flight towards the marshes.

And his heart leaped at the sight, and the moth-like beauty of it, and where he had been out of true with his surroundings, his mood fractious, now something within him adjusted, and he relaxed and was at peace, and at one with the world, and his own presence in it.

He returned in darkness, and several times stopped, able to see no further than a yard ahead of him, guided only by instinct and the faint smell of the sea, and the direction of the wind coming off it, he left the path and stumbled and, twice, fell up to his calves in water and thick marsh mud.

He was not afraid, nor ever for a moment doubted that he could find his way back, was only strangely exhilarated, and without thought for anything, except the rough ground beneath his feet and the direction he should be taking, and for shielding himself so far as he could, his head bent into his collar, from the worst of the wind.

He felt himself completely bound up with the air, the storm, the ground, the darkness, like some bird or animal that had been raised here, to be a creature of instinct, and of physical awareness alone, not an alien, cerebral being, a stranger, come from elsewhere into this wild landscape, but one who in all ways belonged. So that he felt guided home by quite other means than any use of reason or recollection.

He came quite suddenly up to the boat-sheds, saw the wavering light from the inn, and was startled, and forced to wait, out in the blackness and swirl of the gale, and in the heavy rain that was now falling, not merely to reorientate himself at the end of his journey, but to get in touch again with himself, to return, as a thinking human being, back into his own body.

But, walking into the smoky, oily light of the taproom, seeing the men there on the benches, as he had seen them the night before, he still felt oddly uncertain of who, or what, he was.

16

GEORGIANA SAT alone under the lamp, reading of a sixteenth-century voyage to China, and looking, if she could have been seen, surprisingly handsome in the tallow light.

But she was not seen. The house was empty. Thomas was in Norfolk, Alice gone to a meeting of her spiritualist fellowship (which troubled Georgiana, who had been very strict that it should always be kept from her brother. Though of the maid's afternoon seances he had, in fact, long been aware.).

But she read and re-read each paragraph, and could not concentrate, and the usual flights of longing for exotic travels were dulled. She looked up continually, from the emperors and silk roads, to gaze ahead of her, ill at ease, unhappy.

Because of her brother's abrupt departure, and his recent reserve of manner, his coolness, and his greater withdrawal from intimacy with her. And because she looked ahead and saw only late middle age, and senility beyond, and longed for the past, for the boundless joy and close comradeship, the infinite possibilities, of childhood.

And the dry, cracked throat and dulled senses of a head cold, and a hundred petty irresolutions, and the miasmic airs of November.

In the kitchen, Alice had left the tea tray ready laid, scones and a dundee cake, and fresh bread and butter under a plate, she had only to boil the water.

And in a moment, perhaps, would do so.

In the conservatory, beyond the glass doors, the small

birds flew here and there within the cages, on abrupt, bright wings.

And a mile away, old Mrs Gray dozed and snored slightly over her game of patience, and half dreamed peculiar, fleeting dreams, until the maid came in with the evening paper, and rattled the fire irons and raked the curtains irritably shut.

Upstairs, Florence stood at the long mirror, closed her eyes and opened them very abruptly, time after time, hoping to glimpse herself afresh, as another would see her, hoping to admire.

But the face and the figure were inescapably familiar, and what impact she might make, how she might be judged, whether she were handsome or not, she could never tell.

The clock chimed the half-hour. Her mother would be wanting tea.

But she did not go down.

And in other rooms, all over Cambridge, other women sat, alone and with nothing but solitude in prospect.

Only Thea Pontifex, at her desk in the women's college, was absorbed, in her solitude. She wrote steadily, and occasionally paused, to delve into the pile of books beside her, and her cheeks were flushed with the excitements of scholarship, she was lost to herself, and the world outside.

And, because she knew that the maid's ill temper would not last, and that there were muffins for tea, but more, because on the whole she was a woman accepting of life, Mrs Gray was happy enough.

Georgiana in her bedroom, lonely still, her head covered by a towel, over a bowl of medicated steam.

The rims of her eyes burned, but down her back, the shivers ran like water.

And so, turned in on herself, and the discomfort and misery of her influenza, she forgot the time, forgot the assurances made to him. Forgot the caged birds.

Remembered.

Which was how, in the forgetting and the startled remembering, the rush and the guilt and confusion, in fumbling with a latch and fiddling with a seed dish, which she dropped and broke on the tiled conservatory floor, she let a door of the cage swing accidentally open.

Not noticing, aware only of the scattered mess of seed and china-shard, of weak legs and aching head, she went to ring for Alice, and the dustpan, while first one and then several of the small birds found their way out into the freedom of the room.

The bell, ringing suddenly above the kitchen door, startled Alice, comfortable in the rocking chair, out of her worries about life and death, life after death.

For the fortnightly spiritualist fellowship always filled her with an ardent conviction, until a little later in the evening, when the doubts gnawed like worms into her brain.

'But could it not all have been invented?'

(There had been too much just lately in the newspapers, about mediums exposed as tricksters and frauds.)

Yet her friend Annie had wept tears of joyous recognition at the message from her sister, one year dead, had clung to Alice's hand when the medium spoke. It had, she had said, made the whole world perfect for her, and everything right again.

Life and death. Death. Death. Alice worried at it, and the thoughts would not leave her.

Life and death.

But whom to trust?

Life and death.

Perhaps, as it troubled her so much, preyed on her mind for all these hours afterwards, she should not go at all to the spiritualist fellowship.

But what had a man like Thomas Cavendish to offer? There had been no comfort for Annie from the likes of him.

Life and death.

And then the bell rang.

'I was disturbed that you should have left so abruptly, and while there was such unease and ill feeling between us.'

So he wrote to Eustace Partridge, for he could not banish the anguished face of the boy from his mind; and the storm raged on outside, and the light from the oil lamp wavered across the paper.

'In my distress on your behalf, and my own disappointment, I spoke coldly to you, and offered you no help, no comfort, and for that I am heartily sorry.

'But what saddened me most was the impression you gave that you felt no great emotion, no deep and overwhelming love for . . .'

Here he paused. Laid down his pen. Here the wind tore at the casement like a desperate thing. And he was uncertain how he should refer to the young woman.

' . . . the young woman who is to become your wife.'

And which (he would have written) would perhaps have excused it all. But the mere indulgence of the flesh, those cravings, that curiosity about fleshly matters . . .

But he did not write it. He wrote no more. Only sat, in bitterness and resentment that the boy and his folly should have intruded upon him here.

Alice found Georgiana, her cheeks flushed, eyes bright with panic and fever, hysterical among the escaped and fluttering birds, and so, the questions of life and death were for the time being suspended.

And because she saw that they were better left to themselves, and, having cleared up the broken seed dish, could be of no further use here, she simply led Georgiana away to bed, and medicine, and hot water laced with rum and lemon.

In the end, nervous of their freedom, the little birds quietly returned to roost in their cages, and coming in later, and seeing them so, Alice simply closed and latched the door.

But one remained free, one bird Alice did not see, perched high up, close to the skylight, its vivid wings closed, head bent into an iridescent breast.

Georgiana slept. Half woke in confusion. Fell back again into a snake-pit of turbulent, poisoned dreams.

Woke again, with thoughts of death. Death clung to her. But deliberately, knowing that it was the fever, she turned her mind to childhood, as onto sweet, soft pillows, and was at once soothed and made cool.

And the small, vivid bird roosted on alone, close to the skylight, close to the glass, to the air, to freedom.

She started up again, out of her reverie of Ireland, remembering what had almost happened through her own fault, her own forgetfulness. Almost.

But it had not. And Alice would surely say nothing to him and so, how could he ever know?

She was a child again, terrified of incurring his displeasure, for he was the bright, the fixed star in her universe, afraid to confess that she had forfeited his trust.

Thought, almost said out loud, but I am a grown woman,

I am forty-four years old, why must I endlessly look back to our childhood? Why do I still, still see him in the old light, why am I so anxious that he, and he alone, should approve, praise, trust, like, love?

Why has no life since then ever fully satisfied?

What is it I lack?

But then, because of the fever, and the low ebb of her spirits in these ghostly hours before dawn, because of her restless limbs and aching head, she submitted again, and let her mind drift back. To the stories he had told her, sitting before the fire, or on the deep window-seat, looking out at the soft silver veils of rain drifting up across the garden from the Lake. And the books he had read to her, of wild journeys and far countries beyond exotic seas, and their exultant voyages together across ancient maps.

And so, for a time, kept back the visible skull, the vision of death that stalked, grinning over her shoulder.

But life and death and all the troubled thoughts of it preyed upon Alice in her room at the end of the passage, and rattled the window lock, and the handle of the wardrobe door, and would not be denied.

So that in the end, she went down in her dressing-gown to the kitchen, and heated milk, and sat on the chair beside the range and rocked to soothe herself.

Life and death. Life and death. Life and death.

Old Mrs Gray thought of death, too, death more than life now, in the long, wakeful hours.

But then, she always did, and was quite untroubled by it.

Only sat at the half-open window and smelled the balmy, gentle smell of night, blowing from off the river.

And was content. And would not die yet awhile.

17

HE WOKE in the night to silence. The storm had blown itself out.

Thomas went to the window and saw that the whole quayside and the salt flats and the great, still expanse of the estuary beyond, were washed in moonlight, and the face of the moon gazed back at itself, serene in the waters.

And, as he looked at them, he imagined how they would be now, the secret reedbeds and inlets, the mud-flats and saltings, right away to the shoreline itself, seething with birds, feeding, flying, or lying low in the water, and other birds tucked into banks and hollows, knew that what appeared to be so silent, so still, so dead under the moon, teemed with hidden life.

Then, as he stood, he heard the faintest sound, the soft slip of an oar into the water. And the smell of pipe tobacco came up to him faintly, sweetly, on the night air.

The small boats were leaving, the first few gliding away across the estuary, the outline of the men dark as felt against the moon.

The punt-gunners, the wild-fowlers, at the end of their frustration and confinement in the storm, were making silently, stealthily, for their hunting grounds out on the waters, and their secret watching and waiting for the night birds and the dawn birds, their prey.

He would not sleep again now, would not even wait until first light.

For he, like the other men, was restless to be away, to be

out there on the water, though quite alone, and with a less violent purpose.

He dressed and packed his things in the canvas bag, and as he did so, he felt that everything else had dropped away, every other thought or consideration in the world, he felt light and unburdened, and full of exhilaration.

And he was a boy again, the same boy who had got ready like this, furtively, quietly, to go out in the hush of early morning, through the mist that lay low over the Lake, in the fishing boat of Collum O'Cool. Collum O'Cool, who scarcely spoke, only rowed and fished and sat, close and still. And there had been an absolute bond between them, a companionship and understanding such as he had never known in the rest of his life.

Nor did he expect ever to know it again.

He descended the dark, creaking staircase, and, after leaving money on the taproom counter in payment, went out of the inn and across the moonlit quay to the boat-shed, where Abel Sinnett had made the small dinghy ready for him days before.

And the smell of the salt sea blew across into his nostrils and the rich, wet, pungent reek of the marsh, and he felt as if his own body were light enough to rise and soar into the night sky towards the stars pricked out in it, like one of the sea-birds, great of wing.

The island was very small, no more than a few dozen yards across, and marshy, with reeds fringing the outer edges, and thicker grass and some alder and willows towards the centre. On the eastern side stood the hut, with the houseboat moored beside it. And all around, water, flat and still and luminous under the moon.

He tied up the dinghy and for a moment or two, rested there; as the lap of the waves he had made stilled and died away, there was silence again, thin and pure.

Then, in the distance, the faintest of cries, a curlew, passing along the far fringe of the tide.

And soon, that other sound, like no other in the natural world, at first a breath on the air, a movement, rather than a sound, but growing rapidly louder, as the geese came through the night towards him. He could see the skein now, flying towards the sea, white in the moonlight. As they approached, the beating of their wings sounded across the silent water-lands, and then he could hear them yelping, baying like hounds in full cry, their huge, beating bodies directly over his head, he looked up into the heart of the fast-flying pack, before they had gone, over the marshes and the tongue of the estuary, and away to sea, and only the last echo came back, like the faint wash after a great wave, and was absorbed again into the surrounding silence.

With the smallest sigh over the water, the tide turned.

Then the cold, hard crack of a gunshot, from one of the hidden men, and the crack reverberated, around the rim of the night sky, and others quickly succeeded it, and then the ducks rose in panic and clamour, and made away.

Once, he had shot birds himself, in Ireland as a boy, and for a time out here, with the fowlers. But his heart had pulled against it, and he had regretted every bird shot, every airy, feathered body that had plummeted like lead from the free sky. Until finally he had shot a curlew, and felt as if the death that sprayed out of his gun had come instead from his own body, and the smoke of it had risen into his throat and nostrils and he had choked on it.

He had never shot again. But he would not condemn those who did, the men who lay out there now, in punts and hides among the reeds and rushes, and whose harsh livelihood this was.

And now, the dawn came up, pale light seeped into the sky and spread surreptitiously across the waters, and with the first light, a flicker of a breeze, breaking the stillness.

He tied up the dinghy and climbed out and hauled himself, and his bag, up the rungs of the ladder onto the tarred wooden houseboat. Abel Sinnett had opened it up the week before, aired and cleaned it, and left him supplies, food and oil, candles and fresh water.

Now, Thomas stowed his books and few clothes away, and refamiliarised himself with the close, cramped little rooms, the smell and feel of them, set up a kettle to boil on the primus; and when his tea was made, took it out onto the deck, to sit and look out over the wide waters.

And as he sat, from nowhere, as though exhaled by the body of some invisible marsh creature, a mist began to steal towards him, wreathing and unearthly, so that in a few moments, the water below and all around him and then the island, the boat and the dinghy, were swathed in its cold dampness. And with the mist, the silence returned, and pressed in upon his ears, a new, uncanny, muffling silence, quite unlike the clear silence of the moonlit night.

But then, so that it caused a shiver to creep over his flesh like the creeping of the breeze that rippled the water, he heard the strange, ill-omened booming of the bittern.

18

KITTY RIDES out at dawn, at barely five o'clock, and only the servants see her, rides out across the blue plains towards the river and beyond, mile after mile, with the syce for company, because that is the rule. But the syce keeps a few paces behind her and soon, she begins to gallop to try and outstrip him, and he knows it and allows it, though always keeping her in view, in reach.

And it is this that she would miss if she were to leave, the freedom to race across country. Above her, the sky is silver-white but tinged faintly bronze where the rim meets the land, and her head is rinsed clean and clear, as a bowl rinsed in a spring, of any thoughts, any words, there is only the exhilaration and the movement, the rush of the air towards her.

But Miss Hartshorn is awake, as always at this time, she sleeps so fitfully here, sits up in bed with a board across her knees, writing about Kitty's future to her friend in Warwickshire, taking it upon herself to make tentative plans.

Eleanor sleeps, cocooned in her dreams of glory, for she was admired on all sides, and looked magnificent and Lewis basked in it, and still none of it has faded, the satisfaction continues to warm them. And when she does stir and wake, it is only to the glow of happy recollections, like a young girl after a first ball, and then to think vaguely that before long it will be Christmas, which of course Kitty adores, and Kitty will be here with them, and so perhaps, everything else can be left to resolve itself, there are no troubles breaking upon the calm surface of her life.

19

QUITE SUDDENLY, the sun broke through the mist, dissolving and clearing it, flushing the water rose-red, and then, a few feet away from him he saw the bird. It was standing, solitary, motionless, on reedstalk legs, silhouetted against the sheen of the mud which had been exposed by the receding tides, at the island's edge.

And it seemed to Thomas that this place was a sort of paradise and he at the heart of it was in that state of bliss which saints and visionaries and poets attempted to describe. And, looking at the bird, perfectly poised against water and land and sky, he thought that no created thing was ever more beautiful.

20

ON NOVEMBER 22, at St Margaret's church, by special licence. Eustace Partridge to Mary Wimpole.

But it was a glorious afternoon, winter, the trees bare, and yet still flushed with the last of autumn in the air, in the sunlight.

And Mary Wimpole, who was so small, so neat, wore lavender-grey and a hat trimmed with silver silk roses. But there was a puffy paleness about the skin below her eyes.

No one knew them here, the town was miles away from their homes which was what had been thought best; the families had met together and it had all been decided.

After the wedding, there was luncheon in a hotel, champagne had been served, and claret with the game pie, and so, things had passed off well enough, people had become quite friendly. There had been good wishes and a certain amount of laughter.

Later, they had walked the short distance, arm in arm, down to catch the ferry to the Isle of Wight and the late afternoon sun struck gold upon the water. Everyone was making the best of it.

Mary Wimpole – but Mary Partridge now – had smiled, and kissed both sets of parents very sweetly, and held his arm as the boat began to pull away.

And they had waved. Everybody had waved, the figures on the jetty grew smaller and smaller, and became pin figures and still they were waving. And the sea-birds had wheeled and cried and followed in their wake.

It seemed to Eustace that he was, for the time being, for

these moments, really perfectly happy, perfectly content. To stand on the deck looking back to the mainland in the last of the sun, which had a little warmth as well as brightness in it.

Except that he himself was not here, and had taken no part at all in the day's events, there had been a stranger inhabiting his own body, filling his new suit of clothes, while his real self was in suspense somewhere, looking on from outside, and frozen in mid-frame, mid-life. Yet soon, surely, things would be as they were again, and he would be himself and back in Cambridge, the past would reassert itself.

Meanwhile, they walked the cliff paths on the Isle of Wight, and slowly along deserted beaches beside the creaming tide, and the weather held all that week, though the fog-horn blew in the early mornings, and once, there was a frost at night.

And Mary Wimpole chattered to him, and he looked after her with infinite care and tenderness, as he would some object that had been entrusted to him, but temporarily, that was not his but which he was to hand back.

At night, he lay awake beside her, and when she slept, inched his body away, careful not to touch hers at any point, and after that, only listened to her quiet breathing, and the sound of the sea through the window and could neither sleep nor think. Only towards dawn, he became tangled in dreams from which he could not extricate himself when the fog-horn woke him in the muffled night.

On Wednesday afternoon he left her lying on the bed, because she felt slightly unwell, and walked by himself, climbed to the top of Tennyson Down and sat there on the grass beside the cropping sheep, and remembered a holiday spent on the island when he was a small boy. He had come up here then, and sea and sky had stretched away all around and below him, and he had felt himself to be king of the world.

Now, he lay on his back, and felt the earth turn, and

thought that perhaps after all he might make the best of things.

But he did not know her, and though she spoke lovingly, she knew nothing, nothing at all, of him.

And then, realising that, and struck by the truth of it all, he stood up abruptly, and as he did so, recalled the childhood feeling that when the wind blew it would lift him off the ground and he would soar.

As Thomas walks back across the dark heathland and marsh towards the sea, and the gale and the light of the Wherry Inn, seventy miles away, across that flat country, Adèle Hemmings is walking, too, down through the tangle of the neglected garden, where unspeakable horrors lie casually hidden in the grass, to the back gate (whose wood is slimy with rot and whose hinges are eaten away by rust, so that it always hangs half open).

Beyond the back gate, a lane, between high walls, and hedges and fences, and other, more substantial gates, a cutting, a snicket, a ginnel, an alley. And beyond the lane, and beyond all the quiet, respectable avenues, the open fields, the Backs, the river. The world.

Thinks Adèle Hemmings, who has scarcely been into it. The world, under the racing sky. For she looks up, and sees the clouds drift apart like veils, to let out a little of the watery moonlight, before they merge thickly together again and the moon goes out, and she is made giddy, and has to look down.

In the satin parlour, her aunt rings a petulant bell. But Adèle Hemmings is gone, has stepped boldly out into the dark lane, beyond the broken gate, and does not hear and does not care, and even the cats, lying fatly about on their cushions, scarcely twitch, scarcely stir.

Half a dozen dishes, of china and tin and pot, sit about the scullery floor, smeared and crusted with the remains of food, stained with the sour rims of cream (for the maids are paid too little, even by the poor standards of all such maids, and do not like cats, and are thoughtlessly treated, and do not stay. And the present maid is a sluttish thing, and will soon give in her notice.).

In corners, here and there, blobs and skeins of entrail and matted fur, from the day's slaughter.

Adèle Hemmings (whose parents are twenty years dead. But she still remembers them, still weeps) walks out of the shelter of the alley and into the wind, and the wind blows her clothes about and lifts them up, exciting her, her heart takes off and pounds, with the realisation of where she is, alone at night in the silent streets.

In the world.

She is even excited by the silken sound of her own stockings. Thinks that she might laugh out loud, cackle and shriek. Or run about naked.

Though in the parlour of the house, the irritable bell rings and rings, and if she is too far away and too much in the wind and too reluctant, for her ears to hear it, nevertheless, it reaches her, it rings inside her head, the walls of her skull trap and magnify the sound and it cannot be got out.

Adèle Hemmings does not walk very far – fifty yards into the wind, but never out of the shelter of the respectable avenue.

Behind her, a cat follows, slipping along the shadows of the hedge, watchful as a spy sent out from the house.

Later, the clouds began to gather, dark as grapes, bringing rain. Later, he stood on the cliff-top and thought that he might simply jump down, down onto the shingle and dark rocks.

But of course he did not, only turned, feeling the first spatter of rain on his face, to walk back to the hotel, and to his wife.

She has ridden very hard, delighted in letting the pony have its head, she has thrown off the syce and his cautions, his frown of disapproval, galloping, galloping. But the sun is higher now, they have turned for home, sedately trotting, barely disturbing the dust. Sadu is content again.

Exhausted, hot, jubilant, Kitty's head is full of the week to come. There is to be a moonlight picnic, there are no fewer than three garden parties, there is the gymkhana, the social round is unceasing, and suddenly, she sees that it is fun after all, great fun, there are friends, there is so much to enjoy.

Except, perhaps, that it is always Eleanor who is the bright star, glittering at the centre of it all and around whom everything revolves.

They are trotting towards a village, a few houses among the beanfields, for a little way the track takes on the slight resemblance to a road. And in the dust at the edge of the road, but still some distance from the nearest house, she sees a figure, scuttling slowly, crab-wise, bent close to the earth, and, nearing it, looks down at a crippled woman, thin, deformed, with twisted legs and arms, and a hunch on her bent back, like an incubus. And the legs end in stumps and are running with sores, and pus runs out of one of the eye sockets.

She is dragging her body in the ditch, towards the village, and beside her, running easily to keep pace, small boys dance a mocking dance, and jabber and jeer. And then one picks up a handful of dust and stones and hurls it and the others cry out joyfully, and bend to follow suit.

And in shouting at them, cracking her whip to disperse them, in pulling her pony up and round, and calling to Sadu for help, in the swirl of dust and the yelling and confusion, Kitty sees the crippled woman trip and fall half under the hooves of the pony, half into the ditch, she rolls and flails her stunted, withered arms, to save herself.

And Kitty would dismount, do something to help, for the small boys have raced away now. But Sadu rides fast alongside her, bends to take her reins and then urges both ponies on, so that Kitty is obliged to go too and to hold tight to the saddle as they gallop on, she only sees, glancing over her shoulder as she is pulled away, that the woman has begun to move again, crawling slowly, painfully through the dust towards the houses. And though she screams at the syce, screeches at him, angrily, and beats her fists on the saddle in frustration, she knows that it is no use, that he will not stop, but only forces the two ponies grimly on, until they are a mile or more away, and on the last lap towards home, when he releases the rein, gives it back into her control, and then drops a pace or two behind her again, knowing that she will not go back now.

She knows perfectly well what has happened. She is unsurprised. He is a Hindu, and she herself is the daughter of a memsahib, and the cripple is untouchable. That is all there is to it.

In the drive, she dismounts stiffly from her sweating pony and drops the reins for the syce to retrieve, turns her back on him, without looking in his direction.

Impassively, the man leads both ponies off, around to the stables and out of sight.

And, bursting into the house and into her mother's bedroom, where Eleanor is creaming her throat at the mirror, the fury and outrage and frustration swelling up behind her eyes, roaring in her ears like the sea, Kitty says, 'I hate India. I hate this dreadful country, do you hear? *I hate it all.*' And bursts out sobbing, her face scarlet, so that Lewis comes in alarm out of his dressing-room, to demand an explanation for the hubbub.

Later, Kitty sits on the verandah with Miss Hartshorn. She has rested, slept for almost two hours and eaten breakfast, and now they have glasses of lemon tea on the bamboo table before them and suede-bound copies of Keats.

Reading aloud, of autumn and nightingales, drunk on the words, Miss Hartshorn has made herself drowsy, her voice is monotonous and very soft.

Adieu! Adieu! thy plaintive anthem fades
Past the near meadows, over the still stream,
Up the hill-side and now 'tis buried deep
In the next valley-glades.
Was it a vision, or a waking dream?
Fled is that music. Do I wake or sleep?

And as she reads, she remembers vividly, so that it is almost
here, she has almost reached it; for the nightingale sings in
the woodland behind the cottage in Warwickshire, she herself
has heard it.

But now, Kitty stands up suddenly, knocking her chair
over backwards in her passion, and the suede-bound book
falls from her lap onto the floor.

'But what is the *point* of it all?' she is shouting. 'I cannot
understand. What are you trying to tell me? What is the *point*
of all this beauty?'

And storms away, leaving Miss Hartshorn alone, the spell
broken and scattered all around her.

It was one of the most perfectly tranquil weeks of his life.
The last, perhaps.

He took the dinghy out every morning, just before dawn,
and hid, watching the birds, listening, moored among the
reedbeds. Twice, he went out in the late evening, at the turn
of the tide, and remained there all night, lying flat along the
bottom of the dinghy, cramped, cold, silent, content.

Otherwise, he sat on the deck of the houseboat, or else
worked at the little square ledge that let down to form
a makeshift desk in front of the window, recording his
observations, drawing.

He read, the bird books, John Donne's sermons, and Jeremy
Taylor, the Greek Testament.

And after lunch or in the early evening, fell into a deep,

dreamless sleep, lying fully dressed on his bunk for three hours or more, and awoke, deeply refreshed, to the silence.

He neither saw nor spoke to a soul for five days.

But on the sixth day, which was Sunday and the day before he would have to leave, he rowed to where a path led off the marshes, for four miles inland, and walked to the chapel, that stood by itself in the middle of the flat land. There had been a frost, the tips of the reeds and the grasses at his feet were whitened. The sun shone, but with a pale, brittle light, and his footsteps rasped on the path.

The building smelled of cold, cold, watery stone. But it was flooded with light that came through the clear glass of the windows, and the walls were white, so that the light washed over them like water.

There were no other worshippers save Thomas and the priest. He offered up his thanks to God, and opened his heart too, with fervour and joy. And looking upwards, to the wooden roof, that was curved like the upturned belly of a boat, he saw at several corners, where the ribs met and joined, the small carved angels, wings upswept as if at any moment they might break free, and soar.

He would have prayed to remain in this paradise for ever. Except that then, it would become familiar, and the glory, he knew, would fade from it. Only if he left it, would it remain for him, perfect, unsullied, pure.

21

'I T IS,' Miss Hartshorn says, 'simply the most beautiful part of England. It is perfect.'

She and Kitty are strolling around the garden, books abandoned. For they both find it increasingly difficult to concentrate, though for different reasons.

'Our cottage has gardens both at the front and at the back – very neat, you know. Very cottagey. Marjorie works so hard. Marjorie *adores* the garden. Though at the back it is a little wilder, almost overgrown, indeed, up to the fence, for the woods come right down, to the door. Well, as I have told you.'

'Yes.' Kitty stops, in order, somehow, to see it more clearly in her mind's eye. 'Yes. The Forest of Arden.'

'The Forest of Arden!' Miss Hartshorn's voice answers hers, trembling a little with awe.

'It really *is*! Part of the ancient forest. The very same.'

They walk slowly between the flowerbeds, and the soldierly geraniums.

'And the front path leads down to a little wicket gate. But we keep the hedge quite low, so as to enjoy the view – the whole of Warwickshire lying before us, running down towards the Avon. We are only a few yards from the river bank. In the little room in the eaves – the room you would have – you can hear the gentle flow of the water night and day. And the trees – so many, so many beautiful trees, so stately and gracious – elms and beeches and oaks, and then the alders and poplars and willows along the river bank.'

'"There is a willow grows aslant a brook."'

'Oh yes!' Miss Hartshorn beams approvingly, gives Kitty's shoulder a little pat.

'Oh, there is so much of the spirit of Shakespeare all around us. Though Marjorie is the real one for appreciating that.

In the evening sometimes, we just sit quietly on the terrace with our work and we can see the deer coming down to feed at the water's edge, four or five at a time. Of course, Marjorie and I are very quiet. But although it is such an idyllic spot, the cottage really is not too isolated, you must not worry about that, our little village is less than a mile away, and then, we are within quite easy reach of several lovely old Warwickshire towns. And there is a very nice school for young ladies at Leamington Spa. Or perhaps the one at Malvern? The Malvern Hills you would find *very* beautiful. Though that would be rather further, it would mean boarding of course. No, on the whole, perhaps it would be best for you just to stay with us, at least until you are quite settled and have more of an idea. Marjorie and I would teach you and we do have several other friends nearby – Esme Thorpe, for piano and Miss Batt, who is quite a mathematician and, well, the vicar, I suppose, for religious studies. Or the vicar's wife.'

They have reached the verandah again. Kitty stands still before their house, the flowerbeds, the geraniums, the fountains, looking at India, seeing what she imagines to be England, seeing herself at the window of the little room in the eaves of the cottage in Warwickshire, the fields and water-meadows and trees of the Avon Vale stretching away from her.

But thinks that she will want more, wants the world to open out in every direction at once. The cottage in Warwickshire and Miss Hartshorn's friend Marjorie Pepys may not be enough.

And her father and mother have not yet been spoken to at all.

Rain in Cambridge, more steady, insistent rain, so that the river overflowed its banks at last, and all the paths alongside it were under water, and in places, quite unsafe.

Rain pattering onto courts and sliding down ancient roofs, and the sweet smell of the wet earth rising, and a cloud of rain overhanging the streets and gardens, so that breathing made the lungs spongy; and Georgiana, walking through the wet streets, splashed from passing cabs, passing cycles, could not throw off the cold that had settled miserably on her chest.

And she could perfectly well have taken a cab herself, but somehow, had felt defiant.

And had been rather lonely too, indoors, unwell for several days, and her brother in Norfolk, and Alice behaving oddly, she had felt the need to be among others, going purposefully about, the bustle of the street, shops, doors opening and closing, cheerful faces. And all the young men.

She was on her way to Lady Lawne's house, to a meeting of the Committee for Moral Welfare.

And now, round the corner of Petty Cury, one of the young men, who had almost collided with her, raised his hat and said, 'Good morning' – smiled at her, gown flying, arms full of books and brown paper bags – and, smiling back, dismissing his apology, she thought suddenly that that was what she had been missing, and that when Thomas was back, they must have some of the young men in, to tea, to sherry, to Sunday luncheon. For she greatly enjoyed it, their graceful, yet at the same time, clumsy bodies, all over her drawing-room, their legs under her dining-room table, and their voices, and their politeness, and the way she could coax them out of themselves. And there was always one very difficult one, who hung back, and one too boisterous, but charming. Oh, always. Yes, the young men must come again to tea.

So that the rain, running off her umbrella suddenly, and down her neck in a cold channel, and the pile of leaves in a mulch in the gutter, making her slip and almost fall, did not put her into a bad humour, after all.

And at Lady Lawne's house, she found that she was early, the first, in fact, her Ladyship was not even down, and so, she could dry and warm herself by standing very close to the bright fire. For the walk had tired her, she was glad of the pause, the breath rasped in her chest. She was not yet by any means well.

He woke to the sound of rain, water dropping softly on water, and tapping on the wooden roof of the houseboat. Above and all around him, it was grey, pale, dull, undefined. There were no birds to be seen.

And the rain soaked his hair and his shoulders as he rowed away, and the oars made perfect furrows behind him, and before he was halfway to the jetty and the Wherry Inn, the houseboat and the island itself were lost in the veils of rain and mist and greyness. It was not yet cold, yet the damp air felt chill, it penetrated to the bone. There was no wind. No sound, save the sound of the rain.

By eleven o'clock, he was on the road, wrapped in a rug, sitting up behind the brisk little pony. And all over the flat fields, rain, rain and greyness.

But he carried Norfolk with him, and the sights he had seen, the moonlight on the water, the stock-still heron, the graceful curlew, the cries of the geese, carried the whole place, and the peace and silence and beauty of it, in his head and in his heart.

The road turned inland. He was to spend one more night away, before returning home.

Running up the stairs to change – for she is late, she is to accompany her mother to the shops, to Whiteaway and Laidlaw, and then to the bazaar – Kitty stops dead.

Thinks, and cannot imagine why the thought has not occurred to her before, but then how did she ever come to leave her friend and the cottage in Warwickshire? Why did Amelia Hartshorn come to India at all?

22

AFTERNOON. THEY have had a light luncheon at the club. And tonight there is a reception. Afterwards, they will go on to a dinner, and for the first time, they are to take Kitty. Her new frock hangs in the great, mahogany wardrobe.

But she will be brought home early.

And the shopping expedition has been a great success, though they have bought far too much.

(Though the shops in Calcutta make Eleanor long, sometimes, for those in London, for Piccadilly and Knightsbridge and St James, just once, every now and then, it comes over her, like a craving for something very sweet.)

But it is all great fun.

Now, they lie together on the bed, Eleanor and Kitty, mother and daughter, as they used to lie when Kitty was small. But do not sleep. Kitty has been talking about the cottage in Warwickshire. Eleanor listens, listens. Strokes her child's hair.

Thinks, with a dart of pure anguish, but I cannot, I *cannot* let her go! And loves her passionately at this moment. And fears too how things would be with her, if Kitty were gone. For what purpose would there be in her life then?

She sees herself, getting older at the receptions, parties, dinners, visits, weddings, gymkhanas, balls. And all the afternoons and evenings at the club.

Turns, to look again at Kitty, quiet now. But her eyes are not closed. Pulls her closer.

Thinks, an abrupt realisation, but she has already gone!

In the garden, the fountains cascade, up and over and down, up and over and down, so gracefully.

The rest of the shooting party, his father and brothers-in-law, went earlier.

Now, Eustace Partridge walked home alone across the stubble fields, his gun beneath his arm, wet through, chilled.

But his mind was not tired, his mind would never be still, all day long, there were pictures in his head. Scenes, glimpses.

The past.

It was barely six o'clock, but dense dark.

He stopped to get his bearings. And became aware, all around him, of the night creatures, the cowering birds, the secret fox, the wild-eyed, palpitating rabbits.

But almost at once, plodded on again in the direction of home. (For of course, a house had been found for them, on the estate, it was all perfectly in order, perfectly satisfactory now, things have been accepted.)

He had begun to grow accustomed to not thinking, diverting his attention. Though his mind would never be still, night or day, and the pictures, the glimpses, ran on of their own accord through his head.

And at home, his wife sat beside the drawing-room fire.

Or was with his parents, and seemed contented enough.

'It has all turned out better than we dared to hope.' Or so his mother had said.

It began to rain again. There was no moon, the owls lurked, huddled down into themselves, in the heart of the woods.

He walked on.

The long windows of the parsonage gave onto a terrace, and then, to the sloping lawn.

The proportions of the house were perfect, he had always thought so.

And by the time the trap had turned into the drive, the sun, a fuzzy, reddish sun, was just shining.

And they all came out to greet him, or so it seemed, there were small children and young people everywhere, and his friend Cecil Moxton standing shyly behind – for he was the shyest, the most diffident of men. Short, sturdy, with a pale, bald, domed head.

But Isobel was nowhere to be seen.

They climbed up onto the trap, patted the pony, hung onto Thomas's arms, took his bag, danced backwards up the path before him.

He was their favourite visitor, the honorary Uncle.

He did not know about children, was inhibited with them – though now some of them were growing up, it was perhaps easier. But in any case, they ignored his inhibitions, refused to notice them, brushed them aside, as if they were simply of no account.

And so, they were not.

Later, after tea, the two men walked in the fields, the terrier dog running before them.

The sun was low, poppy red.

'Isobel seems – seems rather better?'

Cecil glanced up. Stopped, looking around vaguely. Watched the terrier dog bolt away towards the far hedge.

Thomas had known him for twenty years. And in those years, eleven children had been born. Two dead. After each one, Isobel had been unwell, had grown melancholy, nervous, hidden herself away.

But today, she had lunched with them, had welcomed Thomas with unusual warmth, clung to his arm.

In the hedge, the terrier dog was crouched forward on front paws, nose frantically probing.

Cecil Moxton said, 'There is to be another child in March.'

The sun dropped half below the far horizon, flushing the grey skeins of cloud.

Thomas stood, watching it, watching the dog. Silent. Appalled.

Yet at dinner, seeing all their bright faces around the table, and aware of their closeness, their mutual, loving concern, in spite of his own misgivings, he envied them.

23

'THINGS HAVE been coming to a head. I know that. You think I don't notice things, but that is simply not true. So we must discuss it and settle something. I do so hate it when you fret.'

'Miss Hartshorn . . .'

'Wretched woman.'

'No, it is *not* her fault.'

'Well, she'll be off soon after Christmas and I for one will not be sorry.'

'Taking Kitty with her?'

'*What?*'

'That has been the talk. You know I have said this to you before – that Kitty is restless – she longs to go to England . . . to . . . to reconcile it with her own dreams. And to spread her wings. To be better educated.'

'Yes and that is all very well.'

'*I* don't want her to go. Of course I do not. I shall hate it if she goes. But it isn't a question of my needs, my wants. My selfishness.'

'So I suppose it has all been decided.'

'Of course it has not. But it must be.'

'You think she should go for a spell, a holiday . . . why not? Yes, let her go.'

'She seems happy enough now.'

'Superficially.'

'You think she should go.'

'I wish you would not simply jump at a solution and then

dismiss the whole matter from your mind, Lewis. I need you to support me.'

'You know I always do.'

'Miss Hartshorn has a friend . . . a Marjorie Pepys. They have a cottage in Warwickshire. There has been a good deal of talk about that. Kitty would live there – that is her idea . . . she would continue to tutor her, but there is also a girls' school, apparently. In Leamington Spa.'

'Well then, why not let her go?'

'I do dislike having to conduct a conversation like this through the open door of your dressing-room.'

'Well, I suppose you've discussed these plans with Kitty – and so forth.'

'I've listened.'

'It sounds perfectly reasonable, for a month or so.'

'If you want to know what I think . . . I think it sounds *sapphic*.'

'Good God!'

'Oh . . . and . . . and narrow . . . and after all, we don't really know . . .'

'No. No, I suppose not.'

'She is still a child – she will not even be sixteen. I want the best for Kitty. The best education . . . and care . . . the best environment – the best future.'

Eleanor stands, tall, her hair long and loose on her shoulders. Beautiful hair. But this way, it makes her face look older.

'I thought that I would write to Florence. In Cambridge.'

'Yes,' he says at once. Turns on his side. 'Yes, of course.'

Which she sensibly takes for his approval.

And so, the following day, she does write.

And so – and all, really, very quickly, and easily – and so, it is arranged.

The Turn of the Year

DECEMBER. The snow fell early. It was a white Christmas, for once in a lifetime. People even skated on the river. There are photographs in attics, to prove it.

And out on the fens, the birds froze quietly to death and the reeds rattled together in the bitter wind, and then were still.

Snow all over England. And in the midst of the snow, the old images, the old words, spoken again. But to some, they sounded freshly.

And it came to pass in those days, that there went out a decree from Caesar Augustus, that all the world should be taxed.

On Christmas Eve, Florence dined with a bishop and was bored, but not disagreeably, and later, went to church, and, hearing the old words, bent her head suddenly, and vowed to work for good.

Old Mrs Gray, waking at three on Christmas morning, made up her mind to go to Scotland again, and well before the spring, and so lay awake, planning, dreaming, remembering, listening to the clocks, excited as any child.

In the college chapel, the candlelight shone on the great scene of the Nativity, and on the face of the one, rapt, kneeling figure of no importance and Thomas recognised it afresh, and, reading the old words aloud, admired their beauty. But no more, perhaps, the beauty did not pierce the heart.

Snow fell. Eustace Partridge walked the fields, gun under arm, and hares fled and shrews stiffened, cold in ditches, and he went on doggedly, and did not think of the college chapel, nor of the narrow streets, the books, the firesides, the friends, his own, once dazzling future.

And in another country place, Cecil Moxton spoke the old words, too, before trudging back towards his parsonage through the snow. And, seeing the lighted windows ahead of him, was lifted up a little in gladness for the child to come, and turned his face aside from the gathering shadows, the same ones that always darkened around his wife, after a birth.

Snow fell. The year turned.

Impatient with the meanderings of the Committee for Moral Welfare, Florence abruptly offered most of the money for the house in the country from her own purse, and got the rest out of rich Miss Quayle the brewer's daughter, who was ill, and anxious to buy off death by almsgiving.

And so, the purchase was quickly secured.

On the second day of the new year, Eustace Partridge's wife miscarried her child.

The snow melted.

A pair of wagtails scurried and bobbed about the grass of the Fellows' court, beneath the little fountain.

Florence and Georgiana had talked of a week's holiday together, walking in Switzerland, made tentative plans.

But now, of course, that had all been set aside, because of the letter from India.

And so, everything to do with the house in the country being for the time being accomplished, Florence turned her mind to the arrival of her young cousin, Kitty Moorehead.

The weather turned mild. The new year wore in.
  Just perceptibly, the days began to lengthen.

Part Two

1

AND QUITE suddenly, there it had been. The land. Home. The cliffs and then the green, green fields. Just as they had talked of, just as they all remembered.

And at once, everyone had fallen silent, had withdrawn into their own thoughts, and intense emotions, and simply stood, leaning on the rails, and stared, stared. And the sight of it began immediately and perceptibly, to change them. They drank it in desperately, home, the green land, the white cliffs, and the little red-roofed houses, and were themselves like parched, cracked, long-dry land, drinking in water, they relaxed, softened, began to blossom. And then had to come to terms with what it meant.

And who am I? thought Kitty, standing on, as the ship sailed slowly, and the later afternoon light flushed the fields pink and gold.

Who am I now?

And she, too, was overwhelmed by the thoughts and feelings that poured in, confusing her, was uncertain how to sort them out, and so, simply stood, alone, and received them.

With the first sight of England, it was as though she had indeed entered into a new world, a new existence. But she realised at once that it did not have anything to do with the past, and her childhood, or with anything at all that she remembered (for in fact, she remembered very little, there were merely flashes, still pictures illuminated here and there, but unrelated to one another. They were tableaux, and of little interest.)

Kitty had a profound and shocking sense that her own life was beginning, here, now, as if she were somehow wakening to real consciousness for the first time. India, the heat and the brightness, the people, that way of life, were behind her, and had receded not merely in distance but in time, so that already, they belonged to another consciousness altogether, to memory.

And the voyage had come between, and now, sitting here, watching the shadows slip over the land, and the darkening water, she felt utterly different, and strange. Older. And that anything was possible. And she was afraid, and shrank from it, yet excited and went boldly forward to embrace it.

Who am I?

The thoughts were grave, cold, solemn.

She shivered. The air smelled faintly sweet and damp.

Now, in the little houses among the folds of the dark hills, lights were coming on. But then, spaces, and silence in between.

Who am I?

And the future rushed to meet her in the furrow at the prow of the ship, and she welcomed, yet could not think of or imagine it. She looked down at her own hands, pale as ghosts on the rail before her.

And the voyage, too, had been terrible. Terrible and wonderful and shocking and it, too, had changed her, in ways she had only just begun to recognise, and could not yet understand.

The voyage and what had happened on it had overwhelmed her.

But not the sights. Those she had taken for granted – the schools of silver flying fish, the porpoises, the hot nights thick with stars, the seething ports, with naked children clamouring at the docksides, the endless yellow and brown land and the heat and then the unexpected cold, and the blueness of the sea, and the slowness of it all.

None of that.

Life at home, in the past, had been like so much of that.

But all the rest of it.

Below deck, Miss Amelia Hartshorn, on the bunk in her cabin, was overwhelmed too by the confusion of emotion. She sat, straight-backed, and absolutely still, and all around her, the boxes and suitcases and bags, neatly packed and labelled, so that the little, dark, stuffy place that had been her home, her refuge, was once again bleak and bare and unfamiliar.

When the siren had sounded, and she had heard the voices from above calling out, 'Land!' and 'Home! Home!', she had been among the first, heart pounding, scurrying up the iron staircase, pushing her way to a place at the rail, desperate, like the rest of them, for the sight of the cliffs, the coast of England.

Home.

The reality of it, the actual, rather ordinary sight – and yes,

yes, of course, it was so green, and all was as it should be, yet, so much *smaller* than she had expected – the land itself, had made her tremble, and a rush of memory, a whole flood of recollection, of times, events, and words forgotten, pushed deliberately down into oblivion, had rushed over her, so that, after only a moment, she had gone back down the stairs alone, and into the silent cabin. And the crowd at the rail had parted slightly to let her through and then closed together again at once, her agitation had gone unnoticed.

She thought, it is here, it is now, that I have so longed for, and the rest is over.

For a second, she felt absolute joy.

But what she had had was her own adventure. Now, somewhere, stood the cottage in Warwickshire, behind the woods and overlooking the water-meadows. The words of the psalm ran through her head, as they had done so often in India, filling her with longing.

Like as the hart panteth after cooling streams.

She had forgotten why she had ever gone there, why she had made her escape. Had forgotten, once there, how like some bright, glittering mirage it had always seemed to beckon. Endlessly, she had read the stories, the legends, the descriptions, and her head had been filled, waking and sleeping, with dreams and visions, of vivid birds flying and jewelled turrets, of mountain peaks and hot plains and teeming bazaars. All the romantic things of elegant society.

In the cottage, where the rain dripped endlessly off the trees and the river ran swollen and brown and the darkness gathered and was never pierced by the sun for day after day, Marjorie Pepys held her book up rather close to her eyes, and the room smelled faintly of dog, and the clock ticked, ticked, ticked.

Well, then, Amelia Hartshorn thought, so it is over.

But did not look up and out of the small porthole at the cliffs, gliding by in the dusk.

And at least, the voyage was almost at an end, too, there was that relief.

2

ELEANOR NO longer weeps. There are no tears left. And she must comfort Lewis, who cares more than either of them had expected and is shocked by it, the grief is unceasing, and harsh, and leaves him vulnerable, shaken, guilty. They reach out falteringly for one another, and cling together, though they speak very little.

And the cool house is empty, and all the rooms seem silent, the dust in them lies undisturbed.

But after a time, they allow life to reassert itself, and Lewis works and Eleanor, of course, is always busy.

And they know it is the best for Kitty, and soon, very soon, there will be letters. Apart from that, there will be the arrival of the Hot Season, and all the business of the move to the hills.

At the club, the social round grows more frantic, now that the end is in sight.

Eleanor finds other women with whom to talk intimately, about the sending away of children, of parting, and agonising and worrying and waiting for news and making the best.

'At least,' she says, over and over again, in one way or another, 'at least we had her childhood. And she is almost sixteen now, after all, we cannot hold onto her for ever. She needs to stretch her wings. But at least, we have so much to remember.'

The other women stare at her with large eyes in which

tears almost always stand, and see not hers but their own children's faces, and gaze and gaze, for fear that they may fade and be impossible to recall. Their own children are very young, much younger than Kitty Moorehead. They listen to Eleanor's words and find themselves hating her.

And Lewis wakes in the night still to find that he has been weeping.

3

TO BEGIN with, naturally, they had been absolutely necessary to one another, because of the strangeness of the shipboard life, and of their fellow passengers, each had been the other's only refuge. And Miss Hartshorn had felt her own responsibility keenly.

They had shared a cabin, they had eaten quietly together, they had sat out on deck, through the hot days, and late into the beautiful, star-filled evenings, reading aloud from Miss Hartshorn's books, discussing poetry, and drama and prose, ideas and images, they had done crossword puzzles and played elaborate games of patience, and walked up and down, up and down. And Miss Hartshorn had talked.

Kitty had not allowed herself to think, to dwell on home and the past, or to speculate about the future, and the enormity of what she was doing.

But after a week, of restless, cramped nights in the close, dark little cabin, perhaps even less than a week, she had grown restless, had looked away from the books, and up and about her, wandered off alone sometimes, had hidden on the far side of the ship and leaned on the rail, and watched the flying fish soar past like flights of silver arrows, catching the sun, and felt by turn tremendous energy, and surges of excitement, so that she thought she might have leaped up like the fish and touched the sun; and fear, terrible fear, that threatened to obliterate her.

On the eighth day, she had asked for a cabin of her own. But there was not one, of course, to spare, so that instead, she had had a mattress and blanket brought up on deck and slept out, through the tropics, in defiance of Miss Hartshorn. It was not until much later, on reaching the Mediterranean, that the sudden coldness at night had driven her back below.

On the tenth day, the young officer, whose name was Hartley Hanson Kay, had come to stand beside her at the rail, and after a while, invited her to play a game of deck quoits.

And perhaps Kitty had liked him or perhaps she had not. But either way she had enjoyed herself hugely, hurled herself into game after game, and others had joined them from among the younger passengers, junior civil servants, young wives, there had been boisterousness and laughter. Later, they had sat on deckchairs, Kitty and Hartley Hanson Kay, talking a little, laughing at rather feeble jokes.

Miss Hartshorn, finding them there, had intervened at once, had taken Kitty down to the cabin, admonished, warned, reproved.

'You are not yet even sixteen,' she had said, over and over again. 'And you are in my charge, my care, I am solely responsible, until we arrive in England.'

(But after that, at the quayside, one presumed, her responsibilities would be over, she would hand Kitty over and that would be the end of it. She resented that, resented the whole matter of the cousin, and the arrangements for Cambridge which had been made behind her back.)

That evening, she had gone up alone and spoken to several passengers, and finally, to the young man, who was amiable and pliable and stupid enough, and wanted no trouble, certainly, and, so, the next day, had ignored Kitty, and kept to the other side of the ship entirely, among his own crowd.

Kitty felt bewilderment, and a profound sense of injustice.

As well, perhaps, as a certain relief. Thought fiercely, standing once again, quite alone, that she had not come all this way, had not left her home, merely to find the company of some young man attractive. She burned with a hunger for learning, real learning, far above Miss Amelia Hartshorn's little books, for knowledge, and the desire to do good.

So that the time was exactly ripe for the meeting, which took place by chance the following day, with Miss Lovelady.

'A missionary,' Amelia Hartshorn had said, dismissing the woman with the grey hair rolled up like a tight fat pincushion at her neck.

Not that she herself was irreligious.

Only, she had picked up, on the voyage out to India, a certain knowledge of the hierarchy of the ship, the unwritten code which was the guide to how things were done.

Missionaries were not regarded. If they travelled together, they kept together. Travelling alone, they were left alone. Which was to say, shunned.

Not that she had anything against missionaries.

(For governesses, she was aware, came scarcely any higher up in the order of things.)

'A missionary, a Scots person, I daresay.' (Though Miss Lovelady was not.)

And so, the little, dumpy woman had passed by and out of sight and they had gone on with their reading of Swinburne.

And then, there had been the incident over the young man, Hartley Hanson Kay.

The following day, the weather had worsened, after the progression of so many calm, still days and nights. There was a storm – discomforting, though not particularly serious. And Kitty had felt exhilarated by it, the rough sea and the wind, the turbulence matched her own mood.

But Miss Hartshorn was prostrated. She lay on her bunk in the cabin and was scarcely able to raise her head, from the appalling seasickness. She had no energy left at all to attend to Kitty, was barely even aware of her existence.

So Kitty went up on deck, thrilled by the rolling, boiling

sea, and the wind whipped her hair into her face and she tasted salt on her lips and felt that she might sing and dance and shout with exhilaration, it was as though she were riding the ship, and her own body was part of the wild movements.

After a moment or two, she became aware that the little dumpy woman, the missionary, was on deck too, standing with her face turned upwards to the rain and the blown spray, wrapped from head to foot in a long mackintosh cape like a grey cloud billowing up and around her.

They smiled at one another. But words were shouted, yelled out, yet still went unheard above the din. In the end, exhausted, they were obliged to retreat, and then, naturally, came together to talk, in a corner of the passenger lounge, which was entirely empty.

And the woman, who was a missionary, introduced herself as Editha Lovelady. And so, the friendship was begun.

For the next three days they became inseparable. Though for two hours every afternoon, Miss Lovelady rested in her cabin, and then, Kitty wandered about disconsolately, picked up a book and did not read it, stared at the water, thought about their conversations. And Miss Lovelady retired quite early to bed. She had been seriously ill, it was a heart condition that obliged her to return home earlier than she had ever planned, from the missionary field. Indeed, she had never planned to return at all.

'I would have hoped to remain there. To die in India. That has been home, there is no other. And I am only sixty-two. I dare say that seems very old to you. So old! But I could have worked for, oh, another ten years at least. I feel I am still needed, that I have something left to give. But we do not always choose, Kitty. And I have accepted it.'

Though there was nothing for her in England. She had been one of only two daughters of a clerical family. But they were all dead, and there were no relatives, none at all. There was just the house, let for years, but empty again now. It was to the house in Norfolk that she would go.

'And you are to be with your cousins in Cambridge and that is not so very far away. Perhaps our paths may cross again.'

They sat in Miss Lovelady's cabin. It was early evening. Miss Hartshorn was still prostrated.

'I love it here – it is like a little sitting-room. Like a home.'

There were beaded cushions, and brass ornaments neatly set out, and an Indian spread over the plain ship's blankets, there was a little canvas stool and an embroidery frame, a crucifix on a stand with a religious picture beside, rows of books, and a little spirit stove on which Miss Lovelady had made tea. And a fruit cake, and shortbread in tins. All through the late afternoon and evening and again in the morning, walking out on deck or when the weather calmed, sitting there once again, they had talked. Kitty had talked about home and her childhood. and about herself, her plans, feelings, longings, bewilderments, desires. She had told stories, about the friends in Calcutta, and life at the club, and poured out her anger, at the cruelties of India. She had never talked so much, or so intimately, never wished to do so, before.

And Miss Lovelady had listened, and nodded and sometimes spoken. But mostly, let her have her head, and only sat, sewing.

Books had been discussed, too, taken down and riffled through. But it was not like the lessons with Miss Hartshorn.

'Have you read *Pilgrim's Progress*? Do you know Stevenson? *Kidnapped? Dr Jekyll and Mr Hyde*? I feel you would so enjoy something that stirs the blood! Such storytelling! And then you should be ready for Dickens now, you have such a passionate heart, Kitty, such a sense of injustice. You would find so much fuel for your righteous indignation in the pages of Dickens – oh, and such vigour and humour. Such life!'

But several times a day, she had admonished Kitty to return to Miss Hartshorn.

'She may need something – or else just want your company.

She may be feeling a little better, now that the storm has subsided. You must be sure to attend to her, Kitty.'

For Miss Lovelady was strict in her sense of duty, and Kitty was not to be indulged.

But Miss Hartshorn lay, drained and weak after the appalling bouts of sickness, and wanted nothing. Though she resented the presence of Miss Lovelady and the holds she had on the girl's attention, she would have liked Kitty here, in the cabin, quietly sitting. But did not know how to insist.

Miss Lovelady had cards. She taught Kitty the game of piquet, and then they played, engrossed, for hours, at the same time listening to operetta and the music of military bands on an old wind-up gramophone.

She talked only a very little of her own life in India, the country in which she had lived and worked for thirty-two years. There had been long spells at various mission stations, in the Hills, and very remote places. She had loved it completely, and unreservedly, had never had a day's unhappiness, she had loved everything about the country, the people, the life.

She would never see it again. The pain of that thought was the greatest she had ever had to bear. She could not bear it. And so, it was easier, not to think, not to speak.

'I shall be interested to see the house in Norfolk again,' she said, 'we spent holidays there, when I was a child. I wonder if I remember it aright?'

And looked at Kitty, across the cabin, and Kitty seemed to her to shine like an angel, all innocence and hope.

'And you have everything before you!'

Kitty looked up, hearing the note in her voice, and smiled. But did not, of course, fully understand.

Only that night, for a long time she could not sleep. But lay, aware of the gentle motion of the ship, and thought of Miss Lovelady and how it must be for her, and perhaps realised, then, the extent of her loneliness. And, she herself seemed to be looking from some great height at her own future life, which was spread out like a new country below her.

She felt herself, and yet not herself at all. And then thought quite calmly of home, and saw that, too, as if it were a picture being unrolled, saw the house, the gardens, and the fountains arching up and over and against the immaculate sky. Her mother, walking elegantly. And she was suspended here, between them, and had no part in any of it, but she was perfectly calm, perfectly content.

The ship creaked and settled within itself, sailing on.

In the opposite bunk, Miss Hartshorn, still weak, her limbs aching, thought of nothing, nothing at all.

Kitty slept.

And in her sleep, in her dreams, Editha Lovelady wandered about the house in Norfolk, went from room to room without faltering, and found that she remembered it all perfectly, and in every detail, it was simply as it had always been, and nothing was forgotten, the grittiness of the sand on the floor of the hall, and the soft, pale mounds of it, pushed into the crevices of her shoes, as she slipped them on, and the muddle of nets and walking-sticks and racquets half propped, half fallen over, in the green painted porch.

As she moved about the house, she opened windows to let in the sunlight, and the sea air, for although she was alone, in her dream they were all expected, everyone was coming down.

She took down books from shelves, old, faded story-books, and banged them. But there was scarcely any dust, there had never been dust here.

Beyond the windows, the short front garden and the path that led onto the lane and the lane that led down to the flat shingle, pale pebbles stretching all the way to the rim of the sea. The smell of the sea, and the sea-shore, pungent, salt, came to her nostrils. On the sandy patch of front lawn, a solitary grey plover, running, stopping, running, stopping, making its little, low whistle.

But it seemed in her dream that she waited alone in the house for hours, going from room to empty room, and that no one came after all, and the tide lay far out, far out, and she knew no way of reaching it.

In corners and cracks, spiders' webs, and the nests of tiny mice. And when she touched a curtain to draw it back, the faded fabric fell apart, soft as a cloud of powder in her hand.

Waking the following morning, Miss Hartshorn felt better, able to sit up and wash and perhaps even to eat a little breakfast. Later, she might dress and sit in the chair. So that Kitty was obliged to remain with her, to talk and ring for tea, and tidy the cabin a little.

Beyond the porthole, sky and sea were limpid blue with scarcely a blur between.

But at eleven o'clock, she was able to escape, for Miss Hartshorn was very weak after all, she must lie down again on her bunk and rest, though the sickness had gone.

There was a good deal of activity on the ship, people about on deck to enjoy the air again, for it was warm now, a calm spring sunshine.

But the passage that led to Miss Lovelady's cabin was quite silent, quite deserted, and when Kitty walked down it, a steward barred her way. For Miss Lovelady was dead. Had died in her sleep, in her dreams of wandering from room to room of the house in Norfolk.

Kitty stumbled back, up the iron staircase, and stood on the deck, staring, staring blindly, at the unbroken surface of the sea.

In India, there had always been death, casual death, anywhere, all around her, she had lived with it, grown up with it, and it had scarcely touched her. Eleanor had visited the woman with the dead baby, and there had been other women, with other children, dead of some sudden sickness; a friend at the club had died of smallpox and Father's clerk had fallen down dead of apoplexy, there were bodies, sometimes, in the ditches, on the streets, and the wailing from funerals and the smoke from the pyres hanging acrid on the hot air, and sometimes the bodies were removed and sometimes they rotted.

But still it had never truly touched her, never caused her heart to falter in its beating, its chill had never rested upon her.

Editha Lovelady had been her friend for four days, she had found her by chance and yet by choice too, for and by herself, the closest in the world, she had told truths, welcomed Kitty and her confidences, yet somehow kept at a distance from them, had respected her. She had made Kitty begin to recognise and understand her own self.

In so far as it was possible, Kitty had even loved her.

And all the doors she had opened still stood so, giving onto new rooms, new worlds.

But she herself was dead, and they would never talk again. An image of the dumpy body, of the pincushion, of grey streaked hair, lying still and stiff on the bunk – was she on the bunk, was she still in the cabin at all? – stood between Kitty and the view before her.

And Miss Lovelady had been alone, entirely alone.

'I would have wanted to die there, in India. But we cannot choose.'

Kitty began to shake, so that she was forced to hold her hands together tightly until the bones cracked.

She felt terribly afraid, as though she herself might dissolve and disintegrate.

People sat, or stood at the rail, in pairs and little groups, murmuring. People knew. But no one looked at her, no one spoke.

'What will happen? Oh, what will happen?' she wanted to cry out to someone. But only stood, her throat constricted, and did not, could not, move one step or speak at all.

'What will happen to her?'

For she had not the least idea.

It was all over rather quickly. It seemed that the death had scarcely been discovered than it was dealt with, for it caused a shadow to fall across the ship, it discomforted them. It was best got out of the way.

Miss Hartshorn did not feel able to attend. And would have prevented Kitty but did not know how, felt helpless, weak. Afraid, perhaps.

The funeral was at four o'clock in the afternoon.

People kept away, on the other side of the ship, out of respect, or embarrassment. And because a death, an unexpected, shocking death, is an intrusion, it casts a shadow.

But a few gathered, officials, the chief steward, the chaplain, black as a crow, and another missionary, a Mrs Fanshawe, with her mother, appearing from somewhere. (They had never spoken to Miss Lovelady, nor even been aware of her. Only, hearing of her death, it seemed a duty, to attend.)

Kitty stood apart and alone in the sunshine, and her mouth felt cracked and dry. She was terribly afraid. Thought that she might faint. But did not.

The ship's engine was stilled.

Somewhere below, a small child, crying, crying.

'We therefore commit her body to the deep, to be turned into corruption, looking for the resurrection of the body (when the sea shall give up its dead) and the life of the world to come, through our Lord Jesus Christ.'

No, she would have cried out, oh, oh no, wanted to lunge forward and somehow hold back the grey bundle, for the sight of it filled her with horror and dread, and anger, a terrible anger.

No, I am here, you shan't go, you are not alone, they must not, no.

But she did not speak or move, and Miss Lovelady, shrouded, quite alone, slipped over the side and was gone and the ship scarcely paused, scarcely faltered in its step, the smooth surface of the water was scarcely broken.

The sun went on palely shining.

In the night, Kitty awoke, trembling, and in the end, got up and went out into the cool, still night, and stood in a corner of the deck.

Who am I? she thought in panic. Who am I? For it seemed sure that she was no longer the person she had always been, the familiar child. Death had touched her, and changed her for ever, it had awakened her irrevocably to the knowledge of mortality, her own most of all. *I* will die, she thought, over and over again, *I* will die. She touched her own flesh for reassurance, but received none. And the vision of Miss Lovelady's grey body slipping into the water remained before her eyes and would not fade. She felt loss and grief, and all the things she might have spoken of, or might have asked and told the dumpy woman in her crowded, reassuring cabin, swirled about like a snowstorm inside her head, and would not settle. Most of all, she would have told how she felt now, the fear, the anger, the sense of betrayal, most of all, she felt infinitely betrayed, but did not know by what, by whom.

Above her head, the night sky was clouded, there were no stars.

In the cabin, undisturbed, Miss Hartshorn slept.

4

DRESSING TO go out (for it is her forty-first birth-day, they are to dine at the club), Eleanor holds up a scarf of crimson tulle, and for a second, it veils the light and she sees the world as rose-coloured, softened, comforting, and is reminded of some scene from the past, from deepest childhood, and a rose-red shade or curtain, drawn against the light, and her mother coming in to soothe her.

And is Kitty reminded, and in some such chance and casual way, of her?

But the scarf falls, floats down onto her open palm, and rests there, and it is too hot for the late afternoon, the weather has changed. She thinks wearily of all the business of getting ready for the move to the Hills.

5

BUT INDIA might never have existed, except in dreams. And the afternoon darkened to evening and night, and a light drizzle began to fall, but still, Kitty stood on deck, watching, waiting. And Miss Hartshorn waited, too, but did not watch, only stared at the floor, alone in the cabin, surrounded by boxes and cases, packed and strapped.

Then, the door blowing suddenly open, brought in the smell of rain and river and docks, of Home, and she was filled with joy, joy and then dread. But still, she wanted to jump up and go to join Kitty on the deck, and embrace her and stand watching with her. But did not.

In Miss Lovelady's locked cabin, all the things that had belonged to her, the remains of her existence, waited for no one and were of no significance now. What will happen to them, whose are they, Kitty would have asked; and she thought, ridiculously, of the fruit cake, and the fingers of shortbread in their tins, and the row of brown, sensible shoes. But she could not bring herself to speak about any of it, and whoever would know?

And the house in Norfolk waited, too, windows tightly closed, yet the spring gales battered at them and loosened the locks, and inside, the floorboards moved, curtains shifted, and then, stillness and silence again, and the empty rooms waited. But for whom, for what?

Kitty's eyes smarted, with tiredness and watching, her body felt cramped and stiff, but she could only be taut, alert, it was not possible to relax.

On the quayside, the lamps shone fuzzily here and there through haloes of rain and gleamed in pools on the ground. There was the usual clangour, as the great ship edged in.

Florence stood, under a corrugated metal overhang, sheltering from the rain and the bitter wind, and waited alone, for Kitty.

For there had been a moment when she had allowed herself to look the likely truth of things full in the face, and acknowledge it absolutely, like pulling aside a curtain and staring, just once, straight into a mirror before drawing back.

The truth was, that he would not marry her, that he had no interest in her at all. (But nor had he in any other woman. He would never marry. She might take comfort from that.) She might plot and determine, but her own wants counted for nothing, and had no power.

He would avoid speaking to her, encountering her in any way, if he could. And suddenly, the frustration of it had worn her down. (Though as soon as she had glimpsed and admitted the truth, she had turned aside, and could not bear it, she allowed new hope to flicker up from somewhere, and cupped her hands around it tenderly, shielding it like a weak and fitful flame.)

Well, but at least she had a status, she had been a married woman. When she looked at the other women about her, in their society, that too was a comfort.

So she had determined to throw herself completely into the business of looking after Eleanor's child, and planning out her education. For she had surely some maternal instinct which would serve. And so, for several weeks, she had gone energetically about, letters had been written, visits made.

There were to be classes on certain mornings. Poetry and other literature with Miss Bell at her cottage in Jesus Lane; art appreciation, and some mathematics and natural history, and Thea Pontifex had been approached about finding a tutor for history.

Then, she supposed, religious studies, about which, surely, it would be perfectly in order to consult him?

There must be visits to London, too, to the museums and the galleries, perhaps even, from time to time, to suitable plays. ('She will want more than that. Young girls do nowadays. She ought to be sent to a proper school, she will need to mix with friends of her own age. It is all very different from when you were young.' So said old Mrs Gray. But was not particularly attended to.)

The room was got ready, a very nice room, Georgiana had said so. It was at the top of the house, long and low, with a window at either end. They had chosen pretty new curtains and a wallpaper. There were painted bookcases, and a small armchair, and the chimney had been swept out to allow a fire to be burned in the grate again.

Beyond the windows the Backs, the meadows, the river, and on the other side, all the rooftops of Cambridge, and the great college tower, whose bells would tumble her awake.

And a mirror on the dressing-table and a desk and chair and a new quilted cover on the bed.

It is what this house has lacked, Florence thought, looking round at last, young footsteps on the stairs, a lighter, brighter voice, energy, interest, eagerness. It is what *I* have needed. For she had never had anyone but her mother to care for or take trouble over.

She will bring a breath of fresh air into our dreary lives.

6

THE WIND blew, great gales marauding across the bare land. Branches of trees snapped off and whirled away.

Out on the fens the birds fled, or hid, huddled, and were battered about.

And with the wind came rain, and where a slate had blown off the roof of Miss Lovelady's house in Norfolk, the rain drove in like nails, and seeped through the ceiling, gradually staining a circle, and ran in a channel down the scullery gutter, and drip-drip-dripped steadily onto the yard.

But who was to know or care, what had it to do with anyone at all?

Crossing the gardens late in the afternoon, under a scudding sky, Thomas Cavendish saw, because his head was bent, aconites, yellow as butter and a clot of snowdrops on fragile stems, pale beneath the branches of the copper beech, and on the grassy rise close to the hedge. And stopped, his coat flapping in the wind, and looked down with sudden pleasure at the first faint marks of spring.

On the table in his rooms, a private letter from Jonas Daubeney, the College Dean.

The hotel was rather dark, with heavy oak furniture and lace curtains thick as curd cheese and drapes and covers and cloths of maroon-coloured plush.

People spoke in low voices or not at all, only sat staring into the fire, or turning the pages of newspapers.

Kitty was pale, almost silent. Tired. Beyond the windows in the darkness it rained a chill, thin rain. She could not believe it was possible for India to exist.

But the dinner was good, plain and hot and substantial, and Florence encouraged her to drink a little wine.

'It will all seem much better in the morning. Not so strange. And you will feel fresh again.'

She looks like a child, she thought, *is* a child, among so many dull elderly people. And felt sorry for her and reached across to press her hand.

Kitty smiled, pushed apple pudding onto her spoon. Thought, who am I? What am I doing here? And glanced round the stuffy little room in panic, searching for something familiar, recognisable, to comfort her, and unexpectedly, found it, in the sight of a small brass gong, embossed with figures, and a frieze of animals around the base of the stand.

'Oh, everyone has those!' she said to Florence, 'they are always on the sideboard. In our houses in India.'

But then, trying to swallow the food, she could not, because the tears spurted up, into her eyes, her nostrils, her throat, they filled her mouth and threatened to choke her.

Calmly, gently, Florence led her out.

It had been a long walk, longer than Georgiana had anticipated, out to the old hospital, if she had realised, she would have called a cab. Only she supposed that the exercise would have done her good. Except that the wind had beaten her about the head, pushing against it had exhausted her completely. So that, arriving in the cold, dark entrance hall, she had been obliged to sit down for several minutes on a wooden bench. She was wet, too, the wind had driven rain into her face all the way.

She sat listening to footsteps echoing sharply down the tiled corridors, and the sound of wailing, and the incessant coughs.

Nowhere, Georgiana thought suddenly, nowhere should be like this, so dark, so bleak, so chill. The faces she saw were hard, preoccupied, closed, they had dead eyes.

And then, eventually, on reaching the ward, she was told simply that Mary Dundas was dead, since the previous day. Mary, who had been their housemaid all those years ago, until she had grown lame, and wayward, and unreliable, so that they had been obliged to let her go.

And where had she gone? Georgiana thought now, and the truth was that she had never known, never enquired where, had, perhaps, not wished to be told.

After quite a short time, Mary Dundas had been all but forgotten. But last week the letter had come, that she was old and very ill, dying even, in this hospital, and had asked if she might see Miss Cavendish.

And now, Georgiana had come at last and sat in shame and distress on a hard chair in a cold corridor outside the door of the ward and all around her, the wails, the cries, the moaning, and the brisk, impersonal footsteps.

Mary Dundas was dead. Were there relatives? Friends? A later employer? She did not know, could not ask.

No one should die in such a place, in this way, she thought, and gripped her hands tightly on the sides of the chair. But how could she have prevented it? What could she have done?

Somewhere, a bell rang, and then fell silent, and after that, for a few moments, there was only the sound of the rain pattering against the uncurtained windows, and onto the skylight above her head.

Lamps were lit and glowed in the corners of the room. The fire burned, rich red at the deep heart of the coals.

The Dean's face was scored over with fine lines like cracks in a map. Now and again he spun the globe that stood on the table beside him, touching the tips of his fingers to the coloured countries spread over its surface. Africa. The Australias. China. The Indian Empire. Thomas followed them round.

Africa. The Australias . . . and ocean upon ocean.

As a young man, looking through the windows into this room, this scene, he would have looked upon everything he wanted.

And now?

The wine gleamed golden in his glass.

'You are poised,' Daubeney said, and spun the globe again. 'But of course you realise that. Unless, you were looking to a bishopric? In which case, I would say . . .'

'Good heavens no.'

'No. I imagined not.'

Thomas stared into the fire. Whatever Daubeney had wished to discuss with him he had not expected this. Though he supposed that, had he been asked directly, he would have agreed that the Master of the college must wish to retire some day. He had simply never given it any thought, it had not concerned him.

'You would be the clear choice of the majority. That is not in doubt.'

'But you yourself? . . .'

'Will be seventy-one this year, Thomas. Besides, I have no such ambitions.'

And have I? The fire cracked like a pistol, shooting a blazing cinder onto the hearth.

Africa. The Australias. China. The Indian Empire. Africa. The Australias . . . and ocean upon ocean.

Georgiana sat holding a new book on the history of the Trojan Wars. It was a pet subject of hers. But did not read, only walked the cold tiled corridors again in her mind. Tried to recall Mary Dundas's face.

But she had left her address, insisted that she wished to be informed about the funeral; at least, she had done that.

As he walked back through the empty town streets, the wind came roaring at him down alleyways and around corners, tearing at his clothes, and along the quiet residential avenues, the trees thrashed madly together.

It was very late. There was scarcely a light in any window.

In the end, when the fire had almost died out, and the globe had ceased to spin, he had gone back to his own rooms, intending merely to collect some papers and his coat. But instead, had sat on in the darkness, going over what had been said, trying to come to terms with it. Only the cold, and the last clocks chiming through the courts had driven him out.

Above all, he could not understand why the offer – or at least the suggestion of an offer – had not raised his spirits. Why he did not feel pride, vainglory even, the thrill of ambition satisfied.

Only, looking ahead, he had seen himself in those rooms, beside those fires, for all the years to come, until death.

But what other dreams had he? Where else would he want to go?

The wind yowled, racing down the road, hurled itself at him and wrenched the gate from his hand, and then, for a second, the clouds parted to let out the moon, and turning, he saw some wild, fleeing figure, on the far side and ahead.

But, trying to focus on it, looking again, there was nothing, no one.

He let himself very quietly into the house.

Kitty woke from a nightmare of suffocation into darkness as thick as felt. The room smelled faintly of must and moth and airlessness. She had sunk down into the depths of the feather bed and the wad of quilt lay like lead over her body.

She had forgotten – if she had ever known, how this felt, to breathe in air that was cold and damp and yet to be stifled at the same time under the weight of bedclothes.

In India it was always hot, and the single sheet was always light (but in the hills at dawn the air was cold and fresh as spring water, and then, you woke and leaned forwards to roll up a blanket that waited ready at the foot of the bed).

And, struggling awake from the dreams of drowning, choking, she sat up and could not make out anything around her, could not see her own hand when she held it before her face. And together with relief at being awake after all, being alive, came the thought that she must die. She, Kitty, would die, nothing more certain. The *only* certainty. She touched her hand to her own face. Die. *Be* dead.

And what was 'dead'? And where? How could that be?

Miss Lovelady had said, 'We are in the hands of the Lord. We must be on His side, on the side of the Right, we should "put on the whole armour of God".'

And she had responded to that, with all her heart. To take up a sword and fight on the side of Light and against the forces of darkness, to stand up, for the poor, the hungry, the oppressed, the imprisoned, the sick, to do battle, to right wrong. All of that had sounded an echo in her heart.

Now, alone in this dark room of a strange hotel, so many thousands of miles and light years from home, she felt only fear, fear and dread and bewilderment and weakness.

And where was Miss Lovelady now? She who had spent thirty-two years of her life spreading the Gospel? Who had so stirred Kitty's brave imaginings, who had said, 'We cannot choose.'

With God. So she would have said. But if not, then where? Nowhere. Nothing.

The image of the grey bag, drifting down through fathoms of dark water, bobbed about in her mind, it was anchored there, and would never float away.

She wanted to call out to her cousin in the adjacent room. But did not, for the cousin was a stranger still, and what would she be able to say or do? And the journey across to the window, between the humps and knobs of the unfamiliar furniture seemed too perilous to make.

Then, and strangely, it was for the first time, she thought of her mother, saw Eleanor, standing against the light and the softly sifting curtains, smelled her as she lay on the bed beside her.

She did not cry, but turned over into her waiting arms, and, sighing, fell asleep at once.

But she is old, he thought, stopping suddenly in the doorway. She is an old woman.

Georgiana, sitting beside the fire, reading, her spectacles slightly askew on her nose. The lamp cast shadows under her eye sockets, and in furrows down the sides of her mouth, and, seeing her so, he remembered what their mother had looked like, for there she was before him.

He was shaken. For this was his sister, who had always been a child, a young girl to him. And he felt a spurt of anguish and of guilt, too, thought, what life has she had, does she have? She is alone. She will grow old, is doing so, and I have not noticed, barely thought about her. Does she worry? What does she care about? What dreams, hopes, does she still have?

He realised that he did not know, had not known for years, nor ever thought to enquire.

She saw him, or sensed that he was there, laid her book down. He stepped into the room.

But did not, that night, speak of his conversation with Daubeney. He was not ready, did not know what he thought of it himself, what he wanted. He could not yet discuss it with her.

And so they simply sat, side by side, close to the fire, and Alice brought in the tray, and outside, the wind roared and beat upon the windows, and the sudden draught made the fire blaze.

He wondered if she would care to move into the Master's house, in the college, to leave here, after so many years, to continue to subdue her own life to his. Did she resent him? Perhaps so. Perhaps with reason.

But he said only, 'So the plans for your holiday were quite abandoned.'

Georgiana set down her book, leaned back in her chair, eyes closed.

'Oh yes. Florence has gone today to fetch her niece. The ship will have docked now. I think they travel back to Cambridge tomorrow.'

'I see. I had no idea how much it was all a great disappointment.'

'Florence's niece?'

'The holiday in Switzerland.'

'Oh no.' She made a slight, dismissive gesture. 'No.'

For perhaps it would not have been very satisfactory, they would have quarrelled, or the weather would have been too cold, or else she would still not have felt completely well. Something. Anything. Perhaps it had never been a good plan.

'You seem tired.'

'Yes.'

'Perhaps you ought to see Hannon again? Your cough . . .'

'Oh, that will linger until the warmer weather, you know that it so often does. I am perfectly resigned to it.'

'Yes. The year is at a low ebb. But there were aconites and snowdrops out in the Fellows' garden today.'

'And a terrible wind. I walked a long way against it. I daresay that is why I am tireder than usual.'

'Walked?'

'To the old hospital. I was sent for by Mary Dundas.'

'Mary Dundas . . .'

'The maid. Years ago. You will not remember.'

He did not.

'But she was dead. Since yesterday. I must have meant something to her all these years, for her to send so urgently. I failed her. She was already dead.'

'But you were not to know, of course, you . . .'

'I should have gone at once. I did not, and the fault is mine.'

Her voice was flat and dull. He recognised the depth of her self-blame, and did not try again to dismiss it. Said nothing.

But, after a little while longer, got up and went into the conservatory, where the small birds had gone to roost, and only stirred, fluttered a little, as he entered, before quietening and settling back again.

He closed the door, and sat down among them in the darkness. In the small parlour, Georgiana stayed on, thinking of nothing in particular, before the dying fire, too weary, for the moment, to face the effort of going up to bed.

Adèle Hemmings walks alone through the dark avenues, past all the shuttered, respectable houses, and the wildness of the wind delights her, excites her, the wind lifting her clothes, and the rain running down her face and finding a way beneath her clothes to her body, and sliding, cold over her skin.

For she goes out every night now, or almost, very late, after her aunt has gone to bed. And if her aunt does not want to go to bed, but sits up, demands cards and tea and the serial story read aloud to her once again, and conversation and company, then she is scarcely able to bear the frustration, she feels her restlessness like an itch, the desire, the need to be out alone in the darkness, walking, walking, blots out all other thought.

But in the end, the old woman does go, heavily, painfully up the stairs, in the end, the lights are out, and the cats, too, slipping away from the house, down through the garden, and Adèle Hemmings is one of them, but they are intent upon their own secret, malevolent business.

And no one sees her, no one is aware, except perhaps one man, returning late, glimpses a figure, running before the wind, or a nursemaid, up to a restless child, and, glancing between the curtains, down into the night streets.

Or perhaps after all it is only shadows moving in the wind.

And so she ventures further, away from the shelter of the familiar avenue, out from under the protection of the walls and overhanging trees, into the lanes that thread the town, under the old buildings, and away towards the open spaces, her feet soft on the grass, nearer to the river. Here she is not alone, here are others, hidden among the tree trunks, in the shadows, alone or together, and perhaps she sees or senses them, perhaps not. But either way, does not care, she is exhilarated simply by being here in the wind and rain and darkness, far from the stifling house and the smell of more than a dozen cats and the snores of her porcine aunt. Who, if she wakes, breathless, sweating, unwell, afraid, and fumbles for the bell that is always close to hand, and rings loudly, demandingly, and calls, calls, will not be answered, not be heard.

But perhaps, for now, she sleeps. And Adèle Hemmings walks along the path beside the water towards the mill, and her heart pounds with pleasure and the sky races ahead of the wind, and the sound of her footsteps, like the calling voice and the desperate bell, will never be heard.

7

THE TWO friends, Amelia Hartshorn and Marjorie Pepys, faced one another again, sitting on either side of the hearth in the cottage in Warwickshire. It was as though there had never been any interlude, any parting. Except that things were in one respect, so terribly changed.

The room, though, was precisely the same, nothing had been disturbed or moved, been taken away or added, since Miss Hartshorn had left. And the woods still came down almost to the back door and the river ran through the water-meadows beyond the sloping front garden, as they had always done. Now, the wind crashed through the trees, and somewhere in the midst of them, ripped one, old, and weak and rotten, out of its socket, and hurled it to the ground.

It had rained for days, the river was running fast and rising, rising up the banks.

'There was no wind there. I missed the wind. Wind in the trees and rain on the roof. The sounds were all quite different in India.'

She would have said. But did not. She found she could not bring herself to speak of India at all. The two years were blown away like scraps, flimsy and inconsequential and so forgotten, to speak of them, to try and recall, reminisce, evoke, seemed scarcely worth the effort it would cost. The things she had seen, the beauty and the strangeness, and the horror of it all to her, became like dreams or fantasies, far away and fading farther.

'So, I was wrong to go, quite wrong. There was too much boredom, and too many terrible sights; the heat was too stifling, the dust too thick, the brightness glared in my eyes. I was made to feel subservient, I had no friends, I should have listened to you. I should not have gone.'

She would have said. But did not.

Nor ask, 'And you? What of you, alone here for almost two years? Tell me that.'

But did not.

The cottage had not changed, nor this room in it, nor the wood behind it, nor the water-meadows that led to the river.

But Marjorie Pepys had changed. Seeing her, first, at the door, Miss Hartshorn had almost recoiled, with shock and distress.

Now, she sat opposite to her across the hearth and saw that she had missed the last years of her friend's life, and must soon lose her, and then, be alone here, to come to terms with her death, and her own burden of guilt.

Marjorie Pepys's sight was failing, the eyes rheumy and vague. She had been a plump woman and now, she was thin, thin as a bird, with fragile, brittle bones sticking out through the stretched, dry, parchment skin.

She had been dark, and now was grey, the hair like fluff; had been confident, definite, certain, her movements sure, and now trembled and fumbled and shrank back into herself.

Yet she had said nothing, given no hint of illness in any letter, and so, in what way could it be referred to, this terrible, final change, what words would encompass it? There were none.

Only, within her, Miss Hartshorn's voice called out, for an answer, an explanation, and tried to comfort and reassure.

But aloud, they merely spoke of the wind in the trees and the rising river and the dog, which lay on the hearth-rug between them and still smelled chokingly, and Miss Hartshorn unpacked a little and brought out a gift or two, trivial things. Wondered fleetingly about Kitty. But did not care.

Only once, as she passed close to her chair, on the way out of the stifling little room, Marjorie Pepys reached out and perhaps tried to touch her hand and hold it. But the gesture was vague and made in the wrong direction, and came to nothing, after all.

8

ND THE sun shone and the air was mild, and suddenly, miraculously, for this one day, it was already spring. The light bathed the stones of the buildings and sparkled on the river and played on the arches of the bridges that spanned it.

Waking at dawn, in the pretty new room, and drawing her curtains back, Kitty saw a new world, in a soft, pale light of a kind she had never seen or imagined, rare, beautiful; and at once, all the greyness, the cold and rain of her first days here were swept away, and with them her own apprehensions and low spirits.

'Oh, but it is beautiful!' she said, walking up the avenue with her cousin, under the boughs of the bare trees. 'Oh!'

They stopped. Ahead of them, across the green lawns, King's chapel soared to heaven, riding, like a great ship moored. Birds wheeled in the sky, above the towers and turrets and pinnacles and tree-tops all around.

'It is the most beautiful thing I have ever seen.'

And Florence, looking at her rapt face, caught Kitty's delight and saw it all anew herself and gloried in it and her own spirits rose, too.

They walked slowly on. At their feet, the open cups of crocuses sprouted from the new grass, maundy purple, white and egg-yolk gold. A thrush delved between.

On the river, and in the mud beside the river, ducks dived,

and bobbed about in pairs, moorhens swam and the willows were hazed yellow-green.

'Oh!' Kitty said again, and again, 'Oh!' and turned this way and that as they walked, looking in amazement around her.

And so they went about the whole morning, walked and walked in the limpid sunshine, under archways and through gateways, in and out of courts. Went into a tea-shop to drink hot chocolate (for, out of the sun, the east wind still blew cold down passageways and across the grass from off the far Fens), came out again, among the horses and cabs, young men and the bicycles, to walk further still, Kitty's head a kaleidoscope of everything she saw, her eyes feasted on it in jubilation, it seemed that she could walk and look for hours and never tire, and so, Florence, walking with her, did not tire either.

And the spring sun shone on old Mrs Gray, sitting in the bay window, who felt it warm on her face, and closed her eyes and dozed a little in pleasure, and Georgiana opened the doors of the window that let onto the garden and went out, lighter of heart than for weeks past, to look for signs of the upturn of the year, among the shrubs and plants.

It was, for this one day, as if the world stood quite still, suspended, between the gales and cold and lowering skies of the long winter and others, perhaps, to come, and within this frail capsule of warmth and new light, people blossomed briefly, and were soothed, smiled at one another and spoke and strolled more quietly through the streets and stood companionably in groups on the paths beside the grass and running down to the river.

At the house in the country, which had been taken over at last by workmen, by joiners and tilers and painters and boys carrying hods, the sun shone through empty window sockets and lay in lemon-coloured fans across the bare, dusty boards, and at noon, the men took their bread outside, to sit on piles of stones and planks about the derelict yards and cobbles, snatching what they could of this unlooked-for spring, before going back, to prepare the place for so many as yet unfallen women.

And other women stood in the open doorways of cottages and for a few minutes, took the sun, and the babies played in the dirt at their feet, and out on the Fens, the warmth briefly stirred men and birds and plants and all the rest into new life.

But in the end, after all, they must return for lunch. Though Kitty protested, feeling that she might walk, or even dance, in the sun here for ever.

Only, in King's Parade, Florence met a friend, newly returned from away, and must talk, and so, Kitty went on ahead, through the gateway and around the paths, slowly, in the direction of the river, and felt, at once, very, very young, new-born on such a morning, and altogether adult, to be here, for these moments, quite alone.

Which was how Thomas Cavendish saw her, standing quite still on the curved stone bridge.

(And he, head down, was preoccupied, going over and over his talk with Daubeney, and all that might follow from it. Though he was also aware of the day, that it seemed to be spring.)

He did not know her. There was no reason why he should know her.

It was simply that, stepping aside to make way for someone or other, and looking up, he saw her there.

She wore a pale dress and coat and her hair was off her

face. Her hand rested on the parapet. And he was reminded of some still, entirely graceful bird, glimpsed on the margin of the shore.

She did not look in his direction.

And so, after a moment, he walked on, towards the streets of the town and the college at which he was to lunch.

And it was not for ten minutes or so more that Florence came, hurrying to rejoin Kitty, he and she did not meet then at all.

Why does the weather affect us so? Georgiana thought. She had carried one of the basket chairs onto the terrace, and sat there, her hands idle in her lap. Why should this sun, this unexpected warmth and how the earth smells, the cloudlessness of the sky, make such a difference to everything, to the way we feel and hope and behave towards one another?

The previous day, and for some weeks past, she had been tired and bleak-spirited, there had seemed to be so little point to anything in her life – in all their lives.

Yet now, in this first spring sunshine, there seemed nothing wrong that could not easily be put right, and she looked to a new future, new prospects – though how, or of what, she could not have told.

And of course, the previous day had not only been cold still, cold and wet with a harsh wind blowing about the curded grey sky, it had been the day of Mary Dundas's funeral. Georgiana had followed the coffin, had stood in the dark little chapel, and at the burial ground, beside the open grave, and been entirely alone, save for the clergyman and some hospital official, a bald man in a dun-coloured coat, to whom she did not speak. And feeling the harsh, spiteful, pins of rain on her face, she had wept, tears of anger and bitterness and guilt, as well as of sadness, that anyone should have lived through their last weeks – and how many others before? – and died and now should be buried so, without family or friends. Even I, she had thought in shame, I am only here when it is too late. For Mary Dundas sent for me – though I scarcely remembered her – and I delayed and did not come, until after she was dead – and was there any good reason for that?

There are too many alone, she said. And as she stood there, looking down at the crumblings of earth on the bare coffin, had thought of so many. And then of Florence, alone, for all there was her old mother, and Adèle Hemmings, with no one save for the unloved, unloving aunt. And she herself, too, she realised, she and Thomas, for whichever of them died first would leave the other quite alone.

Unless, she supposed vaguely, her brother were to marry. But dismissed the idea at once, knowing that he would not.

She thought of Alice.

So that, as soon as she reached home, she had gone to talk to her, for a long time, sat on the chair beside the range in the kitchen, and told her about Mary Dundas's funeral, and then, for something else to say, about Florence's cousin, Kitty Moorehead from India. (Though Alice, used to being left to herself, was disturbed, and looked at Georgiana oddly from time to time, uneasy until, in the end, she left. For Alice had her friends, the others who went with her to the spiritualist church as well as those awaiting them there, and who were always with her now, presences, voices, so that Alice never felt truly alone.)

There was warmth and balminess in the air until late in the afternoon, though the shadows were long, and the sun had gone off the garden. Georgiana walked up to where the clumps of daffodils were bright – brighter even since that morning, against the dark leaves of the laurels and rhododendrons, and the last of the snowdrops hid beside the first of the crocuses, at the foot of the trunk of the great old beech.

And her heart was lighter; she had prayed for the soul of

Mary Dundas but then, put the memory of her, and of the previous day, behind her, for she could do nothing else now.

She looked forward to a meeting of the friends of the Missions to China, later that week, and a visit she was to make to a Home for Moral Welfare in London, and to Florence's coming to dinner with her cousin Kitty Moorehead. She looked forward to the summer and the shouts of the young men as they rowed down the river and the garden parties and the music that would float across from summer balls. Life seemed suddenly to be springing up again all around her, there was brightness and laughter and hope in the world.

So that, arriving home a little early, while she was still outside in the last of the late afternoon light, Thomas saw the change in her at once, something lighter, younger in her face and her eyes, and his own spirits were lifted by it, and he laughed with her over some story, as they took a last, slow turn around the garden, and the sky above the bare trees was streaked rose and violet and gold.

'I have not spoken to you until now – there was so much to think of.'

'Of course.'

'And I am still thinking of it – I have not yet come to terms with the idea.'

'So you have made no decision?'

'No, no. And naturally I had to consult you in every way. It is only that you have seemed rather – rather tired. I thought it best not to trouble you.'

'Yes. I have been very low-spirited. Not completely well. So many things have oppressed me.'

'But it is not like you to give in to that – you have so much energy, you always face things with such vigour . . . you know I have always admired that in you – admired your courageousness.'

She looked up at him in astonishment, and flushed a little,

for pleasure. Praise from him now was as much her lifeblood as it had ever been, she felt at once prouder, stronger in the light of his approval.

And, looking at him across the room, she began to consider him already as Master of the college, and it seemed to her an inevitable thing, though the idea had never, in truth, occurred to her before now. He had the stature for it and the gravity.

'Oh, it is what you *deserve*!' she said in earnest.

'Deserve? Why so?'

'Because you are – oh, you are a fine scholar, you have good judgement, you are *wise*. You have served the college faithfully . . . and because . . . because it seems natural and right.'

For a moment, he smiled, as he had often smiled at her when she was a girl, and had been extravagant in praise of him, believing him, as she had, to be a giant, a hero, a god.

'And you are exactly the right age, you have many more vigorous years ahead.'

'But you are speaking as if the matter is settled, decided, and of course you know that it is not. Daubeney has raised the subject . . .'

'And told you that you would have the clear majority of the college in your favour.'

'Yes.'

But then, for a long time he was silent, staring into the fire – for the evening had grown suddenly cold, it was not yet spring after all.

Was it this? Georgiana wondered. This, knowing it, some-how, even before I knew it, *this* which gave me new hope, and stirred some interest in the future again?

Strangely, she realised that the idea of leaving this house, in which she had lived so comfortably for so many years, did not trouble her at all. They would, she supposed, simply let it, and it would be here for them to return to in old age, at the end of it all.

She thought of the Master's lodging, tall, finely pro-portioned, gracing the corner of the inner court, went through what rooms she knew in her mind, and around the beautiful garden, whose lawns ran down to the river.

She had never been ambitious for herself – never, even, to marry and have her own family, she was content, so long as she had a few of her own useful activities, to live through him. But she would enjoy being the mistress of that house, she thought, now, and felt a stirring of excitement, pride even, at the prospect of their new station. And was surprised at herself, and sufficiently human, sufficiently detached, to be a little amused, too.

Thought, suddenly – but Florence would want it. Yes.

Then, looking at her brother's face again, said, 'But you are not sure at all.'

'No.'

'You don't doubt your own abilities – or that you would be a fitting man for the position?'

'No. I think not.'

'Then what?'

He stood up, and went to the window, drew the curtain back a little. The moon had risen.

'Perhaps . . . I am very happy as I am. I have all I have ever wanted. I am simply not ambitious in that way.'

'No.'

'Should I be?'

'Oh, you are as you are, Thomas . . . you should be true to that. Only . . .'

'It is what *you* want for me.'

'Only do not dismiss it because you are comfortable . . . would rather not be disturbed.'

'Afraid to change?'

'Yes.'

'Slothful?'

'No, no. But . . . I am only asking you to consider it carefully . . . look ahead.'

'I do.'

'And . . . and it is an *honour*, surely?'

He glanced round, hearing the note of pride in her voice, warmed, as he had always been, by her love and support for him. Remembered that she had devoted herself and her life, to him. Perhaps she deserved this. He should think of that.

And he could not pretend that he had not been flattered, and, perhaps, would revel in it all, in the authority, the power even.

But, after a few minutes more, he put it out of his mind, unable to reach any conclusion, and unwilling to fret over it longer, and went into the conservatory, to see to the little birds. And afterwards, worked until very late, on his bird book, and drew more than his usual joy and satisfaction from it, drinking it in like cool water. For this was what he wanted, what he did best, loved best, to be here, in this quiet room, among these books and maps and drawings and birds. Here, or else out on the marshes in his boat. These were the only places.

Everything else, he thought, must resolve itself as it would, but he would not trouble himself greatly with it.

But, at the back of his mind, there was something else, some other half-remembered thing, some sight, or awareness or emotion. But he could not recall it or name it. It was simply as though there were some area of warmth and brightness which, from time to time, as he worked, he felt himself close to, as he might row out of the shadows into a patch of sunlit water, and it was, in some strange way he did not understand, an inexpressible source of joy and absolute content.

But what? What?

9

LATER, THE weather would change again, later, clouds would bank up and gales rush in, driving rain before them from the west. Later, only a little later, winter would return, and the one bright day of spring be scarcely remembered.

But now, it was a still, mild night, now the moon rode, and shone on the grey houses, the calm fields.

On Florence, sleeping a satisfied sleep, for now she felt that it was her mission to guide her cousin Kitty, and help her take full advantage of England, for the time being, she was happy and full of good purpose.

(Though every night, she remembered the words of the Professor of Fine Art: 'A woman can make any man marry her, if only she will go about it in the right way.' For she was not deflected from her purpose.)

On old Mrs Gray, awake, as always, and eating biscuits from a rose-patterned tin, and drinking Malvern water, and contemplating Kitty Moorehead, Eleanor's child. Plain, she thought, a plain girl, and yet hovering on the brink of beauty. A child, and yet a child no longer.

Well, she would do to occupy Florence, who had had too little to do with the young, never having had children of her own, and might soften her.

Though the diversion would not last. For she was thoroughly aware of her daughter's desires and frustrations.

She selected another biscuit, and listened with pleasure to the owls in the trees on the far side of the river. The old, she thought, can do anything, say anything, and be indulged, forgiven. Like children. It is our reward, we should make the most of it. But how many did, how many did?

Now, the moon rode higher in the sky. Rode over the parsonage, where Cecil Moxton lay asleep and his wife lay awake, heavy with child for these few, last days, and over the house where Eustace Partridge slept fitfully, though not in the same bed, or even in the same room, now, as his young, bewildered wife. Who was no longer with child and would never be so, again, and who was not to blame but could not believe it. And the gulf between them was wider than any dividing wall, wider than continents. Though he treated her kindly, and with infinite concern, and so, in a way, she was happy.

Rode over Miss Hartshorn and Miss Pepys, in the cottage in Warwickshire, where a rabbit screamed in terror of a stoat, in the woods that came up to the house.

And on the empty house in Norfolk, and the grave of Mary Dundas, that would never be tended, never be dear to any heart, and over the sea, which was Miss Lovelady's grave, where no gravestone would ever be.

Over the colleges and the chapels, the river and the meadows and all the fields around, out to the house in the country, waiting, waiting.

And on Adèle Hemmings who tonight slipped out of the house and out of her coat to walk naked through the dark streets and over the sweet, cold grass.

The moon rode, until the first of the clouds came over it, and the rain spattered on the wind, as, far away, the storm gathered.

10

AT FIRST, as he came suddenly awake, it was his mother who filled his mind, and he was taken aback by it, for he thought of her so rarely – of either of his parents – he was not a man who had ever dwelled greatly on the past, though sometimes, he allowed himself to think fondly of Nana Quinn, and of the holidays at the house in Ireland, remembered with a spurt of joy his days out in the boat with Collum O'Cool. But he never thought – as he suspected that Georgiana did think – of the past as being a perfect place, for ever to be mourned and yearned for, always to be preferred to the present. That seemed to him something like a weakness, a kind of ingratitude. He would have said, always, I am perfectly content to live here, in the present.

But now, coming awake, he remembered his mother, and perhaps he had been half dreaming of her, too, and the vision of her was clear to him. But it was not the sight of her that was so strong, so much as the whole aura of her presence, her smell, her sound, the texture of her clothing, the movement of the very air that surrounded her.

He was a small boy, five or six years old, and he had fallen down the stairs. He lay at the foot, not badly injured, after all, but bruised and frightened, and she had been coming along the upper landing, and seen him fall but been quite unable to save him, had only come flying down after him, and sat on the bottom step beside him and gathered him up to her.

And it so rarely happened, because she was so rarely there, he saw very little of her, it was Nana Quinn, or one of the maids, who usually saw to him, and whom he would have expected.

But now, in the midst of his hurt and the confusion of it all, when the world had suddenly slipped from beneath him and thrown him upside down, now, it was she, his mother who was miraculously here, and he clung to her in relief and in rapture, buried his head in the woollen material of her dress, and inhaled her sweet, particular smell. The pain and shock of falling were not so much obliterated as welcomed, because they had been the cause of this, and he had held to her in desperation, knowing that once she moved away, set him at arm's length from her, she would not take him to her again, nor allow herself to be persuaded or cajoled. But for a few moments longer, they had sat together, and the memory had burned into him, so that from time to time, for the rest of his life, it would surface, and he could savour it.

Now, he lay and it was with him again, the strong sense of his mother's presence, her closeness, and the strength of the joy it had given him was remembered too.

The memory did not disturb him, he did not puzzle over or try to repress it, felt no guilt. Though why it should have been with him now, he could not tell.

But, as he came more fully awake, he was aware of something else, some other recollection.

He shifted about restlessly in his bed.

The night was very silent, very still. The moon shone.

He got up and crossed the room. And, pulling back the curtain saw, thought he saw – what? Shadows? A figure? Some movement between the trees, at the bottom of the garden. A pale shape. Then, nothing. And a cloud slid in front of the moon.

But, just as he turned away, he could tell that it was a cat, caught the gleam of its eyes as it slunk across the grass towards the shrubbery. He shuddered, hating cats as he did, irrationally, violently, not merely for fear of what they might do to his birds – what, indeed, they did daily, nightly, to all manner of small creatures. His fear was darker, more primitive, so that he was alarmed by, even ashamed of it.

He half turned, wanting to go out of the house and drive the animal away, to lash out at it somehow, banish it for ever from his garden. But restrained himself, did not move. And after a few seconds, looking back, he saw that the cat had gone out of sight into the shadows.

Then, as he let the curtain drop from his hand, and settle, it came to him, as unbidden, unexpected, and bewildering, as the sudden vision of his mother to which he had awakened.

He saw the girl on the bridge, standing, still, poised as a bird in the sunlight, looking down into the water.

And with the sight of her, came a strange suffusion of emotion that he did not recognise, but which dissolved and dissipated all of his violent rage and revulsion from the prowling cat, calmed and soothed him, yet disturbed him too.

He lay down in the darkness.

Did he know her, after all? Perhaps it was so. Carefully, he went over the young women known to him – Cecil Moxton's daughters, those of the Dean and one or two other members of his college. But they were very few and although he scarcely knew them, he thought he would have recognised their faces. She was not one of them.

He knew nothing about her then. Had simply come upon her by chance, had never seen her before and would not, in all probability, ever see her again.

Then why did he recall her?

Without realising it, he allowed himself to retain the image of her as he went to sleep, and the contentment that it gave him. And because he was still wholly ignorant, wholly innocent, he felt nothing else, neither anxiety, nor alarm, nor any distress.

11

ELEANOR BENDS her head and splashes the water from her cupped hands, over her face, again and again. And it is cold water, wonderfully, icily cold, and she remembers once more this intense simple pleasure which awaits her year after year.

In Calcutta, the water is never cold, always tepid, luke-warm, and in the last few weeks, as the weather has grown hotter again, at the end of the season, so the water has seemed suddenly intolerably warm, and somehow slimy, one can never be refreshed by it.

But now she is installed at last in the bungalow in the Hills. It perches on a ledge, high up, above and below other ledges, other bungalows, and the streets and avenues run along and slope a little, and everywhere, there are the views, the amazing sight of the far mountains.

And there has been the usual long trek to get here and before that, the weeks of planning and packing, supervising the household move, Eleanor is quite exhausted.

But it is all worth it, as always. Worth it, because of this, the wonderful coldness of the water, and the sharp, sweet freshness of the air, which she also drinks in, in great draughts at dawn, and dusk. Oh, and the flowers, the cottage gardens, and the sight of the banks of wild rhododendrons growing up the slopes, and the Scotch pines, and the blue-mauve haze of the near hills, the floating snow-caps of the far.

And to have escaped the heat and dust and the staleness and the raw brightness and the smells of the hot weather on the plains. It is all worth it.

Or would be, if it were not that she wonders now, what is the point of it all, the point of any of her life, there or here. And instead of feeling refreshed and exhilarated in anticipation of the spring and summer, she already feels jaded, weary in advance, bored before it has even begun, the social round, the calling and the rides, the picnics and parties and mornings at church and afternoons at the library and teas at the hotel and drinks at the club, and then all the nonsense of fancy dress and theatricals.

Worst of all, it is the thought of so many women together which depresses her. There are men, of course, men on leave and the men who work up here, for a lot of them move up for the whole season, as Lewis will move up, in a month or so. But still, many of them do not come, many are obliged to sweat it out in the heat on the plain, it is too much a society of women, and the younger children.

Yet it would not matter, she could still plunge herself into the life and the months to come, and not only make the best of them, but enjoy them thoroughly, and feel them to be worthwhile – if it were not for the stone-heaviness that lies on her heart, and the pain of anxiety, if it were not, quite simply, for the terrible absence of Kitty.

She sits now, at the open bay window, overlooking the verandah and the opposite hills, and hears the whistling of some servant or other, and the hooves of horses, echoing across the valley. But sees nothing, hears nothing, for her mind is full of Kitty, Kitty's presence fills the room. Where is she now and with whom? Is she happy, homesick, well or ill? Does she also sit at a window and dream of and long for, another place?

It seems to Eleanor an insane, an unimaginable thing to have done, let Kitty go, after all the years of keeping her close, defying the custom, earning the disapproval of all those whose children have, naturally, been sent away.

But she did not weep. Had not. Weeping was too facile a thing. Only sat on, looking out and seeing Kitty, seeing England, Home, and longing bitterly for them both.

But a little before four, she is obliged to dress and walk out, to return a call on the wife of the District Commissioner, and, just for having done her hair and made herself look well, she feels better, more willing to face the day.

And she meets this person and that person, all women, all strolling along the Mall, for all the world as if it were the promenade at Eastbourne, and the air is fresh and quite delightful. And she does, she reminds herself, have a certain position here, and being here, has a duty, too, to represent Lewis.

So that, when she catches sight of little, subdued, wan-faced Myrtle Piggerton, whose child died, she crosses over the road to greet her, and, seeing the relief and gratitude in the young woman's face, feels encouraged, by having done the right thing, and makes an arrangement to have luncheon with her the following day.

And Kitty, for the moment, steps back a little into the shadows.

12

'OH, BUT the spring!' Georgiana said in bitter frustration. 'Whatever happened to the spring? I had begun to feel so much better, really quite uplifted. Oh, treachery.'

For they sat huddled in the little parlour after lunch, over a fire that smoked and would not draw, and outside, the wind blew a gale again, that lashed rain at the windows and had already brought down the early boughs of blossom, scattering them all anyhow onto path and pavement, had battered the first daffodils, and sent the rest of the world scurrying back to its lair. Now, the wind was strengthening again, the two women sat, hearing the trees lash together like waves of the sea. They had eaten mutton and capers and coconut sponge, but then, Georgiana had planned a walk, around the garden, and perhaps further, up the avenue towards the Backs in the sunshine. Instead, they could only stare at the awful fire, and talk of raising a subscription to pay for the furnishing of the house in the country, going over and over the old names.

And Florence had had a letter from the matron of St Faith's Shelter, in East London.

'We are welcome to visit any weekend, to suit our convenience – the late morning would be the most suitable.'

Georgiana glanced out of the window at the grey sky. 'Perhaps – in a week or two. Perhaps we should wait until there is some prospect of our enjoying the outing.'

'And we shall make it an outing! Travel up by train and stay overnight – perhaps two nights? – at a good hotel. There are no end of things we might do – theatres, galleries – the shops in Piccadilly . . .' Florence stood up and walked to the window, waved her hand dismissively at the outside world.

'Never mind about the weather. We shall simply ignore it. We have far better things to consider.'

Georgiana looked up at her, tall and stately against the light, her hair coiled. Thought, yes, she should be the wife of the College Master, the mistress of his house, she would become the position so well, give it such style.

But since Christmas, or before, since feeling so unwell and having so many things that weighed so heavily upon her, she felt that she had gradually lost what desires she had had, for her own independence and freedom, more and more she wanted merely to settle back and live the quiet, dull life she had, after all, always lived here, her energy had drained away, and she was in retreat from the thought of any challenge, any change.

And so, the idea of giving up this last prospect, of a comfortable life as her brother's support, when he became Master (for there was no doubt at all in her mind that he was surely destined for that), the idea of Florence's marrying him and so supplanting her, depressed her intolerably. For where would she herself be, in that event, where would she go? She saw herself in a dim little back sitting-room of the Master's house, growing dowdy, disregarded and patronised, as his spinster sister. Or else remaining here, rattling around in this house alone.

'Yes. London,' Florence said energetically. 'Let us fix a day, and I shall write to the matron. In any case, London has been on my mind, for I must take Kitty there, too, she has such a desire to see everything, quite a hunger for it. It is rather touching.'

'She is not homesick?'

Florence returned to her chair.

'She scarcely speaks of home – of her parents or India, at all. It is really impossible to know what she feels. She is such – such an *earnest* little thing, so serious, so solemn. She says that she wants to "do good in the world". I daresay that was something she learned from the missionary woman on the ship.'

'But that was a terrible experience for a young girl – to be so close to sudden death.'

'She is not *pretty*,' Florence said, 'and she is in many ways very *gauche* – a child still, after all. But she is very composed. Quite self-contained. My mother has greatly taken to her. They play piquet.'

'And you are enjoying her company too, and it is very good for you.'

'Well – I intend to organise her education, that is my role, that is why she came to me – I plan all manner of things, trips, art classes, and some socialising – I am trying to round up some companions of her own age. Oh, it will all be great fun.'

'And you will bring her here to dine? I had thought of next Saturday.'

'Thank you. Yes. I am so anxious for her to make new friends.'

But she did not, dared not, mention Thomas, ask whether he might be present. Only stared at the rain on the window, and listened to the wind, and willed, willed that he would join them, that she might be given another chance.

And then, after a while, they bestirred themselves, and the bell was rung for Alice to bring in coffee, and they began to discuss the subscription list in greater earnest.

'Now you have the ace of clubs, so you must set it down.'

'Oh – so I have. But how did you know?'

'If you were a small girl, I suppose I would say that I had magic eyes and could see through the backs of the cards.'

'But as I am an older girl, you will say it is because you have been playing this game since long before I was born.'

'Correct. So, set down the ace . . . so . . . my Jack . . . there!'

'Oh, how vexing!'

They were playing in the drawing-room after tea. The lamps were already lit, it was so dark outside, dark and wet, had been like it the whole day. England was grey again, there had been one glimpse of spring, one sunlit day. Nothing more.

'Is that how you would describe yourself?'

Old Mrs Gray peered at her over the top of her half-spectacles, over her hand of cards.

'An older girl?'

'I suppose – or a young woman?'

'You are both. You are of an age when you may be anything. Like me. I would tell you to make the most of it but I need not, because, you see, if you are lucky, it all comes round again.'

But she saw that, of course, Kitty did not understand.

'Whereas Florence . . .' and she selected a ten of clubs and laid it carefully, deliberately down. 'Florence is what she is and can be no other.'

'You mean she is a grown woman?'

'Florence has always been a grown woman. She was one when she was six. I used to think that if she had had children of her own, she would have had the chance to become a child herself after all. But now I am very doubtful.'

'It is very hard to imagine people as children, once they are not.'

'Even me?'

'No,' Kitty smiled. 'No, not you.' For it was perfectly true.

'You are remarkably like your mother when you smile. So you will be as beautiful as she is. I suppose she is still a beauty?'

'Oh yes. People say it all the time. In Calcutta it is what she is known for. But cousin Florence is beautiful too, do you not think?'

'No. She is handsome perhaps, but her jaw is too square and forceful for beauty. You see, I do not think my goose a swan – though she is my only goose.'

'But you do love her.'

'Ah. Love.'

'You must.'

'Not all mothers love their children. Did no one ever tell you that? Have you not observed it for yourself?'

'No.' Kitty felt suddenly disturbed, upset in some vague way that made her feel physically uncomfortable.

'Well . . . it is true. An unpleasant fact. But you are quite old enough to have to face some unpleasant facts.'

The cards rested between them on the low table and limp in their hands, the game was apparently suspended.

'Do you wonder when life will begin? I daresay you do. You didn't cross half the world to play cards on a wet afternoon with an old woman.'

'I like to do it.'

'Life will begin when Florence decides. She is busy trying to fix up classes for you, lessons in this and outings to that, and then, she will go about finding you some friends. She will succeed, too, she is a very good organiser, when she sets her mind to it. She has organised that Home for fallen women into existence. Has she told you about that?'

'Fallen women?'

'Good heavens, don't tell me you haven't any idea what I mean. Has Eleanor kept you in complete ignorance? How very foolish I always think that is. Girls should *know*.'

'I . . . I think . . .'

'Fallen women are women who are not married but who are going to have babies. Well, it is all very natural and what happens in life, for all the world likes to pretend otherwise, and of course they have to go somewhere, poor things. Though why should they necessarily be poor, I wonder? Because they so often *are* the poor? Often, but by no means always. Well, so Florence has been putting all her energies into that. She has bought a house in the country to be

(184)

converted. Did you know that she was extremely rich? Her husband left her a fortune. *I* have no money.'

She talks to me as if I were simply another woman, another adult, Kitty realised. And if I were six, she would have done the same. I daresay she always talked to cousin Florence like it, too, and that explains why she was a grown woman at that age, if only her mother knew it. (And was rather pleased with herself for the deduction.)

'You will be very good for her,' Mrs Gray was saying now. 'Perhaps *you* will make her young.'

She stared hard at Kitty again, and then looked away, into the fire. 'Except that you seem to be travelling in opposite directions.'

'I'm not sure that I understand.'

But there was no reply, the old woman sat, brooding, silent, and, perhaps, half asleep, so that in the end Kitty went, very quietly, out of the room and upstairs.

And the light in her bedroom was pale, soft grey, less dark, because it was so high up, the window let in so much sky, and she stood, watching the rain slide down the grey roofs, not happy, not unhappy, nothing. Waiting, perhaps, for life to begin.

Of India, of her mother and father, she neither thought nor avoided thinking, they were, simply, there, she carried them with her, and could turn towards them, stretching her arms out to them at any time, and so, in a curious way, she did not need to miss them. Nor did she ever speculate about what they might be doing, at this moment or that, or try to picture them here, or there, or even to work out what time of day or night it might be with them. It was all somehow frozen, suspended in time, as when she had left, and they were doing nothing, the move to the Hills, for example, had not taken place, no changes had been made whatsoever. It was simply like a silent, motionless, bright tableau, framed, expectant.

After a while (for she had a headache, and her throat was slightly sore) she lay down on her bed and, eventually, slept, as old Mrs Gray slept, as usual, before the fire, so that neither of them heard Florence when she came sweeping, flushed, buoyant, into the house.

13

BECAUSE, QUITE suddenly, at the end of the afternoon, as Florence was putting on her hat, Georgiana
had blurted it out.

'They have asked him if he will allow himself to be put
forward as the next Master. He is the choice of nearly all the
Fellows.'

(But, the moment it was out, the moment she saw Florence's face, the eyes bright, she thought, I should never have
spoken of it, it was entirely wrong. Then why, why had she?
For now, surely, she had changed everything, spoiled her
own future.)

She had stopped the cab, dismissed it, and then walked alone,
slowly, up the avenue between the trees, in the pouring rain,
and had not minded it at all, had welcomed it, stepped across
the curved stone bridge (but did not pause, did not linger
there, as her cousin Kitty had lingered), and so, on towards
his college. It had been dismal, dark now, as well as wet, the
lamps blurred in the early evening mist, but she had walked
slowly, savouring every step, through the gateway, and under
the arch, into the outer court, and then, stood, in the shadow
of the walls, imagining, planning.

For he would be the Master, there was no doubt in her
mind, it was surely all quite settled. As soon as Georgiana
had spoken, it had seemed to her inevitable. And then, of
course, he must marry her, that was inevitable, too, he would

need to be married, in that position (though others were not, but she chose not to think of them). And whom else might he marry?

But it should not merely be for convenience. She thought, he will love me. Want, as I do.

'A woman can make any man marry her, if only she will go about it in the right way.'

She believed it absolutely.

And, after a time, of standing, and then of walking, around the courtyards, of looking up at lighted windows, and across the squares of grass towards other archways, other doors, she turned, and so went home, through the rain, her heart thudding, knowing what must happen, tense and bright with determination.

But perhaps, after all, he will say no, for he likes his life as it is now. Or someone else will be preferred, Georgiana thought, sitting in front of the mound of writing-paper and envelopes, at her desk. 'Dear Lady . . . Dear Canon . . . Dear Miss L . . .'

For she should not have spoken. He would be bitterly angry, if he knew. She had seen Florence's face change, with anticipation, excitement, and a sort of greed.

'Oh, Alice, I will only have some soup and perhaps toast. My brother is dining in college.'

But Alice, setting down her spiritualist newspaper, clucked and fussed, and would cook a little dish of baked eggs, or an omelette, and then there were some poached pears, Georgiana was not to let herself go down again, and so, she sat in state, at one end of the dining-table, obliged to eat a meal, and hearing only the tick of the clock and the scrape of her knife against the china, thought suddenly, in dread, and how often will it be like this in the future? How many evenings will I spend eating alone in a silent room, there or here, in this house still, if it happens, if he becomes the Master of his college, if he marries Florence, as I have always planned that he would?

14

THE WEEK went by. It was milder, but still wet, wet and grey. Daffodils came into bud, but did not break.

Kitty had a feverish cold, and lay in bed, or hunched in a chair beneath a rug and, for the first time, missed India, and could not turn her mind away from missing it, and from the recollections that filled her; of the gardens of their house in Calcutta, with the scarlet and orange flowers blazing from the beds, and the fountains splashing, up and over and down. She lay and let the pictures come before her eyes and gazed at them.

And now, Eleanor would be in the hills, and so, she let herself imagine them, too, the snow-line and the mauve-blue of the nearer slopes, and the echo of voices, calling, singing, ringing across from the other side of the green valley.

But her dreams and her visions were curiously unpeopled; nor did they upset her. She felt no sense of homesickness or loss or longing, somehow those feelings were quite absent, as though they had been extracted, like the painful nerves of an open tooth, so that it was now dead.

She merely looked on the scenes of India, through the grey, dank Cambridge afternoons, and they gave her pleasure. For the rest of the time, she sank down into the miserable depths of her cold, and allowed Florence, and Louisa and Ena, the maids, to bring her hot drinks and inhalations. And saw the doctor twice – for Florence took her responsibility seriously – and looked at journals and picture papers, idly. And waited for life to begin.

And sometimes, remembered the dead Miss Lovelady, saw her more vividly than any of those people she had known all her life, so that she half expected that she might walk into the room; and thought about what she had learned from her, and vowed to live by it. And was shocked and bewildered, all over again, by the suddenness of her dying.

The letters about the subscription to the house in the country, went out, batch after batch, fell onto the doormats and letter boxes, of Canon – and Lady – and Miss –.

Onto the doormat of Adèle Hemmings and her aunt. (For Georgiana believed in perseverance.)

In another part of the country, the child of Cecil and Isobel Moxton, a son, was born, and his mother lay and stared blankly out of the windows onto the bare lawns, and was consumed once more by the old familiar despair, despair and terror, though of and for what she could not have told.

But the baby was right enough, welcomed, and made much of by the rest of them, the baby did not suffer.

The week went by.

Alice made elaborate plans for the dinner on Saturday night, wrote out menus and lists, and went very early to the markets, talked at length to the butcher, before placing her order. She wanted to do her best, and for it all to be a challenge, for she had trained in the kitchen of a far grander house, the seat of a viscount, and was bored by cooking plain food for one or two, only.

Old Mrs Gray observed Florence, saw the brightness in her eye and the set of her jaw. Speculated, but did not speak.

And Florence chose a new dress, and two spring suits, with hats, and spent a great deal of time and trouble, not to say money, over it.

The week went by.

The letters were opened, and some ignored, others destroyed, but some replied to at once, with promises, or even cheques, as is always the way. It was a tedious business.

But that addressed to the aunt of Adèle Hemmings lay unopened, with a good many other letters, in the hall, among the mess and squalor of dust and cats. (For the maid who had given in her notice and left had not been replaced.)

At lunch on the Friday, several people had approached him and expressed support, urged him to allow himself to be considered.

Now, just after six, he sat alone at the table in his rooms, in the light of the reading-lamp. There were books open before him, an undergraduate who had read him an essay on Tyndale had just left, his feet clattering vigorously down the wooden stairs.

But Thomas had hardly heard the essay, would not have known whether it had been good or bad, he had not attended to the young man at all and he was ashamed of that, for he prided himself on being dutiful, on teaching his pupils with care, perhaps the more so because his enthusiasm, his heart and soul, were never fully engaged now, his real work was elsewhere, had been, in truth, for years – how many years?

He thought, I am living a lie, then? I am dishonest. I am interested, yet it is no longer of first importance to me. I teach the young men Latin and Greek and New Testament studies, because that is what I have always done, what I am trained to do, and perhaps, I do it well enough.

But it does not *live*, does not stir me.

How much did that matter? How much was private to himself and affected no one else? He could not tell.

Now, he walked to the window, and looked down into the quiet court. Thought, and am I to be Master here?

Then, for a few seconds, he was gripped with passion for the idea, it burned up and consumed him, he felt a flush of pride, ambition, desire – and was taken aback, for he had never been a man interested in power or position. Yet he saw what he might do for the good, and longed to do it, to have the right; and was tempted, too, to imagine himself walking across the court, into Hall, or taking his stall in the chapel, and was appalled, that the idea so excited him. Thought in panic that after all he did not know himself.

And went, then, to the chapel, to kneel down in distress in the silence and darkness, hoping to still his confusion, to come to terms with his discovery of himself. He did not pray, formed no thoughts or words in his mind, merely knelt and waited, hoping, gave himself over to God. And wished, in his heart, that the matter had simply not arisen, that he had never been suggested as the possible Master, and the calm tenor of his days had not been ruffled.

But as he knelt, his eyes closed, he saw before him, not

any vision of himself going about in glory, that was swept away and altogether disregarded.

What he saw was simply, the girl again, as she stood on the stone bridge looking down into the water, that sunlit, solitary day of spring; and with the sight came, as it had come before, absolute peace, absolute contentment, absolute joy, so that the recollection of it made him tremble.

15

A GROUP of women, a tableau, in the carefully lit drawing-room (for Georgiana, like Alice, had gone to a great deal of trouble).

Florence in parma violet, falling full from a tight waist, to show off her hair, her height, her figure.

And Georgiana in claret, with pearls (suddenly full of presence), a match for anyone.

Old Mrs Gray, in black with a plaid stole, upright on the best chair.

The door opened. He saw them, as if arranged for a portrait, and the room as he had rarely seen it, glowing, formal.

And beside the fireplace, stood the girl. Quite still, her hair back from her face, her dress pale.

But her head was slightly turned away, and in shadow.

He stopped dead. And panic and confusion rose to overwhelm him.

The tableau broke. Florence laughed, Georgiana stood, old Mrs Gray's eyes were keen upon him. The girl turned her head, he saw her full face and of course, she was not the same. She was a child, after all, this cousin Kitty Moorehead, and plain and pinched and rather hollow-eyed, with a cold and her hair not loose, but tied back in a neat single plait.

But taller than a child. A girl then.

A different girl.

There was delicate soup, and a glazed, decorated salmon. Alice's face was smooth with pride, as she stood back from the table, admiring, confident. She had extra help in the kitchen and her friend from the spiritualist fellowship had lent the new little parlourmaid, Ellen, the family for whom they worked being abroad.

And they settled Mrs Gray on Thomas's right, a good deal of fuss was made of her.

Kitty was opposite.

Looking round, at the silver and the candles and the dresses of the women, at Alice and the parlourmaid, white-starched, seeing forks raised, heads bent, hearing the murmur of conversation, he thought that this is how it would be in the Master's house, night after night, people dining formally, guests, elaborate meals, evening dress, and how could he bear it? He was not that sort of man.

But Georgiana was enjoying herself, she would rise to it, embrace it all.

He caught Florence's eye. Looked away.

Looked across at the girl, whose head was inclined, listening to old Mrs Gray, and saw then that she was, quite certainly, the same. And, being certain, felt a miasma of disappointment seep up through him. For the sight which had been so extraordinary, and the memory he had carried with him, was ordinary, after all. It had merely been this plain child, standing on the stone bridge.

Kitty thought, Miss Cavendish is nice but there is something not quite right, it is as though she is playing a part, not being her usual self. But nor is cousin Florence, who is giving herself airs (for she had taken in more of human behaviour in India than she realised. She had seen airs before.).

(196)

And the room is so small, I had expected something much grander, and old Mrs Gray says wise things and mad things and disturbing things and now she is dozing. And they are all so *old*. For she had not seen a young person here, apart from the undergraduates, who did not seem to be very young, and some small children with a nurse bowling hoops along a path.

The Reverend Mr Cavendish was talking, for some reason, about bicycles. 'And now young *women* on bicycles, clothes flying, I was almost mown down by two of them yesterday, bowling along quite out of control.'

And for a moment she despised him, and dismissed him, and would have been afraid of him too for he seemed coldly angry, except that he spoke quite quietly.

But then he looked at her across the table and his face softened. 'But there, I daresay Miss Moorehead would love to bowl along the streets of Cambridge on a bicycle. And why not? It would be the very thing. You must arrange it. Have you some friends yet, to bowl along with?'

And at once she was grateful to him for including her, for being aware of her at all.

Florence said, 'Now that is one of the things I must talk to you about. I have been busy this past week, arranging what Kitty will do, and of course she should have friends, we will find those for her – though I am not altogether certain about bicycles – but she is here to have her education completed, that is why Eleanor has sent her. I have been looking into the matter of classes. Only it all takes time. And we shall be visiting plenty of galleries and museums. She should see as many objects of beauty as possible, do you not agree? And then just mix in intelligent society. I am sure she will find friends in due course, she will . . .'

Thomas glancing across at Kitty again, saw her downcast. Said, 'But I think we should let Miss Moorehead speak for herself.'

Kitty flushed, would have said, oh, this and that . . . everything, there was so much she wanted to say. But suddenly, could not, did not speak at all, and, indeed, was almost near to tears, without at all knowing why.

Was saved by Mrs Gray beside her, who woke from her doze. 'I should like some more fish. It is excellent fish. I am very fond of fish, I was brought up on it as a girl in Scotland.'

And so the talk broke like a wave, swirled and changed direction. Moved away from Kitty.

The table was cleared, for a crown roast of lamb, ludicrously frilled.

He had opened the doors to two of the cages, so that after a while, some of the small birds came out and flew up to the roof, or here and there above their heads. Kitty stood absolutely still, entranced, and at last, one, emerald of wing, alighted for a few seconds on her outstretched hand.

She said, 'We have them in India. They are everywhere. But free.'

Disturbed by her voice, the bird flew in quick darts into a high branch of the tree that grew up through the centre of the conservatory.

The others were taking coffee in the drawing-room.

'Well, they are released like this as often as is practicable. But it is true, of course, and you are right, they should be free.'

'Oh, I was not criticising. You must not . . .'

'No, no.'

She went to the cage of moon-yellow weavers.

'These fly in the garden.'

'You miss home. India.'

'It is so strange – you see, I do not . . . it is as though it is, not just another place, another world, but somehow . . . not real. A dream . . . it is there but not there. I can't explain.'

He was silent. The birds fluttered softly. Kitty turned back.

'You see, I have come here because I want to learn. I chose to come. I am so pitifully ignorant . . . I want to know about, oh about everything. I don't want only to visit picture galleries and improving exhibitions in that genteel way, like . . . like a young lady. I want to learn about . . . about the stars and planets and Darwinism and the Greek gods and heroes and the history of religion and calculus and . . . oh, so much.' Her peaked face was transformed, shining, eager.

Moved, Thomas asked quietly, 'And then?'

'Oh, then I want to do good in the world. No, you must not laugh at me.'

'I would not dream of it.'

She sat down on the circular seat that ran around the trunk of the tree and a cloud of the birds rose up in a bright panic, above her head.

'I had wondered . . . I had *known* there was so much in the world . . . I . . . that is why I came here. To be educated. India is only tea parties and tennis and balls . . . which I quite like, but . . . And then there would have been marriage, I suppose. Cousin Florence says I must meet girls of my own age, and she is right, and of course I would like to have friends. But it must not be the same.'

'The same?'

'I mean, the same as India.'

'I think you can be sure that it will not.'

'Mrs Gray says I should certainly meet young men, too. She is very modern, for such an old person.'

'We must all seem very old to you.'

'Yes.'

'You must take care . . . take care not to lose anything.'

'Lose?'

'Oh . . . freshness. I suppose I mean simply – the joy of being young.'

'But Miss Lovelady was right. I have thought about it so much. Life must not be wasted.'

'Miss Lovelady?'

'She was a missionary . . . on the boat. I . . . she became my friend. She was a saint, I think. I learned everything from her in a few days only. I think I am quite different because of

(199)

her. And then she died. I went to her cabin and . . . but she was dead. She had been ill . . . that was why she was returning to England. She didn't want to. She wanted to die in India.'

Kitty looked up at him.

'Where is she?'

'Where. . . ?'

'Oh, they buried her body at sea. I know that. I watched it. But *where is she*?'

He knew he should say, with God, but he could not speak.

'She was such a good woman. And she only wanted to stay and die in India. Is she in heaven? I expect that is what you would tell me.'

Thomas shook his head, turned away in distress. But she sat quite composed, clear-eyed.

After a moment, he said, 'We should go back to the drawing-room now. The birds must be left to roost.' And led her out.

In the hansom going home, old Mrs Gray, having dozed contentedly on and off during and after dinner, was wide awake.

But in between, she had watched them, and missed nothing.

Now, she would not sleep again until the early hours.

She sat very upright in the corner of the cab, the plaid stole drawn around her.

Said to Kitty, 'You should be dancing. That is what all young girls should do. Dance until dawn. I danced until dawn from being seventeen until I was married and left Scotland for good.'

'But she is not seventeen, Mother, she is not yet even sixteen. There will be time enough for all that. It was because of the dancing that Eleanor thought it best she should come *here*.'

Mrs Gray ignored her, turned a little, to pat Kitty's hand.

'Dancing,' she said, again, 'dancing until dawn.'

Kitty smiled, liking her.

But felt dazed, heavy-headed, her cold suddenly worse again. She did not recall much of the evening just past, did not think at all, only let the movement of the cab soothe her.

But she had liked very much to see the birds, fluttering free. And had expected to be tongue-tied then, but was not. She realised that she had told no one else about Miss Lovelady, until this night.

She closed her eyes, which were smarting with cold and tiredness.

And Florence dreamed, like the young girl that Kitty was, and saw herself descending a staircase, entering a room, sitting at a glittering table beside Thomas Cavendish, and knew that she was envied, that she commanded the scene. Knew that she had seen his eyes, admiring, upon her.

And now could think of no possible reason why he would not eventually marry her.

Georgiana, returning from the kitchen where she had been to congratulate Alice, paused in the doorway of the drawing-room and saw the whole evening spread out before her, felt the air still seething with their presence, their finery, their conversation. There, Florence had sat, and there old Mrs Gray, and Kitty, leaning back into the shadows a little, deep in her chair. (But Kitty, she thought, had done very nicely, had been quite composed and not too shy. Kitty, for all her peakiness, had made a pleasant impression.)

Flushed with the success of it, she wanted to hold on to the evening, a little longer, to have time pause.

Thomas stood beside the fireplace. The embers had slipped down low in the grate, and were almost out.

He said, 'I have decided not to allow my name to go forward for the mastership.'

And the bubble of the evening burst and lay in fragments around her. She sat heavily down.

'I have been foolish to entertain it. Of course the position, the way of life would not suit me – it would be wholly alien.'

'If you are sure,' she said, and could not argue, could not think of it at all, she was suddenly exhausted, barely able to form the words in her mouth. 'If you are sure . . .'

But of course he was not. As he spoke, he was again thrown into confusion and indecision.

After a while, he said, 'But now is not the time to discuss it.'

Georgiana did not move. The room felt suddenly cold.

She said, 'Well, it is for you to decide.' And then, 'But at least I am glad we welcomed the little cousin Kitty Moorehead. It was the right thing to do.'

'I hope she will not be a bluestocking.' He spoke harshly. 'She is certainly plain enough.'

And did not say anything more, and after a pause, left the room.

16

THE HOUSE is quite empty.
(Apart from the servants, of course. But they do not count, they live their own, separate, alien, impenetrable lives.)

Lewis leaves at dawn, and returns as late as possible from the club, and then only to sleep here. (Though there is no real sleep, the nights are scarcely less intolerably hot than the days now. Only the glare of the sun, the brightness is gone, there is relief from that. Otherwise, one lies choked by a thick blanket of humid heat, under a net on the verandah. And still it is too hot.)

He will sweat it out here another month, and then join Eleanor in the Hills, for the rest of the Hot Season. The Hills are ahead of him, a cool, blue mirage. Sometimes, waking out of a turbulent half-sleep, he hallucinates the sound of running water from the endlessly trickling streams.

But the worst of it, this time, is not the heat. He has endured that before, will do so again. You simply get on with it. Ignore it.

The worst is the loneliness. The absence of Kitty.

He has never imagined it, nor realised, the single-minded desperation with which he loves her. Has always. He dreams of her every night, and she is always floating away from him, just out of reach.

Once, he dreamed that she was dead somewhere, and

woke, flailing, calling out in terror. Lay, hearing the thudding of his own heart, above the terrible screaming of the jackals that always fills these nights.

And once, coming home early, to change for dinner, he went aimlessly round the empty house, and, coming into Kitty's room, had a sudden, vivid recollection of doing so once before, when she had been a baby, a few weeks old. There had been no one else here. She had lain in her crib, under the veil of netting, awake, eyes open and following the slight movement of light and shadow. He had looked down at her and been so startled by her transfixed perfection, by the beauty of her head, her fingers, the mauve-blue of the skin above her eyes, that he had knelt down and . . . what? Adored her? Prayed to her? For she had been far more to him than simply his child, at that moment.

Now, he stands in the same doorway, looking ahead into the same room. And it is empty.

Asks, where is it? That time past? And where is she? Where is *that* child? And where is Kitty?

17

THE WEATHER turned mild again, the wind veered and then dropped altogether. Spring returned and would, it seemed, settle.

Everything came into flower at once, daffodils and tulips together, with late blossom and early blossom, and the buds were fat and ready to burst on the horse-chestnut trees along the avenues.

But it was still too early, everyone said, it could not last, it was not natural. The weather had been so peculiar lately, the seasons all anyhow. Because of course what people wanted was the story-book year, everything in place and as it should be, sun all summer, snow in winter, green spring, golden autumn, just as they remembered it, from childhood, when the world went aright.

The grass grew and was cut for the first time, and the whole city smelled of it, of spring.

The sun shone, gentle on the old buildings, sparkling on the water. Just as it should. And the young men rowed and the young women rounded corners, wildly, hilariously, on bicycles, skirts ballooning out.

On the marshes, the spring migrants returned, and the over-winterers were long gone to their cold northern places, and the birds paired, now, and began to build their secret nests, and the larks sang their seamless song, spiralling upwards until they were invisible. But still heard, still heard.

And at night, in the corners of gardens, under bushes, cats yowled.

Florence went about with a great purpose, fixing up this class or that private lesson, trailing Kitty in her wake, and Kitty looked about her, and tried to make sense of it all, to understand what she would have to do. And grew a little less pale, and blossomed, and relaxed in the spring sunshine. Saw the young women on bicycles and was stirred with her own ambition.

And from time to time, some young man became aware of her, in the street, and glanced back.

But Kitty did not notice.

A week passed. Thomas, deep in work, avoided people. Shut the door of his study, so that Georgiana sat every evening quite alone.

On Sunday, he preached in the college chapel and, as he stepped down from the pulpit, thought, and is this death, to step down and into the abyss? Is there perhaps, no more than this? And shuddered, and at once, turned his mind away and listened to the Testament, and, later, read from it, and recited the Creed, took shelter in the familiar words. But not, perhaps, comfort.

But the work steadied him, and he did not look beyond it, though he was aware that he had made no decision still, that his future was uncertain, and he changed his mind daily, and saw things differently. And sometimes, as he walked across the Backs, or down the tree-lined avenue, the spring thrust itself to his attention, and then he stopped momentarily, and turned his face towards it, and the vision of the marshes and the still water came to him, soothingly.

And somewhere, too, not in his present consciousness, but

hovering, waiting a little out of sight, out of reach, there was the picture of Kitty, the girl on the bridge. Or rather, not the picture itself, it was not so exact, so clear as that. Rather, it was the awareness that the picture would be there, and all the emotions that surrounded it, if he chose to look.

But he did not.

18

IN THE Hills everyone dresses in the latest fashions,
after the patterns sent from London and Paris, everyone
promenades. And it is wonderful, they are like flowers
revived, in the cool air, they sparkle in conversation, pay
visits, make plans, regain appetites, with new energy and
vigour. And if they ignore this or that – the bazaar, the
servants, and do not listen to certain noises, they can imagine
that this is not India at all, but Home, Home.

But it is not Home, and Eleanor knows it, lying on her
couch in the afternoons, listless, bored, and she does not share
the liveliness, the bubbling talk and excitement, for once, she
would rather have stayed in Calcutta, with Lewis. Or so she
thinks.

But at last she must get up and dressed, and go to tea with
Myrtle Piggerton, for they seem to have become close friends.
And they will talk desultorily, and sometimes, it is of doing
something worthwhile, perhaps starting a little morning
school for the native children, or some practical classes, for
the women. Perhaps putting on a theatrical performance, in
aid of the Mission, a play, something with a greater intellec-
tual substance than the usual frivolous comedies that are so
popular here.

Or perhaps Lewis will take her for a week's holiday, a river
trip up-country would be stimulating.

She remembers her stay in a wooden houseboat on Lake
Kashmir, years ago, before Kitty was born, remembers the
pink mist over the water at sunrise, and the terraced gardens,
rising up behind, the tranquillity of the place.

And Myrtle drinks her tea and chatters, chatters, to conceal her desperate longing for another child, and her unassuaged grief over the loss of the first, and brings news of a midnight picnic, with Chinese lanterns strung about the trees, and dancing, flirtations.

But Eleanor thinks she will not go.

Says, 'We have to do so much to please men. Why else would we be here at all? What else is there?'

And thinks of the alternative, of Miss Hartshorn, and the whole procession of sad governesses.

And the days pass, and some have affairs. But nothing to be taken very seriously. And soon, Lewis will come, and Myrtle Piggerton's obtuse young husband, and the Hill season will be at its height. And at the end of it, the packing, and the awful journey back, the winter in Calcutta. And so the world turns.

Eleanor thinks, I cannot bear it, I can no longer live like this. And resolves absolutely to return to England. To Kitty.

19

FIRST THERE was nothing. Blackness. Complete unconsciousness. And then, as though he had walked onto a stage or into a lighted room from a dark hall, there was the dream.

But it did not feel like a dream, there was none of the usual strangeness about it, everything was as usual, and as it was in life. Almost everything.

It was spring, of course, the first day of spring, the sun shone, and there was even a little warmth in it, though it was so early. The catkins and the velvet willow buds were out, and the crocuses, maundy violet, egg-yolk yellow and white upon the grass, and the delicate primroses hidden deep.

Thomas walked at leisure up the Avenue, slowed, taking pleasure in the sunshine. There were people about, faces upturned, smiling at one another, and at total strangers, because of the beauty of the day.

And so, he came towards the stone bridge that curved over the water. And glancing up, saw the girl, standing still, poised as a bird in the sunlight, her head bent, looking down into the water. One hand rested on the stone, and her hair was tied back from her face.

He stopped dead.

In life she, Kitty – for, of course, it was Kitty, he knew that now – (and yet, still it was not) had stood exactly so. And worn a pale dress.

But in the dream she was quite naked.

He came awake in blind terror. His room was dark.

Kitty, who was not Kitty, the girl, stood on the stone bridge, pale as marble.

He looked, and could not look, but the vision would not fade. The absolute beauty of it gripped him by the throat, choked and suffocated him.

He could not move.

And afterwards thought that death at that moment would have been the best, the only possible thing, would have saved all that came after.

But he could only lie on his bed in the darkness, pouring with sweat from shock and terror, unable to form any coherent thought, any words, mesmerised by the vision, by the dream that did not, would not fade, as the memory of the real sight had never faded. But the two only merged together and were suffused in a clear light.

He did not sleep again that night. But after some time, he had no idea of how long, switched on the lamp, and made to take up the prayer book. But when his fingers touched the cover, drew back at once, and could not, dared not.

Only left on the light, hoping that the vision of the girl would somehow be obliterated.

But it was not, it remained steady before him. The difference now was that he had no feelings of joy or peace in the presence of it, could not turn to it for warmth and comfort. There was only fear, of what lay in the depths of himself, and of what it had done, might do. And fear of his own powerlessness.

He would have read but could not, would have prayed, and dared not.

And so, gradually, the silver-grey line of dawn crept around the curtains and into the room, and he lay revealed in it. And then for a few moments, he did sleep a strange half-sleep and held the dream again before him and wonderfully, the dread and horror were suspended, dissolved, and he knew only thankfulness and joy, and could rest a little in the light of them.

So that, opening his eyes as the sun rose, and shone onto

his face, briefly he was filled full of what he knew quite certainly was love, before the terror engulfed him again and he fell down into all darkness.

Above all, he must avoid encountering the real Kitty. (For they were separate still, the girl on the bridge, and the cousin, Kitty Moorehead, though he knew them to be the same.)

He took to staying all day in his rooms, or at least within the boundaries of the college, and only returning after dark. And even then, took a route quite different and farther round than usual.

Georgiana, left alone, was concerned, bewildered, and went wearily back to the begging letters about the house in the country and when she raised her eyes from them, supposed that it was still the question of the mastership that troubled him. For her own part, she no longer thought of it at all. Let it be. Whatever he decided, she would accept for herself, for what other choice had she?

'Dear Canon X . . . Dear Miss de Y . . .'

His work he undertook mechanically, listened to the essays read aloud to him by the young men, went over their translations, explained this, emended that. Took refuge in Homer, soothed by the ancient story, which did not touch at any point upon his real life or concerns. And the birds, late at night – for he avoided going to bed as long as possible, he sat among them for hours in the darkness, comforted.

From time to time, he took out his notes on the sea-birds, stared at them, but wrote no more. All of that seemed far away, unrelated to him. And all day and all night, went in fear, and had no ideas what he might do.

But the picture was always there, waiting for him to turn to it. The girl on the bridge. Kitty. Not Kitty.

20

A ND FOR the next two weeks, the dream came again and again, until he was distraught. He thought that he should talk to someone. But there was no one, it was out of the question.

Once or twice he went into the chapel. But the chapel was cold and bare and empty of all help, there was nothing for him there.

And the nights came, and after the nights, the beautiful, sunlit days, full of birdsong and the greening of all the trees. It was full spring, but he scarcely knew it.

In the end, there had to be some resolution.

It was after nine o'clock in the evening, quite dark. The air soft, and smelling sweetly of grass.

He had dined alone, in his rooms, spoken to no one.

He came out of the shadow of the college. Walking briskly as he did he would be home within minutes.

But at the top of the street, he veered off suddenly, cutting down first one, and then another side lane, keeping close to the high walls, until he came out again in a different part of the town.

And after a hundred yards slowed his pace.

There was no moon, and yet he was afraid of being seen. Once or twice, a cab went by and he shrank towards the hedge.

And then he saw the house. The curtains had not been drawn, and the lamps were lit and shone softly out of the wide windows of the drawing-room.

At first, and for some time, there was no one. The house stood alone, the room empty. Thomas stood motionless on the pavement, not thinking, not knowing why he was there, or what he expected to happen. No one walked past him. If they had done so, he had not imagined what he might do.

Somewhere, a dog yapped. Again. A door closed.

And then, a shadow crossed the light and looking up at the window, he saw her. She was standing in profile beside the lamp. Her hair was drawn back. He could not see her face.

But after a few seconds, she turned and then he did see her. And at that moment, Kitty and the girl on the bridge merged and became one, reality and memory, his dream and the picture before him were now the same. He stood transfixed, and he knew love, pure and absolute, as he had never known it in his life before, so that he struggled to catch his breath. And then, he could only half run, stumbling, away, and after a long time, found himself walking fast down one of the straight roads that led between mean dark little houses, and so out of the town, towards the open country.

21

FOR IN the open country he could breathe again, he felt better with space on every side of him.

The cottage in Warwickshire was in the country, and far further from any town. But that was not open, it was closed in, the woods came down to the house and seemed to press upon it, to drain the air.

Miss Hartshorn felt choked, stifled, when she stepped outside, to stand for just a few minutes at the front door, or briefly into the garden, her lungs seemed to fill up with moisture, her head ached dully.

But she had scarcely been outside these past weeks. Had been nowhere at all.

And now, tonight, her friend Marjorie Pepys was dying.

It had come so soon.

Once, they had made plans, discussed what they might do together in retirement, where they might venture. But the plans had been shelved, had not been referred to at all, they had done nothing, everything had become subservient to Miss Pepys's dying. Day after day, Amelia Hartshorn had woken to the recollection of it, and to notice, as she had never done before, the darkness, the claustrophobia of the cottage.

They might have talked, there was much they could have said. But they did not, they said almost nothing, for talk exhausted Marjorie Pepys, and in the end, where was the point of words?

And so, they sat on opposite chairs, across the little, crowded room, and later, Miss Pepys lay on the sofa, and at last, in her bed, and dozed, and from time to time, opened her eyes, which watered constantly. But saw almost nothing.

I should read to her, Amelia Hartshorn thought, and gathered piles of books from shelves about the house, and set them on the table beside her. Now, she might read again all those writers they both loved, and which she had remembered in India, Stevenson, Thackeray, Shakespeare, Lamb.

But did not. Sometimes, picked a book up, turned a page. But could take nothing in. And Miss Pepys slept and was far away. Only watched, guiltily, helplessly, the slow business of her dying. Except that it was not slow, it had been quick, so quick, she had scarcely arrived home, had not been given time to get used to it, to come to terms. And how long had Marjorie had? And now tonight, suddenly, it was here. Death. It was almost over.

She had pulled her chair a little away, towards the window, the lamp was low, and threw shadows onto the ceiling, and in the light of it, Marjorie Pepys's face was tallow, dry.

Through the window, slightly ajar, came the night smell of the garden, the trees, the river, and from the wood, the night sounds. She remembered the horror of the night sounds in India, and how she had longed, prayed, to be back here, longed for the owl and the barking vixen, and the sound of rain sussing down through the leaves.

From the bed, a stir, half sigh, half rasp in the throat. Words? Miss Hartshorn went to her.

The bedclothes were scarcely raised, she lay, flat as a leaf or a sheet of paper beneath them, she might have had no bones or flesh at all. The skin was transparent over her wrists, bone gleamed through, bluish-white. She was a stranger, unknown, no longer familiar. Yet alive, the pulse still beat in the cords of the neck.

The noise again. Words. Yes. Amelia Hartshorn bent her head. 'Open the window wider.'

She did so, and the breeze blew in, drifting the curtain about.

Now her eyes were wide open, and very blue, bright again, as they had always been, and struggling to see.

Now, she smiled.

Miss Hartshorn touched her hand, dry as a moth's wing, she thought it might crumble to dust beneath her fingers.

And then she wanted to cry out, why did you not tell me? Why did you not write? Was it to punish me? I would have come home. I would never have gone.

Should never.

The voice came very clearly, startling her in the quiet room.

'We are barren,' Marjorie Pepys said. And then, her eyes closed, and for a long time, there was silence, she seemed scarcely to breathe.

It is death, Miss Hartshorn thought, and felt a leap within her of something like dread and excitement mingled. Death.

But the night drew on, and death lingered outside the door and in the end, the lamp flickered and failed and so she sat on in darkness beside the friend she no longer knew, and thought of India again. But without feeling. And once or twice, of Kitty. But without interest.

It was not until five or so that death came at last into the room, along with a chill, damp breath of air from off the river, and the first, sour, parchment light of morning.

'And a window is always left open, even in the depths of the harshest winter.'

Mrs Gray's fingers darted in and out, in and out, the crochet needle cocked at an angle.

'For the soul to escape, and to fly away from the body at the moment of death.'

Kitty was half asleep, curled in the armchair beside her, like a small child listening to the last story before bed. (For at last she had settled, after wandering aimlessly about the drawing-room, or simply standing, still, beside the window, close to the lamp. It was the evenings that dragged and were dull here.)

'Have people seen the soul at death?'

Dart, dart, dart. 'Oh, many have. Those with the second sight.'

'What sort of people are they?'

'It is very common in the Highlands.'

'What have they seen?'

'Some say a bird. Some say a moth-like thing. Or a wee bright insect.'

'Mother, you should not fill her head with your tales. Kitty has come here to be educated, to have her mind sharpened.'

Florence was writing a letter to Eleanor Moorehead, mainly about Kitty. But her voice was mild, she was unable to rebuke anyone, or to be seriously irritated about anything, she felt warm, smug, with hope and anticipation, she had assured herself, past all doubting now, that Thomas Cavendish would marry her.

'I have arranged two classes, in History and the History of Art. With some ladies here who have been most highly recommended – the Misses Lewis. They are sisters, and have taught in schools, and are very widely travelled. And she is to have Mathematics in a class with three other young ladies. She seems very interested in scientific subjects. But I am told that the Classics should have priority.'

She glanced up again at her mother and Kitty, huddled in chairs together, gleeful with talk. Thought, it is good for them both, for the old to be with the young. And all the time, I have something of my own, another life to look forward to, at last.

And she held the secret of it close to her and drew warmth and strength from it, fed off it, as she bent her head, again, smiling, to the letter.

He sat in the darkness, on a stone at a crossroads.

(And the house in the country, the house being made ready for the fallen women, was no more than a mile away, if he had known it.)

It rained a little, damping his hair and the shoulders of his coat. But he was scarcely aware of it, or of why he was here, or what he might possibly do.

But the night sounds, the open air all around him, made him long to be out on the marshes, sitting silently on the dark water in the punt, or on the deck of the houseboat, watching, waiting.

And he remembered his last time there, and looking back, saw it as a time not only of peace and utter contentment, but of innocence, too, like some paradise before the fall.

And he longed desperately for that time now, that absolute lightness of heart.

And he would go, get ready tonight, and be there this time tomorrow. He stood up, began to walk.

Except that he could not. He might never go there again. He was another man now.

But then an image came to him of Kitty, looking out across the water, pointing, turning to speak to him, and he grasped at it, his mind raced ahead. He would take her there, she would see it all, be with him in that place, as he knew that she would surely be with him, in dreams, night and day, if he went alone, and he walked faster down the empty road, in thrall to his fantasy.

It was only an hour or more later, reaching the first of the houses, that he stopped, and came back to himself, and to the harsh reality of things.

The clouds cleared, letting out the moon, a half-moon, waning, not bright, but giving a little light to light his way, as the old clocks chimed two, and he walked, more slowly now, dazed, as though he had been knocked out and come to, half conscious.

And in the darkness around him, there were still sounds, and others walked here and there, in the lanes and alleyways and down the avenues and across the grass that led to the river and the weir. But he heard none of them, saw nothing.

Did not see Adèle Hemmings as she walked, maggot white and naked, between the bushes and undergrowth bordering the houses higher up the avenue, her mind a mass of fragments of strange, bewildered, unrelated thoughts.

Georgiana, awake in her room, heard his footsteps and the closing of the door at last, and was relieved of her immediate anxiety, that he had not yet come home, and yet not relieved at all, but deeply troubled, and unable to speak of it. And so remained drearily awake, hearing the wind, if it was the wind, rustle and stir the branches and bushes in their garden and other gardens along the quiet streets.

22

LATE APRIL, and the first swallows seen, dipping and
skimming over water, the first cuckoos heard. And a
light breeze blows the apple blossom prettily down, to
lie in soft heaps on grass and path, fresh for half a day, before
curling, browning, scattering away.

In the gardens of the women's college, the lilac buds,
horse-chestnuts burst and flare, and the college tortoise, newly
emerged from deep beneath soil and stones, stalks warily,
legs like stilts, across the lawn.

The young women, skirts hitched, were playing croquet.

'There is croquet in India. At the club.'

Kitty sat in a canvas chair, on the terrace, beyond french
windows.

They were taking tea with Thea Pontifex.

'Oh, but then, of course you must play!' Thea sprang up.
'Come, let me take you over, let me introduce you.'

Kitty looked to where the group parted, swaying, laughing.
Already, shadows had begun to lie along the grass. She
thought, and I will come here, I will; be like that, independent,
happy, learning, among friends, it is what I want to work
for. And followed Thea.

She is pretty after all, and she is almost a young woman,
Florence thought, watching, leaning back in her chair.
Though once among them, shaking hands, talking, Kitty was
still slighter, younger-looking, and somehow frailer. For the

young women of the college had already fought battles and emerged triumphant, and were confident, secure in their place here.

She remembered her own recent passion to take up some course of study, and belong in this place, and with surprise, amusement, even. All that was far away now.

But Kitty. Yes, Kitty would do very well here, and she would be more than happy to put all her energies and powers of persuasion into accomplishing that, to live this life through her.

Kitty held the mallet, laughing. They were deferring to her, welcoming, kind. The ball cracked forward, went anywhere. The group parted and re-formed, there was more laughter.

The tortoise had reached the rockery.

Returning, sitting beside her again, Thea Pontifex said, 'Kitty must be properly taught. She is a clever girl. Little classes here and there will certainly not be enough, if these plans for her are serious.'

Mallet clocked against ball, again, raising a small cheer.

'I have made a start on arranging things for her, but it is clear that I simply know too little about the real requirements. I see that now. Kitty must be given every opportunity, be guided in every way.'

'Her parents have given you *carte blanche*?'

'Her parents . . .' Florence paused, remembering the rather vague letters.

'Her parents perhaps see it more as a way of passing the next year or so, until she is grown up.'

'Yes. I daresay they have the usual horror of female education.'

'But I do not. And Kitty is in my charge here. I am to make the decisions as I see fit. And she is clever, you say so yourself.'

'I have said that she seems to be alert and intelligent. Of course, I have as yet no proof.'

'And keen to study.'

'Yet I doubt very much if she has any idea of what study is.'

'Then she will learn. And that is precisely why we are here. Why we have come to you.'

A jubilant shout from the croquet game, and Kitty darted, slender, eager, to retrieve the ball from among the lavender bushes bordering the far side of the lawn.

Thea Pontifex turned her head away from them, to look again at Florence.

'There is something I have to tell you.'

The game was resumed.

'It is that I have become engaged to be married.'

Before Florence could comment, she said quickly, 'I shall leave the college at the end of the summer. Of course, I shall give all the help I can to Kitty until then, and think of who might advise you more closely, but I myself will not be here. It seems right that you should know. You and I are such old friends. I – we – have not yet spoken of it to very many people.'

For a few seconds Florence sat in silence, the garden, the graceful, burgeoning trees, the figures on the lawn unseen before her, as she felt anger, anger and bitter envy rise up like bile within her, and she stared at Thea, plain, dowdy, studious Thea, friend from her youth. But always, until now, somehow inferior, and to be patronised and pitied.

She scarcely attended to what else was being said – Thea's

talk of the future – the husband-to-be, a widower, father of one of the young women – a move to live in Sussex, in a village beneath the Downs, other stepchildren . . . Only felt, after the wave of anger and bitterness, a new determination, bright and strong as steel, with regard to her own situation.

The croquet game was, quite suddenly, over, and Kitty, with two of the young women, coming towards them, stepping onto the terrace from the grass.

Florence said brightly, 'Kitty, our plans are thwarted and all in disarray – but for the best of all reasons. Miss Pontifex is to be married!'

A buzz of interest, exclamation, among the girls.

And under cover of it, quite quietly, Florence said, 'And I, in my turn – though no one must know of it yet – I expect to have news of that kind myself before too long.' And felt her heart leap and quicken, as if the act of speaking it out loud must surely make it be so.

No one must know it. But, glancing up, she saw that of course Kitty had heard, and was looking at her, taken by surprise, and perhaps in some bewilderment.

Florence returned the child's gaze, eyes steady and defiant upon her.

23

THERE HAD never been a spring like it, everyone
said so.

On May Day, the lawns and gardens were
crowded, straw hats came out. The young men sprawled on
the grass or else took to the river. (And some young women
too giggling in groups, delighted with themselves. And some
of them, being kind, invited Kitty, there was to be a picnic
among bluebells under the trees. Kitty wore white, with a
silk sash, her hair down.)

Temperatures neared eighty, or so it was believed.

Now, Thomas thought of no one and nothing else. It was as
if he had gone mad. He had seen her only three times. They
could scarcely be said to have spoken.

He went out, wandered desperately among the young
people, looking, looking. (But turned away and retreated, in
shame, just as he was very near and might have seen her,
laughing, beautiful, among the other picnickers on the grass.)

On the staircase, going towards the library, the Dean.

'Cavendish – I am very glad indeed to see you. I have been
a little – a little concerned.'

It was dim here, cool, private. But still, he turned away
his face. Daubeney peered.

'I should very much like to talk. Will you come and see me? Will you dine?'

'I have been finishing a piece of work. I . . .'

'Of course. But there are things to discuss. Just in a friendly way.'

'Yes.'

'Tomorrow? We would be alone . . .'

He looked round, panicked. He did not know what day tomorrow was.

'Thank you . . . I . . . yes. Yes.'

'You are not unwell?'

'Unwell? No.'

He turned.

'I have a tutorial. If you will excuse me.'

He reached his room. Closed the door. Stood, trying to focus, to come to his senses.

Unwell. No.

Yes.

Was he? What was he?

The vision rose before him again. Kitty on the stone bridge, looking down into the water. Her dress pale. Hair back from her face. And his only thought was that he must see her. Perhaps then, somehow he would be sane again, and this would be over.

He stood at the window, looking down onto the quiet courtyard. Wagtails bathed, fluttering about in the shadow of the fountain. But all the people were gone, to the gardens, to the river. He rested his head on the glass and thought nothing. Nothing. Kitty.

24

IT WAS spring, but it was almost summer.
May blossom curded the hedgerows. At dawn, mist
wreathed, ghostly, over the river and far beyond; at dusk,
the swifts, newly returned, soared around all the towers of
the town.

And the sun shone, every day was cloudless, every day was
hot.

Florence had planned the trip to London, to St Faith's Shelter.
They were to go on a Thursday, returning by Saturday
evening. And Georgiana, anxious, preoccupied, would go,
not having the energy to do otherwise.

They were sitting in the deep shade of the copper beech.

'But it is Latin and Greek which are most important, and
she has done neither, of course, she will have to make up a
very great deal of work.'

'Yes.'

'And Scripture. I daresay those should all go together.'

'Oh yes.'

'But we have so far been unsuccessful.'

'Perhaps – one of the schools? Should she not simply go to
school?'

But having come this far, Florence would go further.

Looking away from Georgiana, watching a bluetit dart into the bushes, and at once, out again, said, 'I would welcome advice.'

'But you have taken advice. Miss Pontifex . . .'

'But this is not her field, Thea is a historian. Besides, her thoughts are elsewhere. She no longer seemed very interested – or committed.'

'Ah.'

'Might you not mention it to your brother? Or perhaps I should simply write him a letter?'

A breeze rippled the leaves above them, so that for a few seconds, they were dappled with sunlight – the detail from some painting, two women on wicker chairs, under the great tree.

Brother, Georgiana thought of him, saw him, his face suddenly older, strained, grey, and almost wept with her own helplessness, shut out. And remembered in childhood days when he had locked his room against her, and she had sat down on the other side of the door, close up to it, touching the cold wood with her hand, leaning her head against it, hating him to be within, private among his own things, unreachable in his own thoughts.

Loved him now as then, surreptitiously and in silence.

Florence said, 'I feel sure that he would be able to recommend someone, solve the problem at once.'

'Yes.' Though she scarcely heard.

Looking at her, sensing her preoccupation, Florence thought, it is illness perhaps; or simply old age already; and felt concerned. But knew that whatever it was could not touch her, she herself was immune, invincible.

The bird, through accident or its own stupidity, had caught its leg in the door of the cage. It was not badly injured, it would not die, he thought, unless of fright.

Thomas stood in the middle of the conservatory cradling

the soft, bright-feathered thing in his hands. Its eyes gleamed bead-bright. Coming to the doorway, Georgiana watched, and felt excluded again, an intruder here.

His face, looking closely at the bird, seemed younger, unlined, and tender. But catching sight of her, he frowned, shaking his head, and so, she turned away, and waited in the outer study, among the other birds, those that were dead, or present only in image, and to which she could do no harm.

After some time, he joined her. 'I am sorry. You wanted to speak to me.'

'You are dining in college?'

'I am dining with the Dean.'

'You are always rushing away. I feel I have to make an appointment to see you. You never settle, now.'

'It is full term, you should know how much there is to be done.'

'Yes, yes.'

'I shall try not to be late back.'

'But then you will be tired and preoccupied, or I shall be tired, and so it will not do.'

'Georgiana . . .'

'In any case, it was scarcely important, it was simply something about young Kitty Moorehead.'

Pain flared, pain or pleasure, anxiety, hope, dread?

'Florence is trying to find tutors for her, and just now, it is Latin and Greek. And Scripture. I am to ask if you might suggest someone suitable, that is all.'

For a second, he paused, his thoughts turbulent, flailed about among them. Then abruptly turned and, going out of the room, said, 'I am afraid I am already late. And I could not possibly advise about teaching at that level, for a young girl. What are you thinking of? How could I?'

Georgiana stared after him in the wake of his ill temper, bewildered, surprisingly near to tears.

And the Dean had almost nothing to say, and gleaned nothing at all from him, it was a fruitless, awkward evening, there were too many silences. Thomas was home a little after ten o'clock. The house was already in darkness.

He went at once into the conservatory. But the injured bird was hours dead.

Daubeney sat alone over a last glass of port.

But after all, there had been nothing more definite at any point than a few words privately spoken, some opinions canvassed. Nothing irrevocable in any way. It would be perfectly easy, if it became necessary, to go back to the beginning and start again.

He thought, I have failed with Cavendish. Or failed Cavendish. But did not know which, or how. Only drained his glass, and turned down the lamps, and went to bed.

In a narrow, cobbled side lane, leading down to the weir, a small church, tucked sideways into the wall. And behind it, someone had half made a garden, though much of the time it was overgrown, you pushed aside trailing branches and clambering brambles, trees arched, meeting overhead now, to form a green shade, roses clung to the wall; in February there were snowdrops, in May, bluebells and lily of the valley. The old gravestones leaned between. There was a stone seat.

He sat on it, in the late afternoon, and thought about love. But he knew nothing of love, or not of this kind. How could he know? He was blind, stumbling forwards in an unfamiliar landscape. For what had he loved in his life?

Places, he thought at once. The house in Ireland, and the low shoreline, and the violet shadow of the mountain. Sky and sea.

The marshes and mud-flats and water stretching to the North Sea. His days alone there. The island. The geese flying. The birds, always.

His mother, he had loved passionately when small. But the passion had faded.

Nana Quinn, he supposed. He could scarcely remember.

(He did not think at all of Georgiana.)

His work. Did he love that? Or was it merely satisfaction?

His God? No, his religion was not of that kind. But he loved the cadences of Scripture. The old words.

None of these things counted for anything at all. He saw that now. He had never thought that he might love a woman. If this obsession was love. And how was he to know? He had no possible way of telling. Marriage he had considered, but always in the abstract. He saw it as necessary for some, for companionship, and the establishment of families, and as the way women were provided for. But he had never felt the need of it.

He had watched the years of patient, single-minded devotion of his friend Cecil Moxton in bewilderment, knowing that what he watched was love of the purest kind. But had never for one moment understood it.

And the case of a young man like Eustace Partridge, who had ruined his life because of the weakness of the flesh, had merely repelled him. And the waste of it had made him angry.

Now, he sat watching a blackbird scurry, close to the earth, head dipping, and knew himself to be utterly changed. Knew joy, felt as a lightness, a quickening in his breast, thinking of Kitty, seeing her in his mind's eye.

But love?

The blackbird rose abruptly and flew low to the ground

for a few yards, before settling on one of the lichened head-stones.

A breeze blew, parting the leaves.

Love?

He got up, and left the churchyard, and began to walk quickly up the lane, away from the river.

'You will have tea, of course?'

'That would be – kind. Thank you. It is very hot.'

'I will ring in a moment. Hot? Yes. Unseasonably so, do you not think? They say it has been in the eighties – surely that cannot be natural? It is only early May. My mother says that we are going to have a glorious summer, the hottest summer ever. Oh, do please sit down.'

'I wonder how one would know.'

'Know?'

'Ever? That we are to have the hottest summer *ever.*'

'Yes, I do see. But in any case, it is only Mother, liking to pretend that she has second sight. Highland blood and so on. It makes her feel interesting. I daresay the weather will break soon and then we shall have rain for a month.'

'It shows no sign of breaking yet.'

'Oh, yes, and you are hot. I will ring for tea at once.'

She rang.

'Of course Kitty does not find it hot at all, after India.'

His heart lurched. Kitty.

But she was not here.

'This would be a day in the Cold Season, she says, and even then, it is never so fresh, the air is never so clear there. She is looking well, do you not think? Our climate agrees with her.'

'Yes. I . . . I am sure it does. She seems . . . yes.'

For a moment, he struggled, her gaze upon him. She sat on a small chair which was upholstered in eau-de-Nil, on the other side of the room. Her dress was a deeper shade of the same green. She had placed herself rather carefully.

But he was unaware.

He looked down at the carpet, counted rosebuds on the intricate border. Felt panic.

It has come, Florence thought. It is now. Now, he will surely ask.

The door opened on the maid, bearing tea.

And so, tea was poured and drunk, and a dundee cake cut, and he felt more than ever out of place in this room, and looked in desperation, at oil portraits that hung from the walls, and china in decorative cabinets, and shelves of the works of the English poets, as if for help. Found none.

And Florence spoke only a little, a few words, and then fell into silence, looking across at him.

(Old Mrs Gray, it seemed, was resting. And Kitty?)

He said at last, 'I understand from my sister that you are in need of a tutor for – Miss Moorehead. That you have had some problem?'

'Oh, for Latin and Greek,' she said, almost without interest. 'I had forgotten that I mentioned it to Georgiana.'

'I gather that she has studied neither subject?'

'Oh no.'

'But someone could be found, I am quite sure. I would be willing to speak to one of my pupils if . . . but perhaps you would not think that suitable?'

'Really, you need not trouble. Georgiana suggested that Kitty should go to school. Well, she will not do that, her parents do not seem to wish it. But I am sure a schoolmistress can be found. I have thought of a way round it and that is, I shall advertise. But it is all very trivial, really you are not to concern yourself.'

'But I would want to concern myself.'

She looked up, hearing an edge to his voice.

He said, 'She must have the best tuition from the beginning. Perhaps you will at least allow me to see any applications you may receive – so much harm may be done by bad teaching.'

Florence stood up and crossed to the window. 'She is only a girl, after all,' she said, with a slight laugh, 'I daresay all this will come to nothing in the end. She is not one of your clever young men.'

'Nevertheless . . .'

Florence did not reply, nor turn back to him.

There was silence again.

He had no idea what else he might do, only sat staring down at the empty teacup and saucer in his hands, a cold, dead misery numbing him through.

He had come only in the hope of seeing her and he had not seen her, and so he must go, back to college, he supposed, or home, or else, to walk without purpose about the lawns and paths. It did not matter where.

Florence's back was stiff and straight as a rule.

He set down his cup, rose heavily.

And, hearing him, she too felt the cold, leaden weight of disappointment.

He had said nothing.

But why then had he come?

But he was simply embarrassed, this would not be easy for a man like him.

Of course he would come again.

She turned, having reassured herself, smiled brilliantly.

In the hall, she waited, as he took up his stick, drew on his gloves, and tried to choose the words to say, '*I* will teach her. Let her come to me, let her . . .'

But could not have spoken them.

And, hearing the sounds, the maid came down the passage to open the front door, he had almost left.

And then footsteps running, and she was there, on the staircase, and seeing them below, stopped, said, 'Oh, hello . . . good afternoon.'

He looked up at her.

Kitty flushed a little, with confusion, as well as the excitement of running.

'I am going out to tea in an undergraduate's rooms – that is, a lady, a woman undergraduate, of course. I have suddenly made a whole lot of friends, isn't it fun, and they have introduced me to others.'

She jumped down the last two or three stairs, hair loose, flying out.

He was transfixed by her, his heart pounding.

Then, she looked at him, and her face became quite grave. She said quietly, 'But you must not think badly of me. I am not become completely frivolous, I have not forgotten what I said to you, you must not think that I did not mean it.'

'No. I did not think it.'

'It is just that the weather is so very beautiful and – but I am to study, it is all being arranged, there is so much I am to learn.'

It seemed to Thomas that they stood looking at one another in the dim hall for hours, then, for a lifetime, for no time.

Yet for only a split second. And that no one else was there, no one else existed in the world.

Then, Florence stepped forward, spoke, the maid put her hand up to her cap, and so, the pieces fell into a different, duller pattern, and he had gone, the usual politenesses said.

It was over.

He walked very quickly until he was out of sight of the house, and then stopped for breath, and clutched at the wall, and held onto it, dizzy and trembling violently.

And Kitty took her bag, and her wrap, too, in case the evening grew chilly. (But it would not, of course it would not, it was a perfect early summer evening. Only Florence insisted, and indeed, was rather sharp.) And by then the friends had arrived, three of the young women, she was swept away by them, she was happy. And later, reminded for some reason, of the scene in the hall, of Thomas Cavendish, felt a sudden, warm impulse of friendliness towards him, and even of complicity, as though they shared some secret from which all others were excluded. Though if she had been asked, she could not have explained the feeling, or justified it.

And then, the afternoon, the new friends, the sudden gaiety of it all, overtook her.

Coming down after her rest, old Mrs Gray sensed the air in the drawing-room sour with dashed hopes and disappointment.

Florence stood looking out of the window again.

'I suppose you want to have tea. Ena has just now cleared away but of course she can make some more.'

'No. I shall not want to trouble her.'

'Don't be ridiculous, Mother, it is what they are for, there is no question of troubling.'

She rang the bell irritably, and then, when the maid did not come at once, stalked out and into the hall.

But in the hall, stopped, and saw it all again, saw Kitty careering down the stairs, hair flying. Saw her stop, saw Cavendish look up at her.

Saw on his face an expression she had never seen before but could not understand or put a name to.

25

IN THE Hills, Myrtle Piggerton has a flirtation, and
perhaps it will become an affair.
    (But such things usually remain quite innocent here.)

And Eleanor watches and is shocked, or envious. But at any
rate, withdraws her friendship a little, and so, is even more
lonely herself. And desperate for Kitty.
    She goes to church a great deal, and volunteers to organise
a Sale of Handiwork, in aid of blind native children.
    Makes plans to go Home.

On the plain, Lewis sweats and works and drinks too much.
    Is lonely. And wakes in the hot nights, out of wild, terrible
dreams, to find that he is weeping, and tries to bring Kitty's
face to mind, for comfort.
    And cannot.

One morning, very early, Eustace Partridge walks four miles,
in the chill, pale mist that lies over the fields, before the sun
has risen, to catch the first train that rattles with milk churns,
through the quiet countryside to Cambridge.

And his young wife wakes in the empty room, not knowing where he might have gone, or why.

But by now she is used to that.

No one opens the shutters of the house in Norfolk. But a little sunlight finds an entrance here, and here, and cuts, thin and bright as a blade, across the dusty floor.

It is dawn when Adèle Hemmings slips home from her solitary spying upon lovers, and hearing voices that speak only to her from the moon and stars, prophesying, urging.

Miss Hartshorn clears cupboards and drawers and wardrobes of her friend's clothes, and parcels them, to despatch them to the workhouse, or to poor relief, and looks up from time to time and out of the bedroom window, which is still open, as Marjorie Pepys wanted, the night of her death. But thinks nothing, dares not dwell upon the past or contemplate the future. Only, occasionally some scene from India flashes unbidden across her mind, surprising her in its detail and brilliance.

For two days, the weather dulled slightly, there was cloud and a little drizzle. But then it passed and was forgotten, the sun rose higher, and May bloomed on in its full glory, of lilac and laburnum, the last of the hawthorn and the first of the elder, and all the fields golden with cowslips and dandelions, thick as stars.

And the flat blades of iris with lavender-blue heads, stood tall against the old stone walls in every college garden.

Georgiana, opening the windows and coming out onto the lawn, saw a cat pounce hard upon one of the first fledglings, and screamed at it and flapped at it and called to Alice and cleared the sad mess of blood and bones and feathers hastily away, before her brother should return home.

But Thomas sat on a bench under the great branching chestnut trees beside the river, and thought, Kitty, Kitty, Kitty, in hope and love and dread, and nothing else held any interest for him or had any meaning at all.

26

H E WANTED to be with her. The thought of it possessed him completely, there was nothing else. Kitty.

But the opportunity came quite soon, and presented itself entirely naturally.

He had the name of a possible tutor in Latin and Greek, the unmarried daughter of a fellow of another college, who lived at home and cared for an invalid mother, and longed for stimulus, distraction and younger company, and would be entirely suitable.

And, of course, he could have written a brief note, would have done so, under normal circumstances.

But nothing was normal now.

Mid-afternoon of an early June day. The avenue was very quiet, some blinds down here and there. It was still hot, the sun still shone and shone.

The chime sounded, far away in the recesses of the house.

He must simply hand in the address, see no one, he had no reason to go inside.

The maid opened the door.

And Kitty was behind her, in the hall.

He thought that his heart, beating so violently, might erupt out of his chest. He held his hands tightly around his stick and behind his back, because he could not control their trembling.

In the drawing-room, everything was in order, formal, neat, the clock ticked into the silence.

He thought, how dull it must be for her here, with the two women, how uninteresting, after life in India. Though he had no real idea of how that life might have been.

'I am so sorry. There is only me. My cousin is unwell, she has a bad migraine headache and is in bed, and Aunt Dosie is always resting at this time of day.'

'Aunt Dosie . . .'

'Mrs Gray. Her name is Theodosia, don't you think that very romantic-sounding? But not very Scottish, which of course she is – and never can forget it. I wonder where the name came from?'

He looked at her in bewilderment. She was a child, chattering on, trying to behave in the correct, adult way with an unexpected visitor. A child, that was all.

But she was Kitty. And her flesh, her hair, the bones of her fingers, as they rested on a chairback, seemed to him rare and amazing, the most precious he had ever seen, she was more beautiful than angels. Kitty.

He did not believe that anyone before this time, this day, could so have loved another being.

'So I am here alone. Almost alone. And all my new friends are doing their examinations, they cannot attend to me just now.'

He said, and heard his own voice sound strangely into the room, 'I have the name of someone who might perhaps be suitable to tutor you in the classics. Your cousin asked me for advice, I . . . it is a Miss Unsworth. I am slightly acquainted with her father.'

He did not know how to order the words aright, how to speak to her at all, he was aware of sounding unnatural, false, stiff.

(242)

'Oh, you are very kind. Where does she live? When might I see her? I am very anxious to begin. You see, it is my aim to be an undergraduate. I have been quite inspired by the friends I have made – those Miss Pontifex introduced me to. I long to live in the college and have people of my own age all around me and a room of my own. Oh, but I do realise how much I have to do, how ignorant I am. But I *intend* to succeed.'

Her face was bright, earnest. Kitty, he thought. And almost groaned aloud. Kitty, Kitty.

'And now you have gone to so much trouble for me, and you are such an important man and so very busy. And I will go to see Miss . . . ?'

'Unsworth. Miss Rose Unsworth . . .'

'Yes. Oh, do forgive me – I should have – may I offer you some tea? Or rather, a glass of sherry. I know that is the correct thing to offer a college fellow, sherry is what they drink all the time.' She flushed, seeing him smile.

'Only, I do not mean that . . .'

'Of course you do not. And you are quite right. About the sherry. On the whole, that is to say. But I will not take any now, thank you.' But at once, wished that he had accepted, needing to stay here with her, to be in this room.

So, he would have tea instead, when she offered it again.

But she forgot to do so.

Faintly, from the street, the cry of 'Rag and bone, rag and bone . . .'

And then she said, 'My cousin was going to ask if you would perhaps show us around your college one day. I have only seen any of them from the outside, of course, from the gardens; and once, I stood in the great court of Trinity. And we walk across the Backs. The women's college is really rather

(243)

new, and very different, there are no pictures or treasures of any kind.'

'Is that what you would like? To look around the inside of a college? To see pictures and treasures?'

He would take them, of course, show them what there was to show, for it would mean he might be with her, it was all he wanted. He would invite them.

He said, not knowing that he was going to do so, 'Then let us go. You have nothing else to do? It seems rather – quiet for you here.'

'Now? This afternoon?'

'Now, this afternoon. That is, if Mrs Bowering . . .'

'Oh, no, it will be perfectly all right, she would not be able to come and I had better not disturb her, she is really very unwell. Her headaches last two or three days sometimes, I am told, she has to have the blinds down and absolute quiet. Shall I need a coat? No, I think it is warm enough. I will just tell the maid to say where I have gone.'

The door opened and closed, stirring the still air, shifting the curtains as she went, hair flying out from her shoulders.

He swayed slightly, reached quickly for a chair.

Thought, Kitty. Kitty, Kitty, Kitty.

Thought nothing else at all, was only carried on the tide of it. And did not at all consider what he was about to do, the propriety or not. None of it mattered. Nothing mattered.

He wanted to show her the treasures of the created world.

And besides, he was old, he was fifty-four years old, and a Senior Fellow, a clergyman, it was perfectly appropriate and acceptable that he should escort her.

The clock ticked on into the silence.

He was never to forget any of it, for the rest of his life he would remember everything, in the smallest detail.

But perhaps that afternoon most of all. For on that day, it seemed, his life began. Before it, he realised, there had been nothing, nothing at all.

(And after it, for however many years there were, less than nothing. But that was a different matter.)

Such paintings, such treasures as the college had, he showed her.

(They took a cab there from the stand at the corner. Closing his eyes, even thirty years later, he could see the hairs on the thick neck of the man who drove it, the seam of grease on his collar.)

There was the great picture in the chapel. The Adoration. He took her to that first of all. Stood, watching her eyes become used to the dimness, and focus upon it, trace the figures one by one, the potentate, the shepherds, the Madonna, the waxen child.

And her own face was grave and still as those portrayed there, and the light from the candles beside the altar gave it the same fine, painted sheen.

He could scarcely breathe.

After a moment, he pointed to the kneeling figure, the rapture on the uplifted, worshipping face.

Kitty nodded slightly.

Coming out of the coolness, and the gloom, they laughed, freed, in some way, by the brightness and the warmth of the sunshine that blazed in their faces.

'It is very beautiful. It is very *grand*,' Kitty said. 'And how old the child looks. And how wise.'

She paused. 'But I did not very much care for the chapel. The atmosphere is so sad. And . . . and crushing. I felt very insignificant there.'

Kitty, he thought.

And here she was.

He wanted to cry out to the four walls.

Kitty, Kitty, Kitty.

Then, there were the corridors, and the staircases, the great Hall, the Gallery, the portraits, the cases and vaults of silver, the chained Bible, King Henry's library, the Elizabethan chest. More staircases. More corridors. It seemed to him dull as the tomb.

On a narrow landing, she half knelt, to peer through a slit of window onto the Fellows' garden below.

'Like looking through the wrong end of a telescope.'

Otherwise, inside the old buildings she scarcely spoke and when she did, almost whispered. Her face was very composed, very grave. As grave, as solemn, as the waxen child. As wise.

She had coiled her hair up, beneath her hat.

Once, as she half turned, he saw the skin of her long neck, pale, and almost transparent with a sheen as on a circle of honesty. He stared, his mouth dry.

But then, coming out from the shadow of the buildings, and under the arch into the full sunlight again, and the garden and paths that led down to the river, suddenly she smiled, and took off her hat and shaking her head, let her hair fall onto her neck and shoulders, down her back, all anyhow, and skipped once or twice, turning to say something to him, eyes dancing.

And he felt it, too, the shadow fell away from him, and rolled off his back, he put the buildings, the walls, the books and the paintings and the treasures, all, all behind him and forgot them, they were nothing, they were as dust, and so, laughing, too, he went beside her towards the river which ran between the banks, sparkling in the sun and where the young men in boaters punted and rowed and the young women sat together, smiling, and glided with pleasure under the bridges, into the rippling shadows, and out again, and the moorhens and coots circled around and about them, and the willows trailed gentle strands into the water.

He looked down at her as she stood beside him, holding her straw hat between her hands, against her dress.

He said, 'Have you been on the river yet?'

Her face, upturned to his, was the face of a young child.

And so they went, walked down to where the boats were, below the bridge, and took one.

He had not rowed on this river for more than thirty years.

Getting in, she reached out her hand to balance, but he would not have touched it, drew back a little. But the boatman was there, she turned instinctively to him to hand her in.

And then, as she settled on the cushions, leaning back a little, put the straw hat back upon her head, and her face was grave again, and quite serene, looking down at the water, and above the water, to the bank, and the bridges, and over and beyond them, to where the towers and stone walls soared to the sky.

He thought only, this time is the most precious there has ever been, all moments have led to this, all moments end here, end now. And then thought nothing more, and there was no more time.

The boat slipped through the water between others, and if he was seen by anyone, he did not know it, would not have cared. After a time, they were downstream, away from the buildings and the Backs, under bridge after bridge, and out of the town altogether, to where the river ran between grassy meadows, full of buttercups and poppies, and tall swaying grass-heads, and the brown cows grazed down almost to the water's edge.

Once, a kingfisher darted low, bright, blazing blue, from bank to bank.

In holes in the mud, a family of young water rats played, peered. Vanished.

Kitty trailed her hand in the water and the ripples spread gently out from it, thinner and fainter, as they receded, and there was no sound except the creak of the rowlock and the dip and push of the oars. And all around them, the birds, madly singing.

He felt unreal, bodiless. He felt wonder. Astonishment. Pure, vibrant joy.

No dread, no fear, no bewilderment now, but acceptance, as of some miraculous gift.

And, looking across at Kitty, love.

Her face was turned from him, shaded by the rim of her hat. Serious. Absorbed.

He could row for ever.

But after a time, hours, or years it might have been, they moored beside a path that led through meadows to a village, and walked slowly there and had tea in a garden, at a table under the trees. There was no one else at all.

'It is like the England in pictures and books, the England

they all long for. I read about it, from being very young, in India. And heard them all talk. This is what they remember.'

'Yes. It is not always like this. But you know that now.'

'Oh yes – the rain, the cold wind, those grey streets. But all that has gone now, hasn't it?'

'Yes,' he said. 'Yes.'

And stared at her wrist as it curved to hold her cup.

From somewhere deep in the far trees, a cuckoo.

'There would be nightingales here,' he said.

In the end, they walked slowly back towards the river, where the boat lay low on the water beneath the sloping bank.

But at the bank, she stopped, and sat down on the grass and leaned back on her hands, smiling, peaceful. Said, 'It is the most beautiful day I can remember. Days like this should never be over.'

He thought that he would weep then.

And, as he looked down at her, she looked up, full into his face.

And looking up, Kitty saw love, and knew it at once for what it was, though she had never seen it in this way before. And, for a second only, she was puzzled, and afraid. But then what she felt was simply adult, fully grown up in that moment, as if she had crossed a bridge or walked through some door and had gained all the wisdom, and the knowledge of the universe and of the human heart, and could never now go back. And, recognising it, she took it upon herself at once, accepted it.

And all in a second. No more.

Slowly, she stood up. Again she did not ask him for a hand to help her. He would not have dared to give it.

She faced him.

He said, 'Kitty.'

And thought to die, then.

Very carefully, she stepped back into the little boat, and sat, gathering her skirts around her, her back straight, eyes wide. He saw the pulse leaping in her throat.

And took up the oars and in silence and stillness, rowed them back, and the sun had slipped down a little in the sky, and shone onto her and blazed round her, and all was different between them, and the world wholly changed for ever.

27

'KITTY?'

But it was the maid, Ena, who was in the room, changing the water jug.

The headache had not lessened, though the sickness was gone.

'Miss Kitty has gone out, ma'am, for a tour of the colleges.'

'With some of her friends? The undergraduates?'

'No, ma'am, with the Reverend Mr Cavendish, who called.'

But she was not well enough to get up until the following afternoon, and then, felt the usual, bruised wariness, afraid that some sudden movement would trigger the headache again. It was like a thunderstorm that has rolled away, to linger dully somewhere in the near distance, and might at any time return.

At tea, she said, 'I hear you visited the colleges? Privilege indeed!'

'Yes.' Kitty spread honey upon a slice of bread. Her hair was plaited tight at the back of her head, her dark linen dress severely plain. She was not the same person.

Would never be.

'It was very interesting.'

But, staring into her face, Florence found it closed, and defying admittance.

Only, the previous evening, it had not defied old Mrs Gray, who had been sitting at the window when Kitty returned and had looked into it, and into his face, too, and seen what was open and plainly written there.

But would of course say nothing.

28

IN THE early morning, Lewis leaves the house and rides, and feels well, strong, vigorous, able, even, to tolerate the intolerable heat. On Friday, at last, he will leave for the Hills.

By noon, he shivers with fever at his desk, and later, is giddy, disorientated.

Later still, before midnight, dead, on the floor beside the bed, where he has fallen, eyes wide open, staring, staring.

29

IT WAS such a short time, to change lives so irrevocably, and all over so quickly.

(For Florence and Georgiana were gone on the train to London, to be taken around St Faith's Shelter for the fallen young women, they would stay at a good hotel close to the park, and go to theatres and galleries, too, and shop in St James's, they would enjoy themselves, it would do them both good.)

It was only three days.

But it seemed to him that it lasted for ever, looking back, it had been the whole of his life.

(Though Kitty, looking back, if she ever did, could barely recall it.)

She had said that she would like more friends, that she had only Miss Pontifex's undergraduates, who in any case were older, and had their own lives, and perhaps had merely been kind.

'I will give you friends – new friends, of just your own age, or thereabouts, they will be glad to welcome you.'

And so they went, on the train for a short distance, and then, through the lanes in a trap, between verges, thick and creamy with the late flowering of cow parsley, and, here and there, wild scabious, pale, chalky blue, and clouds of tiny butterflies, orange-tipped, drifted up as the wheel brushed against the grass.

It was the most perfect of days once more.

(And what old Mrs Gray thought, she did not speak, only wondered sadly, sitting at the wide window in Cambridge, about Florence and all her illusions.)

He had left a note on his door in college, and done no work at all, and seen no one, and did not think of any of it for a moment.

Kitty sat straight-backed, very still, they were quite silent with one another.

But now and then she smiled, at him, or away, at some distant, secret thing.

And looking at him, she felt old beyond her years, and responsible, too. She was not girlish, had no thought of chattering about any of it to such friends as she had, understanding that it was not a thing of that kind. Though she had never until now known anything of love, that had been to do with some distant, possible future, she had not bothered to consider it.

She saw that he looked at her, and saw love, again, and recognised its rarity, its absolute value. But felt quite calm, though knew that he was not, and that for him it was momentous in a way she could only dimly comprehend, that he trembled and was afraid. Felt for him.

But whether she loved in return, she could not have told.

The trap turned into the village, where honeysuckle and the first of the roses flowered and climbed and cascaded over walls and doors.

Corridors, Georgiana thought, it is always corridors. And high, narrow windows, and iron beds, primly made, and girls with sad faces scrubbing floors. Texts on the walls. Bibles. Sheets being hemmed, in a great, bare basement hall.

And the babies taken away from them as soon as born.

And all for what? she thought, for what? Wanting to weep.

In India, the message makes its slow way up from Calcutta to the Hills, passed without interest through a dozen hands.

Eleanor sits on the verandah and looks at the green, green trees on the opposite slope, and is aloof from Myrtle Piggerton (whose flirtation has petered out, but who must still suffer the social consequences), and is lonely, and will be lonelier still, soon.

But rings the bell for iced tea, not yet knowing.

In the garden of the vicarage, more roses, and beds of great, pink, blowsy peonies, and the children, the girls walking arm in arm (for of course, they had taken to her at once, and especially Elizabeth, she was straightaway become a friend), and the baby peaceful in the pram.

Later, after tea, they played French cricket, where the lawn ran down towards unkempt grass and the great hawthorn hedge.

(But Isobel stayed in the house, she felt unsafe in the outside world, vulnerable. And they were used to it, their life continued more or less without her, though several times, one or other of them had gone back to see her, and the sense of her despair hovered around the edges of the day, and the summer sunshine, souring them a little.)

But Kitty did not feel it, Kitty was not soured, Kitty ran and threw and laughed and kicked off her shoes and rocked the baby back to sleep, and tossed her hair from off her face, and the small boys clambered about her, pulling her down, spinning her round, ambushing her with shouts. Kitty, Kitty, Kitty.

She was a child among them.

But once, caught him looking at her, and smiled, bright-faced, joyous, and he saw that, after all, he had no need to speak, that she knew, had long known, and that all was open between them, and then, his heart leaped, in pain and pleasure, then, all things in the world were possible, and there was no hurt or harm anywhere.

Standing beside him, Cecil Moxton saw too, and stared, bewildered, disbelieving.

Slowly, they began to walk away together, out of the garden, echoing with the cries of the children and through the gate that led to the fields, and followed the path bordering the wood, the terrier running before them. They walked for a mile or more, until they were out of sight of the house, the hayfields thick and rich and sweet around them.

But for a long time he could not speak, only looked at the hayfields stretching all around and away from them in the late afternoon light, the faint haze on the horizon, as if the sea lay there. And he had again the sense of time, as well as space, stretching infinitely ahead of him, and yet of there being no time, and of standing here at the still centre of things, the place to which he had been journeying all his life.

In the end, he struggled for some way to speak of it to Moxton, some way of explaining.

But he could only say, at length, 'I saw her . . . I walked from home, across the Backs. She was – standing on the bridge.'

He fell silent, seeing it again, as he had seen it a thousand times in his mind's eye, Kitty standing, looking down into the water.

'You see – my life is changed – utterly and irrevocably changed – and I – I am not the same man – I – it is as though . . .'

Cecil walked away a few paces away from him, and stood, head bent.

'It is all I want – all I – I want nothing more in life. But . . . how can that be? Why should it be?' He was crying for help.

Cecil half turned, but did not look at him, could not meet his eye. When he spoke, his voice sounded tight, strange.

He said, 'But she is a *child*. She is fifteen years old. She is younger than Elizabeth.'

'Yes.'

'She . . . you cannot . . .'

Then Thomas said, simply, 'Why should I not marry her?'

'Marry?'

'Not . . . when she is older . . . a little older . . . Why?' Wildly, as he spoke, he thought it possible.

Knew that it was not.

He said, 'I have never known love. I am fifty-five, and I have not known love until this time.'

'No.'

And Cecil looked at him then and saw that it was true, and that his face was softened and made young by it; it was as though he looked not at a sober, fleshly man, but at someone changed and made altogether new, reborn. And wholly innocent.

And he thought then of his own love, for his wife, as it had begun so many years ago, and of Isobel now, her face blank and turned from him, of the days and nights of despair.

'What am I to do?'

Moxton shook his head, not knowing.

'It is all. There is nothing else, do you not understand that?' His voice was urgent, angry even, yet he whispered and could scarcely be heard.

In the end, Cecil turned and slowly began to walk away, back in the direction of the house and the garden, the laughing children. Kitty. And after a few moments, Thomas followed him.

Whether it was better to have spoken or whether he should have kept altogether silent, he did not know.

But, looking up and seeing Kitty, standing slightly apart from the others, at the corner of the lawn, he cared nothing either, forgot it, everything, in thrall to, stunned again by, love.

Looking at his face again, Moxton felt a spurt of anguish and cold fear, but intermingled with a sudden, mad hope, and the desire to defend him.

The game ended, the circle of figures broke. There were joyful shouts, and then the children came running, laughing towards them over the lawn.

In its pram underneath the tree, the baby stirred in sleep, eyelids fluttering a little. But he did not wake.

And in the trap, driving through the night lanes, Kitty slept, too, and he stopped and laid his coat over her, and then drove on with infinite care, as if the road beneath them were made of glass.

In the little, rattling train, empty apart from themselves, she sat in the corner of the carriage, huddled back against the seat, pale and moth-like, as the moon rose, silvering the countryside. And the train whistled, eerie, ghostly, running through a tunnel, frightening the vixen who raced away from it, back to her cubs in the far spinney.

'You are very tired,' he said, 'I have been very wrong to keep you out so late.'

'Oh no, I am only drowsy. And . . .'

'And?'

But she shook her head, and looking out of the window, he saw the backs of the first, dark terraces, on the edge of the town. And – for time still stood, for them and must never spring forward, nothing must end, said,

'Then perhaps, tomorrow, you would like to go . . .' he hesitated, 'go to the sea.'

'The sea,' she said gravely. 'Yes. I should like that most of all.'

And they looked into one another's faces, one another's eyes, then, and so remained, looking, and never looked away until the train drew into the station.

Hearing their voices and the closing of the door, old Mrs Gray sat on the armchair beside her bed, fully dressed. But did not go down, did not interfere. Only remembered things that were a lifetime away and, understanding what she had seen in his face, and the meaning of it, feared for him.

30

'THE SEA,' she had said, 'I should like that most of
all.'

And so they went, nothing could have been simpler, and if the world stirred uneasily, beneath the bright,
serene, sunlit surface, a calm before the storm, and if he knew,
he was entirely careless of it.

There had not been a cloud in the sky for days, they were
grown used to it, took it for granted, everybody did.

From the railway station, they walked up the hill, past the
granite-faced church, and at the brow, before the slope began
to run down again, stopped, and looked over the rooftops of
the little pink- and white- and lemon-painted houses, to
where the sea lay, flat and smooth and bright blue as a child's
sea in a picture.

Though when they reached the level, and the narrow lanes
that led out onto the foreshore, the houses, those belonging
to the fishermen, were not all so pretty, some were dingy
and mean, with blank windows that let in no light.

And the shingle beach sloped down to the water's edge and
the waves swelled up and tumbled over, foaming and swirling
all around, it was not, even today, a gentle, sheltered sea.

The pebbles were pale, grey upon grey as gull's wings, and

the gulls themselves perched on the breakwater, and rawked from the rooftops, wheeling suddenly about the sky, riding the water, far out. The air tasted salt on their lips.

They walked away from the town, and Kitty took off her shoes and the water washed over her bare feet, making her laugh with pleasure.

He wondered how it could be that he was content simply for there to be this, to walk with her, look at her, have her in this place with him, and be entirely happy, in a state of bliss and utter satisfaction, to need nothing else, nothing more. For all of his past, the old interests and concerns had dropped quite away from him, and his old self was sloughed off, like a skin. And looking about him, he saw the world re-created, all things were strange, new, brave and infinitely rare and beautiful to his eyes. He looked at sea and sky, at the stones beneath his feet, and the shimmer of the far horizon, and the bird balanced on the post ahead, and he had never seen their like before, all were miraculously new to him.

Kitty was standing, her shoes in her hand, the sea water creaming, opaque, green and white as bottle glass, around her ankles.

She turned, 'Oh, it is beautiful here. It is a wonderful place. It is quite perfect.'

And danced then, stretching out her arms, in the sunlight, at the edge of the water.

Behind the town, behind the sea wall, lay the marshes, and the river wound slowly across them inland for mile after mile, under the great, pale bowl of sky.

Later, they came here, and walked again, and as soon as they had left the sea and dropped down onto the marsh path, they left the sound of it, too, the ceaseless rushing up and falling over and sucking back upon itself, rasping down the pebbles. Here it was utterly quiet, save for the odd, haunting cry of a bird and the brush of their legs against the dry grasses.

The water lay low in pools, half dried up, and the river ran like a silver snail-thread.

Farther away, the sky was darker, as though condensing

like a bruise. The air was very close, very still, it seemed harder to breathe here.

And then, as if both had agreed upon it, though neither had spoken, they sat down, on the dry path, overlooking the water, and the wide, pale marsh, and began, falteringly, to talk to one another in the way of lovers, though neither knew it, or knew that this was a common thing.

He told Kitty what he had scarcely spoken of before, not because the things were secret, but because there had never been any chance, or occasion, any other person, to tell. Told of childhood and of the house in Ireland, and his days out in the boat with Collum O'Cool, of his sister and her love for him, how she would follow him about; of his mother, school, the university, the church, his friend Cecil Moxton, his work, his God, his love for the birds, the island and the hours spent alone there, told her his thoughts, feelings, fears, and, in between, the small details, that he did not know he had so much as remembered, and the dreams and the night-mares.

And Kitty told, too, and as she told, relived, and saw it all vividly before her, India, the hot days, the house, the Hills, the servants, the horses, the crying of the jackals at night, the procession of governesses, and talking of it, wanted it again, missed it, and speaking of her mother and father, cried, as she had not let herself cry since coming to England and the tears seemed necessary. But they were not tears of unhappiness.

They sat, a little apart, not touching, looking away from one another, and after a long time of talking, fell silent, and there was only the whistle of a bird now and then, in the silence of the marshes around them.

He said, 'You must eat something. We should go back to the town.' But, looking up, he saw that the sky had gathered and darkened and was hanging heavily over them, there was thunder faintly in the distance, and the first heavy drops of rain.

All around them, the open marsh, save for, perhaps a hundred yards away, near to the river-shore, a half-derelict hut, once used by the punt-gunners, abandoned now, for they no longer came to this part.

But it was clean and dry inside, though quite bare. Through the glass-less window, and the door that swung half open, they looked out at the rain, as it came in soft, pale clouds, sweeping over the marsh, shutting out the line of the land, where it met the sky. The air smelled of earth and salt and of the mud, stirred by the first rain for weeks.

He said quietly, 'Until now, I have never cared for any living creature, as I have cared for birds. A single curlew cry in the midst of the marsh, or a wader standing alone at the edge of the water– I have never ached for any human beauty as I have ached at the sight of those. Until now.'

She listened, her eyes still on his face, and received what he said gently, kindly.

'I saw you first, standing on the stone bridge, looking down into the water. You did not see me – know me then – or I you. And you were like – the most graceful bird, and so, I loved. At once. But not as – and what to do . . . how to . . . what may happen to this love or . . . what you . . .'

He stumbled hopelessly over the words, they made nonsense, he was defeated by them, and buried his face in his hands, his eyes burning, his tongue dry, cleaving to his mouth.

The rain made a soft rushing sound on the roof of the hut, as though a brush were being swept across it, to and fro, to and fro.

Kitty said, 'This is love. It is – it is not as I had thought.'

He shook his head, but did not look up.

But after a moment, said, 'I care for nothing else. You should know that. Will not. There is *nothing else* in life.'

He looked up. 'It is terrifying.'

He wanted to reach out to her, but did not. He was paralysed.

She was standing at the window with her back to him, watching the drifting rain, falling like needles onto the still surface of the river.

He said, 'Kitty,' his voice an odd, rasping whisper.

Then, very carefully, she began to remove her clothes, the wrap, the long, full dress, the petticoats and stockings and chemise, they fell onto the floor and were left like soft, discarded feathers. She stepped out of them and then was motionless, before him, and pale, and naked as a wand, her body not yet a woman's body, not yet formed. But he did not know that, had never seen, nor had any image of it in his mind.

He scarcely breathed.

But then, knelt before her, and gazed and as he gazed, reached out his hand and drew it down her body, an inch away from the flesh, not touching her at all, drew it down to her bare feet, and back and reaching her breast and shoulder, mouth, hair, would have touched. But could not.

Kitty's eyes were lowered, she did not look at him.

And in the end, he rose and stumbled out and half fell, a few yards away, onto the path, and knelt there in the gentle rain, weeping, his head bent, face covered by his hands.

31

LATER, THE rain stopped, and a fine mist clung to the surface of the marsh. But above it, the sun shone through again, reflecting on the surface of the water. The air smelled infinitely sweet.

Kitty stood at the door of the hut, white-faced, and somehow, older. She was dressed, her clothes carefully arranged, so that he wondered wildly if it had indeed happened, if she had ever stood naked for him, or whether he had had some insane, half-waking dream.

They walked back over the mud, between the wet grasses, to the sea and the streets of the town, and felt strange, embarrassed to pass houses, be among even a few people.

At the hotel, they ate, and drank a little, sitting in a dark back room, and Kitty was reminded of her first evening in England, with cousin Florence, after she had disembarked. A lifetime ago.

Then, because his clothes and shoes were soaked through, but more because he knew in his heart that this, today, would be the end of it all, but could not, could not bear the end ever to be, he asked for rooms, and rooms were found, they could rest and bathe, his things were taken away and dried.

He said, 'We had better stay here. It is too late to get back now.'

'Yes,' Kitty said.

And quite early, she went to bed, and slept at once, exhausted. Thomas went out again, when his things were returned, to walk in the darkness along the shingle, close to the sea, despairing, incredulous, joyful, entirely calm.

He spent the night in Kitty's room, sitting up in a chair, and looking over to where she slept, and waiting for the dawn to break on the horizon, along the line of the sea.

When it did, waking Kitty, she did not start, but watched him as he sat, and when he turned and saw her, said, 'Remember this.'

He went and knelt beside her then and buried his head in the bed-cover, and, briefly, she reached out her hand and touched his hair, stroking it lightly as she might that of a distressed child, to comfort.

And it was the only touch between them.

32

FOR NATURALLY, he had been right, those three days were both the beginning and the end of it all, there was to be no more.

But what there had been was enough to ruin him, and the shame lasted a lifetime. But he understood that, accepted it. His only fear was for Kitty. But Kitty was taken away, Kitty scarcely suffered at all. Or so it was supposed. But as she never spoke of it, no one knew.

When they arrived back in Cambridge, it was to find Florence and Georgiana come home early from London.

(Georgiana having felt unwell, and depressed after their tour of St Faith's Shelter, so that she had no taste at all for the enjoyments they had planned, the theatres and concerts, the strolls in St James, she had been such poor company that Florence had agreed quite easily that they should leave. And besides, she was anxious to get back, living as she did in such hope of a proposal, wanting to further her own plans. She had even confided to Georgiana that she had some reason for hope, though Georgiana had said nothing, uncertain what to believe. But perhaps it was so.)

Except, of course that it was not and had never been. And arriving home and finding Kitty and Thomas gone, and when they did not return that night, she saw how things were, the truth was plain, shocking and terrible, before her.

It was not until long afterwards that Florence vented every

morsel of the bitterness and hatred she felt, speaking one night to her mother. At the time, she said only, 'I will destroy him.' And did so, quite easily, by going at once to the Dean.

On the same day, Eustace Partridge had climbed up to his old tutor's room, seeking advice, help, comfort, a welcome, for he planned to leave his wife, and come back here, take up the old ways, somehow, find refuge. But found instead a note pinned to the door, and then, from the servant, and another undergraduate, an old friend, met by chance in the town, heard rumours and parts of the story, and felt utterly betrayed, and most of all by what he saw as the hypocrisy. He had expected nothing of himself, nothing of any other man, but of Cavendish, he expected everything, probity, self-discipline, chastity – perfection.

He left Cambridge at once, not for home, but for London, to lose himself, confused, angry, and, at last, sitting on a park bench late at night, infinitely sorry too for another wasted life.

In the house, Kitty stood at the window of her room, and later, lay on her bed fully clothed. But did not sleep. She felt that a hundred, or a thousand years, had passed in three days, and was grown up and completely adult, it was as if she understood the meaning of all things, had seen to the heart of them, and above all understood instinctively that she had known love, of a kind she would never know again, for the rest of her life, and was humbled by it, and grateful for it, and ashamed of nothing.

But whether she loved in return, she still could not have told.

Much later, after dinner, for which she did not go down, old Mrs Gray came and sat with her for a little, and held her hand in the darkness, and all was well, at least between the two of them.

She had not expected it. But it was to Georgiana that he talked, told everything there was, breaking down several times, as he did so, told every detail of those days and of his feelings, the whole truth. And she believed him without question, and would, of course, remain with him, protect him, defend him, that would never be in doubt.

And only wept, when she was finally alone, wept for the innocence of it all, and his vulnerability, and because of his suffering that must go on, for ever perhaps, and for which she could give him no help, no alleviation. But envied him, too, for what he had known, the love that had so transformed him.

33

EVERYTHING HAPPENED as might have been expected.

Eleanor, having heard of the death of her husband, and written of it to Kitty, and begun all the dreary business of packing and leaving the Hills and returning to Calcutta, and the empty house, the dumb, respectful servants, having bravely begun to come to terms with it, even, and the realisation that her life here was over, and she had no purpose in India now, received the letter from Florence, telling Kitty's story, dealing the new blow.

And so made the arrangements to sail for home, and in time, arrived, and took Kitty at once away from Cambridge, to London first, and, later, to Sussex. (And it was to Sussex that Thea Pontifex went to live, after her marriage, and only a dozen miles or so away from Kitty, and perhaps, eventually, they met. Or perhaps they did not – but Miss Pontifex, at any rate, was happy.)

And night after night, Adèle Hemmings continued to slip out of the back gate and down through the snickets and alleyways, prowling, muttering. But finally, was discovered, wandering naked beside the weir, and taken to shelter, and was fortunate never to have been harmed. Though by now she was quite deranged, and scarcely understood.

For three more days afterwards, her aunt lay dead in the upstairs room of their house, as she had already been, for who knew how long, and the cats, wild with hunger, marauded through the gardens all around.

And, the door of the conservatory having somehow been left open, when the birds were out, by Georgiana, or by Thomas himself, preoccupied, still, a cat, inevitably, found the way in, and there was carnage, which Thomas discovered at dawn. And Georgiana, hearing him, came down, grey hair plaited, and hanging over her shoulder, and sat, as he wept, then, holding him, and rocking him like a child, in the midst of all the small, maimed, broken bodies, and blood, and bright, scattered feathers.

Among the possessions and papers of Miss Lovelady, gone through eventually by lawyers somewhere, a note was found, neatly written, leaving the house in Norfolk to Kitty, who was traced, and so it came to her.

But she could never bear to go to it. It remained empty, winter and summer, for years more, and then was sold for very little. But it gave her some money of her own which, one day, she might be glad of.

There was nothing left for Miss Hartshorn in the cottage in Warwickshire, had been nothing since she had cut herself off from it, by going to India. She had come back, but not to belong. So that she did not know where to go, what to do, and so thought of India again, wondered if she ought to return. For where else was there?

But knew she could not have faced that, and what, in any case, would be the point or purpose?

Instead, on a sudden whim, she closed the cottage, and went in search of the place she had come from, so many years ago, another village, sheltered by a fold of the Cotswold Hills. She had grown up here, but left at the age of seventeen, and never returned, and felt fear, as she approached, in case it had changed beyond all recognition, and she would no longer know it, for then, the last hope would have gone, and there would be nowhere in the world for her to belong.

But nothing had changed, all was exactly as she remembered, as she walked up the hill between the low stone cottages, in the evening light, and stood in the lane, outside the door of the first house in which she had lived as a young child, and knew that the past had been given back to her, and that she was saved, rescued from herself, and all her own mistakes and follies, and not barren, but infinitely rich.

Old Mrs Gray lived on, through the scandal and all its aftermath, and into the years when, for most people, it became old history, forgotten, and still planned her visit to the Scotland of her girlhood. But died eventually without having gone, though not until she was almost a hundred, and by then Florence had begun to age, and be forgetful and ill-tempered, and periodically did not recognise this or that person, which was the start of her illness. (But the romantic way of seeing it was that the disappointment and bitterness had turned her mind, and jealousy and hatred eaten like a canker into it, ruining her.) But whether she would have recognised as much as the names of those involved, was uncertain.

Georgiana resigned from the Committee for Moral Welfare, but others took over, and in time, the house in the country was completed and inhabited by generations of fallen young women, for there was never any shortage. Though none was ever so fallen as those who, in truth, were not.

There were other committees for Georgiana to join, and she was invited to do so, for no one ostracised her. Indeed, a point was publicly made of not doing so, she was welcomed and valued, her life was fuller than it had ever been.

Alice stayed on, and trudged each Sunday and Wednesday evening, to the spiritualist fellowship, and the seances, which seemed to sustain her, or at any rate, to do no harm.

But, for about a year after the scandal broke and spread like a stain, thickening and deepening as it went, life was suspended, because Thomas and Georgiana went abroad, to Switzerland first and then to Italy, not so much because he felt obliged to go, as that he could not bear to stay, and not to see Kitty, and yet to see her everywhere, to walk across the Backs, and towards the stone bridge, where she always stood for him, looking down into the water.

Only, abroad, he saw her too, and had her with him constantly, so that in a sense things were no different.

But their absence gave people the time to talk and be done with talking, and on his return, they were kind and pretended to have forgotten. Most people. And after all, what was the scandal, what exactly had happened? Who knew?

He continued to write his book on the sea-birds, and completed it, and it was published and became a standard work, and that gave him some satisfaction. He even began another. But abandoned it, unfinished, after some years.

Otherwise, he went a great deal to the houseboat, spent days and weeks alone there in the silence, and the tranquillity, the lapping of the water, the open skies, the crying of the birds, the dawns and the moonlit nights, wind and sun and storms, soothed him, rinsed his mind of all anxiety, so that he seemed to float, quietly, on the surface of the shining water, infinitely calm. And read his Bible, and the Daily Office there. But did not otherwise pray.

And Kitty was always with him, the memory of her never dimmed or became cloudy, and the love he had felt he continued to feel, and it was never supplanted.

He regretted nothing at all. He had known a brief time of joy, absolute and unalloyed, and saw it as a foretaste of paradise.

So that many years later, as an old man, standing in the sunshine by the river, which was crowded with the young men in boats, and holding a saucer, and a dish of strawberries, and looking up, and seeing a girl in a pale dress, on the stone bridge, the past raced towards and broke over him and became the present, and he felt what he had felt anew, fresh and raw and vivid. Love, as he had never forgotten for one second of a lifetime since, nor ever once regretted.

And Kitty?